Falling For You

Book Two in the Buckeye Falls Series

Libby Kay

Falling For You
Copyright © 2023 Libby Kay
All rights reserved.

ISBN: (ebook) 978-1-958136-41-6
(print) 978-1-958136-42-3

Inkspell Publishing
207 Moonglow Circle #101
Murrells Inlet, SC 29576

Edited By Yezanira Venecia
Cover Art By Fantasia Frog

DEDICATION

To My Sister, Kathleen.
Much Like The Sisters In This Book, You Make Me Laugh
And Provide Support Through Thick And Thin.
Love You!

CHAPTER 1

CeCe LaRue was wrist-deep in a mound of bread dough when she heard her cell phone ring. The trilling sound grated like a block of aged parmesan over a bowl of pasta. Mumbling a few choice profanities, she lifted her hands and attempted to answer with her elbow as Max's smiling face beamed from the taunting device. After one more attempt at elbow poking, the phone went silent. "Come on," she groaned, knowing the reason her boss called.

"He's calling off again, isn't he?" Evan Lawson asked from the doorway. He shrugged off his jacket and dusted a few snowflakes from his blond curls. Walking over to the table, he picked up her phone as Max called again. "Hey, Max," he answered, watching CeCe roll her eyes from her spot at the table. She tried to push her hair back with her forearm and ended up covering her nose in flour. "Yep, it looks like sourdough this time."

CeCe could hear both men laugh at her morning routine. It wasn't her fault she wanted the diner to have fresh bread every morning. "Put him on speaker," she ordered while thrusting her hands back into the blob of dough.

Evan shook his head and ignored her request. "Sure thing. We'll get everything ready to go. See you soon." He disconnected and put her phone back on the table. His blue gaze finally met CeCe's, and he smirked. The guy had an unnerving ability to disarm her with just one of his goofy grins. *Darn him.*

Now was not the time to evaluate Evan or his ability to short-circuit her brain. Ever since they went to the Christmas Jubilee together, CeCe was unable to bake her way out of Evan's charms. It was just one night out, one night with a friend she thought she knew, but what she hadn't expected was Evan's dance moves, the way he filled out that tuxedo, the way he respected her boundaries yet still made her feel seen, made her feel special. They'd laughed and relaxed like they never had on the clock, and she'd be lying to herself if she thought it was a fluke. Evan was certainly boyfriend material, but she was not about to break her rule. You don't date coworkers—or at least not again.

Despite going back to their former routine of workmates, Evan wasn't perturbed. He'd always been a nice guy, but over the last couple months she felt a shift between them. He'd linger at the end of shifts, taking care to make sure she was in her car safely before heading out. He'd move things off the higher shelves, keeping everything at her level, because it wasn't easy being the shortest one on the team. Not that she'd give him the satisfaction of seeing her flustered by his charms. Nope, not going to happen.

"I could have taken that, you know." She huffed, turning her face down to her work. Slapping the now-formed ball of dough, she smiled as the sour tang hit her nostrils. This was going to be a good batch; she could feel it.

Undeterred, Evan walked over to the sink and washed his hands. Within a minute, he donned an apron and started cracking eggs for the breakfast rush. "I know, but watching you flail around entertains me," he said, smiling through his egg-cracking.

"Ugh." CeCe grumbled as she formed loaves of bread and covered them in a towel to rise. No matter her mood, she trusted the bread-making process. Life was complicated, but she knew that flour, yeast, water, and salt made terrific bread every time. "What's his excuse this time?"

Evan pulled down a few frying pans from above the stove and lined them up by the grill. Without being asked, he grabbed another tray for the fresh loaves and placed it on the counter. CeCe had been trying to reach that before he arrived, but she couldn't find her kickstand. Such were the struggles of being barely five feet tall.

"Does he need an excuse? He's been with Ginny every waking moment since Christmas." There was no malice or accusation in Evan's tone; the guy was a born romantic.

Their boss, and friend, had finally gotten his ex-wife back over the holidays. While it was certainly heartwarming, it threw their usually predictable boss off his game and into the arms of love. Sure, Max was still devoted to the diner, but he'd found the work-life balance he'd been missing for years. In a matter of weeks, he was basically a new man.

"No. You're right. He doesn't need an excuse." CeCe wiped her hands on a towel and started icing a tray of warm cinnamon rolls, the cream cheese icing oozing into the cinnamon swirls. Like clockwork, Evan joined her side and leaned in for a closer look. His eyes practically sparkled as she handed him the pallet knife. "You can have the rest, but don't eat it near the counter."

Evan scoffed, but took the proffered knife. "I'm not a kid. I know not to drool over the customer's food." He took his prize and backed away to the corner. CeCe attempted to ignore the sinful noises he made as he licked the knife clean. *Maybe she should invest in some earplugs?*

Pulling at the collar of her tunic, she tried to cool herself down. "Must be the ovens," she muttered as she ambled into the walk-in fridge for the rest of the breakfast ingredients. As she opened the door with an armful of trays, Evan was there at the ready, reaching out and taking the load without even a grunt, carefully placing everything on the counter. "Thanks," CeCe said as she handed him the second round of trays.

3

Following a familiar routine, the pair stood side by side and chopped, mixed, and prepped what they needed for breakfast. CeCe used to do this routine with Max, but Evan had been taking more of an interest in cooking recently. Their boss getting struck by Cupid's arrow only accelerated Evan's time to test recipes and sharpen his knife skills.

CeCe had been at the diner for nearly three years, the longest she'd ever been at one job. She was a few months away from her thirtieth birthday, and she wasn't too proud to say it got to her. Time never meant much to CeCe, who traveled around the Midwest finding kitchens where she could use her pastry chef diploma. A stint in Chicago and a stop in Ohio's three-C's, and she had somehow found her peace in the small Ohio town of Buckeye Falls.

The peace of their morning prep work was interrupted when Helen, their lead waitress, barged in through the back door. "Did you see?" she practically shouted as she ran over to them, the local paper clutched in her meaty hand.

Evan hurriedly moved a bowl of eggs as Helen thrust the paper onto the counter, which she followed by slapping her hand over the headline. "What's up?" Evan asked, craning his neck to see what all the fuss was about. Helen was usually more sour than excitable.

"He's coming to Buckeye Falls this summer for a food competition. Can you believe our luck? Someone like *him* coming to Ohio?" Helen exclaimed, her enthusiasm contagious until CeCe finally saw the "he" in question.

Glancing down at the paper, CeCe felt her hands go clammy as she dropped her whisk. It clattered across the floor and landed next to Evan's sneakered feet, a trail of pancake batter in its wake. Without saying a word, he retrieved it and tossed it in the sink. He pulled another whisk from the utensil holder and tried handing it to her, but she was lost in a slew of emotions.

Feeling her throat close, she needed to get out of the kitchen and away from witnesses because she was either going to faint or puke. Her happy place had been invaded by a black-and white-image of her past, and she knew she couldn't take it—at least not right now.

"CeCe, what's wrong?" Evan asked, stepping closer and resting his hand on her arm. Despite the warmth of his touch, she didn't register the contact, just kept blinking. Her eyes brimmed with unshed emotion. And CeCe was no crier.

Helen put her hand to her chest, finally picking up on CeCe's mood. "You look like you've seen a ghost." She grabbed a water bottle, opened it, and handed it to CeCe. She took it, but she couldn't bring herself to drink. Her tongue was heavy, stuck to the roof of her mouth like she'd eaten a peanut butter sandwich.

Staring up at her from the grainy front-page photo was celebrity chef Eric Watson. Over the last couple years, he'd moved from his own chain of successful Chicago restaurants to being the biggest star on the Food Network. His TV persona was part Gordon Ramsey and part Jamie Oliver, but with the Midwestern charm only Eric could master. He managed to both school someone in the kitchen and make them weak in the knees. Right now, CeCe was feeling his charms in a very unpleasant way—and she feared she was about to upchuck all over her sourdough.

Before he was a celebrity chef, he was the love of CeCe's life. There were too many conflicting emotions roiling through her in that moment: sadness, fear, and most importantly, disgust. Disgust that this man still had the power to make her feel this small. She was past all this Eric drama. *Wasn't she?!*

"I need some air," she said, forcing her feet to propel her toward the door.

Helen and Evan stared after CeCe until the door slammed behind her. Stumbling out into the cool early March morning, she tried to fill her lungs with air, but she knew it was a losing battle. She paced back and forth, limbs shaking, as she stared unseeing at her feet. She heard the door open and knew Evan was behind her. He had the uncanny ability to be near when she needed someone, but this was not the time.

Evan draped a coat over her shoulders and ushered her toward a bench, her feet faltering along the way. She leaned on him until they were seated. "Here," he said, taking her shaking hands in his. He squeezed them and she felt the strength of his grip, of his presence. "What can I get you? You look terrible."

CeCe chuckled, giving him the reaction he'd hoped for. "You always know what to say to make a girl feel special." His hand raised to her face and gently swiped a dusting of flour from her nose. Ordinarily, she would tell Evan to keep his distance. It was a poorly kept secret that the guy had a little crush, but she didn't have the energy now. "I'll be fine. I'm just a little tired." The lie sounded lame to her own ears, and she fought from rolling her eyes.

"Why don't you go home and rest? I know what to do with the bread, and Max will be here before lunch. We've got this."

CeCe hadn't taken a day off work in a year, and only then because she got food poisoning at the community center potluck. A word to the wise, never trust Mrs. Sander's chicken surprise casserole. Apparently, the surprise was E. coli.

Taking a deep breath, CeCe got to her feet. "I'm fine, I swear. Why don't you help Helen with the coffee maker? You know she always adds too many grounds."

Evan didn't move at first, staring as she struggled to compose herself. She would not cry in front of him; she wouldn't. Squeezing her eyes shut, she tried to picture something happy, something light. Like a perfectly whipped meringue in a pavlova. But it was no use; she felt vulnerable, right down to her core. The sensation made her skin prickle.

"Are you sure you shouldn't go home? CeCe, you work yourself to the bone for this place. The last thing Max wants is for you to faint on the job." Bless Evan for his blind optimism. He took her at her word that she was simply tired, and it tugged at her heartstrings.

"If you help Helen with the coffee, then I'll be on my game. Seriously, Evan. I'll be right in." Her voice hitched at the end, a sure sign she was about to snap.

Judging from the pat to her arm, he either didn't notice or he trusted her. She'd wager it was trust. He approached the world with an openness and eagerness that CeCe didn't share. If she was a bulldog, then Evan was a golden retriever. Over the years, CeCe wore her gruffness like a badge of honor. It kept her focused, and more importantly kept her heart protected. Maybe she was a grump, but she bet Evan was just a more positive, sweet person. Too sweet, like the cinnamon rolls she'd just frosted.

Of all the things CeCe worried about in life, and there was a laundry list, seeing her ex again was at the bottom of the list. Eric ran in a different circle, and when she left Chicago, she knew he'd never follow. Living in Buckeye Falls had felt safe and comfortable. She had her life at the diner and had quickly become a member of the community. She helped cater events and was BFFs with the mayor's wife. CeCe truly was a part of Buckeye Falls. But now her little town had betrayed her, inviting her enemy across state lines.

She knew she needed to get herself together and read the article. She needed to know what brought Eric to Ohio and how long he was planning to stay. Standing and stretching, CeCe felt the coat over her shoulders. It was Evan's coat, oversized and smelling faintly of cedar and too much spice, like his cheap body spray. Sniffing the collar, she tried to ignore what the scent did to her insides. She also ignored that he always knew what she needed.

Evan was a nice guy, that's all. And besides, right now, CeCe had bigger fish to fry.

*

"Here's the Denver omelet for Mrs. Sanders," Evan

announced to Helen, who plucked the plate from his hand. "Remind her I left the ham out," he said.

Helen muttered, "Then it's hardly a Denver omelet."

Evan couldn't disagree. He'd learned so much since he met Max and CeCe.

When he started, he was fresh off a hellish year interning with his father's company. That gap year proved Evan wasn't made for the corporate machine, and he began second-guessing his degree. Despite liking the process of creating websites, his diploma felt like a useless piece of paper. His father had pushed for Evan to follow in his footsteps, but managing a division at the largest tech company in Columbus felt as awkward as a Denver omelet without ham. Standing in a hot kitchen with egg yolk on his pants and bacon grease burns on his forearms, Evan knew his father would die if he saw his son like this. But damn it, he was happy.

When he left home, Evan told his parents he needed to find his own way. So he drove far enough away to feel himself relax. Not knowing what he wanted to do, he had stopped at the diner for lunch and to clear his head. Helen had been griping about being short-staffed to a high schooler who could barely carry a bus bin. Evan looked around the space; it was loud, hot, crowded, and smelled like a cross between sausage and cinnamon. He'd been hooked.

Inquiring about the vacancy, Evan had been introduced to Max, who was warm and friendly, offering Evan a job as soon as the ink dried on his application. It had felt like home from the first time he clocked in, and Evan couldn't imagine being anywhere else.

Naturally, there were other factors keeping Evan in Buckeye Falls, and one of them was standing behind him rolling out dinner rolls. He'd fallen for CeCe as soon as Max introduced them. From her messy blonde hair to her surly attitude and hilarious wit, he was a goner. The only problem being that CeCe saw him as a kid, someone to boss around.

Their dynamic was changing, and he wasn't deterred, or at least not yet.

"Hey, gang," Max greeted from the doorway. His dark hair was mussed, and he wasn't wearing a coat. As he strode toward the group, Evan saw that his socks didn't match. He looked happy and disheveled. He looked like a man in love.

"Morning." Evan waved over his shoulder with a spatula. "Helen's out with the orders, but if you have the grill, I can help."

Max gave him a thumbs-up and headed toward his apron. He threw it over his head and stopped when he saw CeCe, who hadn't looked up from her work. "Hey. I'm sorry to leave you guys hanging this morning. I'll be better about being on time." He waited for her to respond, but CeCe didn't move.

Evan motioned for Max to join him in the dining room, and the pair walked out of the kitchen. Helen had stashed the newspaper by the register, and Evan retrieved it to show Max. "Here," he said as he waited for Max to read the headline.

"What's this?" Max frowned down at the paper.

"I don't know what's up with CeCe, but it has something to do with this." Evan stabbed at the headline with his index finger, smudging the ink with his greasy finger.

Immediately, Max blanched. "Eric Watson is coming to central Ohio?" Max scanned the article, his hands tensing on the paper as he read.

Still not sure what the issue was, Evan summarized the article. "Yeah, sounds like he's doing a Midwestern food truck competition. It's over a long weekend, just before your wedding. Sounds like the winner gets prize money and an item added to Watson's menus in Chicago." Max didn't react, just kept staring, so Evan continued. "I think we should enter; getting endorsed by Eric Watson would put this place on the map. Plus, you always said you wanted to get a food truck for when fair season starts."

Max's expression hardened, and he shook his head.

"We're not joining the competition," he said firmly. "I'm going to help CeCe. Can you help Helen?"

Evan wanted to argue, but instead nodded. Max had never led him wrong before, and Evan wasn't about to start doubting his mentor. As he walked into the kitchen, Max snatched the paper, balled it up, and tossed it in the trash.

"Something is definitely up," Evan muttered as he watched his boss stomp up to the grill. Max was normally so quiet and easygoing. It jarred Evan to see him wound up.

Helen approached with an empty coffee carafe and sighed. "Tables five, six, and seven need more coffee, and I forgot the side of bacon for table four." Taking the coffee carafe, Evan refilled it and got into work mode. He knew there would be time to ask questions about the article, but that certainly wasn't during their breakfast rush.

When the diner closed after lunch, Evan was exhausted. He and Max installed a new tabletop in one of the booths before finally calling it a day.

"Thanks for staying late for this," Max said as he wiped sweat from his forehead. "It's one of those things you put off until it's too late." The old tabletop was propped against the wall, a crack marring its otherwise smooth surface.

"No problem." Evan heard the front door open and Ginny walked in. Max's face lit up, and he quickly joined her by the entrance. Evan felt a tug in his ribcage at the sight. He was so happy that Max had found his way back to Ginny, but he was also envious of that type of connection. Evan yearned to have someone who looked at him that way—someone who couldn't wait to be closer.

Growing up, Evan had seen his parents' marriage ebb and flow. They were still together, but he would guess they wouldn't say they were still in love. Raising four children and spending thirty-five years together shapes people, but it didn't seem to bring them closer together. When Evan did visit home, his mother was her normal self, but his father wouldn't bother with much, if any, affection toward his wife or kids. Evan always knew he wanted more from life, from a partner.

"Hi, Evan," Ginny greeted from Max's side. Her hand sparkled as the light caught her engagement ring. "Thanks for covering this morning. You really are a lifesaver."

Evan flushed at her praise. "You're welcome. You know me, happy to help." He shoved his hands in his pockets and watched Max wrap an arm around his bride-to-be. "Want me to take this out back for trash day?"

Max shook his head and gestured toward the kitchen. "Nah, we got it. You've done more than enough today. I'll see you tomorrow."

Evan nodded, waved to Ginny, and made his way back toward the back. "Wait!" Ginny shouted from behind him. She caught up to Evan and fished in her purse for something. Pulling out an ivory envelope, she handed it to Evan. His name was written in swirls of calligraphy. "It's your invite to our wedding. I hope you can come." Ginny's smile was so sweet it melted Evan's heart a little.

"Wouldn't miss it." He peeled open the envelope to see it was addressed to Evan and a guest. Staring at the plus-one, he wondered who he would actually take. He knew who he *wanted* to take, but he didn't want to make assumptions.

"And you're not working the event," Max teased, joining Ginny and wrapping his arm around her shoulders. It was as if they couldn't survive in the same space without touching. "We're going with a caterer from outside Buckeye Falls."

Ginny interjected, "Highly recommended by Natalie, so we know it's good." Natalie was the mayor's wife and founder of Buckeye Fall's only event planning business. Ginny had joined Natalie's team at the beginning of the year as their head of marketing. Evan knew Max was proud of his wife-to-be for starting over, especially since it brought her back into his life.

"I'm sure it's going to be great. I'll RSVP *yes* right now." Evan beamed at the pair.

Ginny lowered her voice and bowed closer. "You can bring a date too. Just let us know." She winked, and Evan felt his heart sink. CeCe was the only person he wanted to go with, but he couldn't ask her outright. With CeCe, patience was key.

"Uh, yeah, I'll let you know."

Max waved as Evan backed into the kitchen. Expecting to find it empty, he was surprised to see CeCe measuring a spoonful of vanilla and standing over a pot of boiling sugar. "You sure that's a good idea? Shouldn't you be resting?" he asked as he joined her.

CeCe didn't look up; she kept swirling the pan as the sugar turned amber. "I'm fine, just needed to get started on these candies."

Evan surveyed the detritus on the counter, proving CeCe had a long day ahead of her. "What are they for?" He picked up a bowl of something beige and sniffed it, nearly choking on the strong orange scent.

For a moment, CeCe didn't reply. She plunged a thermometer into the molten sugar and pulled the pot from the heat. "I'm trying some candies for Max and Ginny's wedding. I thought it could be their favor."

"That's really nice of you, but the wedding isn't for a couple of months."

Lifting a shoulder, CeCe never took her eyes off the sugar. "Yeah, but Natalie wants to see a few of them to decide what the centerpieces will look like. Now seemed as good a time as any to get cooking."

Evan looked at the clock on the wall. He had hours of nothing ahead of him and hated the notion of CeCe overdoing it. "Can I help with anything?"

He braced himself for CeCe to say no, to wave him away like she usually did. Instead, she gestured to a stack of colored papers on the counter. "Can you cut those into two-inch squares? I'm testing the wrapping as well as the candies."

With a nod, Evan washed his hands and got to work. At

first his big hands were too much for the delicate paper. A few sheets stuck to the pads of his fingers; another had fused to a blob of sugar on the counter. Finally CeCe came over and cut out a template.

"Let me show you," she said, taking the scissors and deftly cutting the shape she wanted on the first try.

When Evan reached to take the scissors, their fingers grazed and a shot of awareness jolted him. It reminded him of the time he stuck his hand in a bug zapper on a boy scout camping trip, the sensation nearly singeing him. He blindly hoped CeCe felt the charge, but she didn't show any indication that she had. Her attention was on the candy, and he needed to focus on the matter at hand. Otherwise he'd be cutting more than paper with those scissors.

Twenty minutes later, the papers were cut and CeCe poured out the last of the candy to cool. "Thanks for your help. That saved me some time." She tucked a lock of hair behind her ear and surveyed her work. A dozen rows of tiny candies shone in the fluorescent lighting. A smug look of satisfaction crossed her lovely face, and Evan had to stop himself from documenting the moment with a photo. Nothing looked as gorgeous as CeCe after a successful day in the kitchen. As far as he was concerned, she was the eighth wonder of the world.

Evan loved watching her come alive like this. Her normally gruff exterior vanished when she created sinful confections. She practically glowed, radiating a heat that brought him—and his appetite—to life. And there was a particular smile CeCe had when she cooked—her nose wrinkled and her bottom lip jutted out slightly. He'd only seen it outside of work a few times, and he'd give anything to be the reason it was on her lovely face.

"Happy to help. Is there anything I can clean up?"

CeCe shook her head and carried her pot to the dishwasher. "I've got it. You go out and be young and carefree."

Her words felt heavy to Evan, like she couldn't handle

their normal banter. CeCe loved to remind him how he was younger, but he wouldn't let it go. She wasn't that much older than him, and, frankly, he didn't care either way. Age didn't matter; it was the person who mattered.

"Well, this young and carefree guy is going home to nap and read a book. I have a feeling you're living it up more than I am." He meant to tease her, but CeCe only looked sad.

With a sigh, she turned on the dishwasher and reclined on the counter. She crossed her arms over her chest and stared down at the tiled floor. "Yeah, I guess."

Evan stepped closer and kept his voice even. "CeCe, if you need something, you know I'm here. Right?"

She kept quiet, following the grout lines on the floor with her eyes. She was a million miles away, and Evan wanted to pull her close and comfort her. Something was clearly wrong.

"Sure." CeCe offered a small smile before turning and continuing with the dishes.

Evan decided not to push things. He wished her a good night and stepped out into the chilly winter air.

The wedding invitation burned a hole through his pocket as he hopped into his beat-up SUV. He wanted to be optimistic, to RSVP for two and tell Max to save CeCe's invite for someone else. Having taken CeCe to the Christmas Jubilee Ball, he knew they would have a great time together. They'd laughed, danced, and eaten way too much. It was the best date of Evan's life. The trouble was, CeCe needed to admit that she had fun in the first place.

Evan turned the car on and waited for his K-pop tunes to blast through the speakers. Pulling out onto Main Street, he lost himself in the cheery pop music. Deep in his soul, he knew CeCe was the woman for him. He just needed to be patient and find a way for her to see it too.

CHAPTER 2

When CeCe got back to her place, she texted her friend Natalie. The candy samples were ready and CeCe needed a little girl time. She invited Natalie over for a drink, since girl time was more fun with sugar and booze. CeCe poured herself a shot of whiskey and plopped down on the couch, her feet kicked out on the coffee table. Beside her sat the whiskey bottle and the crumpled article she'd taken from the kitchen's trash. Max, bless his heart, thought that throwing the article away would save her from herself. But she wasn't beyond a little dumpster diving if the situation warranted it. *And her piece-of-crap ex coming swooping into her life certainly warranted it.*

Slugging back the whiskey, CeCe coughed at the burn before facing her past head-on. With trembling fingers, she smoothed the paper and read the article. Fortunately, it only had one picture of Eric's smug face on it, but even that was too much. Since she left Chicago, she had been very good about avoiding any reference to Eric or his growing restaurant empire. She wasn't on social media and hadn't stayed in touch with most of the Chicago crew.

The article showed that her past was about to intersect with her present, and right before Max and Ginny's wedding. The competition was open to any restaurant or pop-up with a food truck, and the list of prizes was enough to make her mouth water. The publicity alone from participating would entice diners from outside Buckeye Falls, and she couldn't argue with that much free marketing.

As CeCe finished the article, there was a knock at the door. Natalie didn't wait for CeCe to open it, letting herself in and joining CeCe on the couch. Not so long ago, familiar gestures like this would have caused her to bristle, but now she treasured having someone this close. Natalie was a friend CeCe didn't see coming, busting into her life with as much grace as a runaway freight train.

"What's up?" Natalie asked as she kicked her boots off. She was still dressed for work, her fair hair pulled into an artful bun, her designer outfit costing more than CeCe's monthly mortgage payment.

"Candy is ready. Let me show you what I've got." CeCe stood and stretched before walking over to where the boxes of candy waited for Natalie's approval. "I have butterscotch, orange cream, and caramel." She pointed at each confection as Natalie drooled.

"I'm assuming this is a taste test too? They all look stunning." Natalie snapped a few pictures on her phone before plucking one of each candy. Before she dove in, she sauntered back to the couch. With a manicured hand, she gestured to the whiskey and newspaper on the coffee table. "I'm guessing this is the real reason I'm here. Max told Ginny something was up with you."

CeCe didn't begrudge her boss his happiness, but damn, this small town and its lack of privacy. "Yeah." She sighed into her second glass of whiskey.

Natalie eyed her friend carefully, stealing another candy from the box on CeCe's lap. "Want to talk about it?" Natalie asked around a melted caramel. Covering her mouth with her hand, she groaned. "Before we dive into girl talk, it's definitely the caramels for me. I'll bring a sample for Ginny to try, but she's going to love these."

Usually praise over a recipe brought a sense of satisfaction to CeCe, but today it wasn't cutting it. She rubbed at her chest with her hand and leaned back on the couch. Since this morning, she'd had a case of heartburn she couldn't shake. She hated how her body still reacted to him, especially since he'd caused enough indigestion over the years.

The whiskey was finally doing its job, numbing the edges of her brain as she closed her eyes. She listened to the smacking sounds of Natalie devouring more sugar. She'd be buzzing off the walls by the time she left. At least she'd have the energy for her two rambunctious kiddos.

Natalie snatched the paper before CeCe could stop her and her eyes grew. "Wait a minute," she breathed. "Is this Eric? *The* Eric? As in, horrible, lying, cheating, pseudo-stalker Eric?" Natalie dropped the paper like it was on fire, nudging CeCe from her perch on the couch. "Talk to me. This isn't like you to pout and hide."

Her friend was right, but she couldn't quite articulate the problem. How do you open your heart and share the most painful memories? CeCe was the person you went to with your problems. She didn't have problems. Her life was simple—cook, eat, sleep, repeat. The only variation being bake, eat, sleep, repeat. Since moving to Buckeye Falls, her life had found a familiar and comfortable routine, and CeCe clung to it for dear life.

"Max said we're not doing the competition," CeCe finally said. She plucked a candy from the box and popped it in her mouth. The orange flavor coated her tongue as it slowly melted. "And I think Ginny might prefer the orange cream."

Natalie moved the box out of reach and poked the paper with her finger. "Don't change the subject. You're not doing the competition? That's insane."

Raising an eyebrow, CeCe turned to see her friend. "What are you talking about?"

"It's insane not to show up and show off," Natalie

declared with the certainty of a woman who truly never experienced that kind of heartbreak. "You and Max are going to join the food truck event. Weren't you already looking at trucks to rent?" Natalie waited for CeCe's sad shrug before continuing. "Exactly. Don't let this jackass put you off your game. You two are the best chefs in Central Ohio; no, likely all of Ohio. Once that idiot rolls in, he's going eat his heart out when he sees how amazing you are."

CeCe let out a deep breath; Natalie wasn't making this easy. "I thought of that already," she said, reaching a hand up to silence her friend. "But here's the thing, I don't have to show off for him. I don't need to prove anything to him. Being around Eric is going to be too—" She hesitated, feeling the lump in her throat grow three sizes. It was like trying to swallow past a grapefruit. "It's too much. I left Chicago to get away from him. Once I landed in Buckeye Falls, I found my happy place. I don't want to engage with my ex in my happy place."

Natalie huffed out a breath. "I love that this is your happy place. I sometimes take for granted how special Buckeye Falls really is."

CeCe sipped from her whiskey, debating how much of her old wounds to open. There was something to be said for keeping it all bottled up. Judging someone for their actions, or inactions, wasn't possible if no one knew the truth. But then she watched her friend, sitting there waiting on CeCe to open the Pandora's box of her dating history. It didn't seem right not to share a little more of the burden.

"I hated myself after Eric, and I think if I were honest I still hate myself *about* Eric."

Natalie eased back into her seat, resting her head in her hand. "What does that mean?" The question held no judgment, only concern, and it bolstered CeCe to open up more.

"I'm embarrassed that I fell for Eric's crap. He was a two-faced liar, and everyone knew it but me. I dated a married man for nearly a year without realizing it. I mean, how stupid could I have been?" CeCe brought her hands to her face, covering her eyes from her own story.

Natalie wrapped her arm around CeCe's shoulders, drawing her close and mumbling words of encouragement. "You didn't know, honey. And didn't you break up as soon as you found out?"

CeCe wiped at her eyes with the sleeve of her shirt, feeling the dam burst as the tears fell. "I did, but that doesn't change the outcome. I lost my career in Chicago, and I lost a part of myself. I let a man dictate my life, and that's not who I am."

"We all have a story or two from our pasts that we'd like to avoid," Natalie offered, but CeCe wasn't letting herself off the hook yet.

"Yeah, but mine literally crippled me. Nat, I was a different person. I *am* a different person now. I know I don't let people in as much, and Eric's to blame."

"You let me in, and Max. I'm pretty sure there's a cute waiter who is *dying* to have you let him in more." Natalie winked as she playfully nudged CeCe's side. "You do let people in, but you're choosey about it. Guarding your heart isn't a crime."

"Then why do I still feel like Eric took everything from me?"

Natalie rested her head on CeCe's shoulder as the tears silently fell. Natalie didn't offer any more platitudes, just rocked CeCe back and forth as they watched the light outside the window dim with sunset. A quiet hum from Natalie's purse broke the moment, and she shifted slightly to check her phone. "Ugh, I need to get home. Anthony got called into an emergency meeting with town council." She took CeCe's hand and brought it up to her lips, kissing it before cradling it against her chest. "I'm sorry. You're right; you don't have to prove anything to anyone. Least of all that asshole."

Caught off guard by Natalie's complete 180, CeCe blinked a few times. The tears would continue to fall, but she did feel slightly better after opening up to Natalie. There was a lot to work on, but CeCe didn't have to do it all tonight. "I'll remember you said that," she finally croaked. "You never say that I'm right."

Natalie released CeCe's hand and swatted at her with a pillow. "Ha, ha," she said as she got to her feet. Natalie pulled on her boots and headed toward the door. "I'll call you tomorrow. In the meantime, do me a favor?"

"Favor?" CeCe braced for impact, unsure where Natalie was going with this.

"Remember, you're allowed to be happy. Whether it's with someone or by yourself. Don't forget that, okay?"

"Happy?"

Natalie soldiered on. "Yes, happy. I know you like to be stoic, but you're allowed to be happy."

Repeating the word like a mantra, CeCe pulled a blanket from the back of the couch and curled into a ball. Now that she was alone, her muscles unclenched and the tears truly fell, ugly tears that caused her to heave with the release. She hoped the happiness would come after the tears dried, but still, she was uncertain.

It had been years since she gave Eric this type of power over her. CeCe was no-nonsense, both inside and outside the kitchen. She'd broken her rule of not dating at work with Eric, and it ended worse than she could have imagined. "Ugh," she groaned as she stood and paced into the kitchen. Few things calmed her like creating something delicious.

By nature, CeCe loved feeding people. When she cooked and baked, she got satisfaction from other people's enjoyment. But sometimes she needed to get into the kitchen and make a mess for herself—needed comfort food just for her. Opening the pantry and her fridge, she sadly realized it had been ages since she had made it to the grocery store. Messy comfort food would be a problem.

Slamming the door shut, she padded out to the living room and dug around the couch for her phone. Takeout would have to do. As she dialed her favorite pizza place's number, she heard a knock at the door. Freezing in place, she hoped she'd misheard.

"CeCe, are you home?" a familiar voice came through the front door. CeCe frantically checked her reflection and walked toward her visitor. Her eyes were red and puffy, and it was pointless to pretend she hadn't just fallen apart.

Pulling open the door, she saw Ginny, wrapped in a coat and holding a huge paper bag. "I brought you some dinner," she said with a sheepish smile.

Not wanting to be rude, CeCe stepped back for Ginny to enter. "Come on in. Your timing is actually perfect. I discovered I have no food in this house."

Ginny giggled nervously and placed the bag on the counter. "Max said you might need a few things." She kept her gaze down and emptied the bag onto the counter. CeCe recognized Max's famous cheese enchiladas and had to stifle a moan of delight. She was touched because those were Ginny's favorite too.

"Is that what I think it is?" CeCe peered into the plastic to-go box. The heavenly aroma of cumin, cheese, and lime hit CeCe square in the face, and she was a goner. "Let me get you a plate too."

Ginny held her hands up and stepped back. "No, this is a delivery service. I need to drop off another tray to Dad and Mona. I don't mean to keep you."

CeCe studied Ginny for a moment. At first, when Ginny came back into town, CeCe wasn't sure what to think. Max had been brokenhearted and pining for his ex-wife for what felt like an eternity; his loss had been a part of him. Now that they'd reconciled, CeCe saw such a change in Max. She wasn't the sentimental type, but it made her happy to see Max so happy. Plus, Ginny really did seem like a nice person.

Fidgeting, Ginny finally met CeCe's gaze and asked, "Are you all right?" CeCe appreciated Ginny's directness, even though her expression soured. "It's none of my business. Forget I said anything. I'll leave you and your dinner in peace." Stepping back, Ginny nearly tripped on her own feet. "Ack, sorry," she muttered as she made it to the door.

"Ginny, wait," CeCe called out as she met her at the threshold. "Thank you for bringing dinner, and thank Max for me."

Ginny shrugged. "You're welcome. Once we're unpacked, you need to come over to our new place. We want to throw a dinner party."

"Sounds nice," CeCe said, meaning it even though her tone was flat. Supporting Max was important to her.

"Well, uh, good night." Ginny raised her hand as she stepped into the evening.

CeCe watched her walk to her car but called out before she could leave. "Thanks, Ginny. Really, I appreciate you checking in." It was the most she could offer anyone now, but judging from Ginny's growing grin, it was enough.

For the second time that night, CeCe listened to a friend drive off into the night—to their homes with the men they loved. As CeCe heated her enchiladas, she thought about what that would look like. What would it feel like to have someone with her now, helping her set the table and open a bottle of wine? What would he be like?

Suddenly, a flash of Evan crossed her mind's eye, and CeCe gasped. She pictured him chopping vegetables while singing along to a sappy pop song, his voice never quite on key. A smile tugged at her lips at the image, but she quickly shook herself from the moment. Evan wasn't hers, and it didn't make sense to daydream about him.

But since the Christmas Jubilee, thoughts of Evan were coming fast and furious. True to his word, he'd been the perfect gentleman that night. He'd been by her side the entire time, spinning her on the dance floor, laughing with her, helping her with setting up the buffet, never losing his lopsided grin.

"Knock it off," CeCe chided herself when the microwave dinged. She pulled her dinner free and nearly ate it straight from the box. "Max, you did it again." She sighed as she settled on the couch to finish the rest of the meal.

An hour later, her eyelids heavy, CeCe dozed while a reality show played on the TV. Just as her head fell back, she heard a buzz on her cell phone. Checking the text, she saw it was from Evan. *Hope you're having a good night. Let me know if you need anything.*

Another lump formed in CeCe's throat. This time for entirely different reasons. Instead of being sad, she was happy to have someone like Evan in her life. No, that wasn't true. She was happy to have *Evan* in her life.

And that scared her half to death.

*

Evan set up his laptop on his kitchen table while a pot simmered on the stove. It was time for his weekly video call with his sisters, all three of them. They'd started the tradition when he was in college. Every week, they picked a night to eat dinner together via Zoom. Each sibling was in a different part of the Midwest.

Sophie, his oldest sister, was married with two kids and lived near Cleveland. She was the bossiest of the group and took her role as big sister very seriously. Emily, the middle sister, was recently married and pregnant, living in Indiana. Mallory, the youngest and closest to him in age, lived thirty minutes outside Buckeye Falls. They had always been the closest, and since she was also single, they banded together.

Evan poured himself a beer and scooped up some stew for dinner. He'd been trying several recipes with Max, and he was closer to the perfect sauce. Easing into his seat, he heard the familiar chimes of an incoming call. Pressing the accept button, Sophie flashed up on the screen.

"Hey, baby brother," she cooed as Evan rolled his eyes. She waved with one hand, one of her children hanging onto her other arm.

"Hey, guys." He waved back, careful not to knock over

his beer. "How are you doing? And whose arm is that?" He gestured at the screen with his fork.

"It's me, Uncle Evan," a gap-toothed mouth squealed. Jackson was the oldest, and he had recently lost his first tooth. Sophie sent nearly a hundred texts documenting the momentous event, complete with pics of bloody tissues that were better suited for a crime scene.

"How are you, Jackson? How's the tooth?" Evan took a bite of his dinner, eagerly awaiting his nephew's play-by-play. There was a reason Sophie was documenting the tooth, and it had everything to do with the kid peering into the screen.

Jackson held a grubby hand up, opening it to reveal the tooth. "I still have it, but Mommy said the tooth fairy needs it." The boy frowned, clearly discouraged it was no longer his property.

Evan laughed. "It's the way of the world, little man. You gotta do what your mom says."

"But why?" Jackson asked, looking annoyed.

"Because she's the boss," Emily chimed in, leaning back on the couch and rubbing her growing belly. Evan felt his chest tighten at the scene in front of him; another sister growing up and living her life. He was so proud of his family.

"I'm here, too!" Mallory shouted through the computer. "I'm just heating something up," she said over the beeping of a microwave.

While Sophie and Emily were currently stay-at-home moms, Mallory was an ER nurse with a nightmarish schedule. Much like Evan, she was more focused on working and setting up her own life than creating new ones.

"Hey, Mal," he greeted with a salute.

Mallory squinted into the camera, carefully assessing what everyone was eating. "It looks like Evan wins again for best dinner." She sighed as she peeled a plastic sheet off her frozen dinner. "You might need to hook me up again when I visit tomorrow. Those leftovers were the best thing I ever ate."

Evan beamed at her praise as he tucked into his stew. For twenty minutes, all talk focused on the kids and everyone's jobs. Finally, Sophie asked Evan what she asked every week. "So, Ev, any news on the job front?"

Evan tried not to let it bother him that his sisters, at least two of them, thought like their father. They wanted Evan to use his degree and "grow up," as they kept telling him. But he felt he was using his degree, only not like they wanted. Freelance work *was* work.

Taking a moment to collect himself, he sipped his beer. "There's a food truck competition coming up this spring, and I think the diner is going to enter." That wasn't necessarily true, but Evan was going to convince Max. "Plus, I'm working on a few freelance web design projects. You know, keeping busy." Evan lifted one of his shoulders as he finished his beer. If Sophie kept up with her interrogation, he'd need another one for sure.

Mallory, always his cheerleader, smiled and gave a thumbs-up. "And don't forget, tomorrow is kung fu marathon night!"

For years, more years than anyone could remember, the siblings got together and watched a kung fu movie marathon on cable. These days no one had cable anymore, but that didn't stop Evan from finding a barrage of movies on Netflix. A few clicks, and he was in kung fun heaven. Sophie and Emily were too busy, and far away, but he and Mallory kept the kung fu tradition alive. They'd stock up on food and drinks and spend a whole night watching their favorite films.

"You're damn right it is. I'm all ready for you, Mal." Evan winked and collected his dishes.

Emily offered a playful eye roll as she adjusted herself on the couch. She grimaced and rubbed her back, and Evan wished he was there to help her—even though he wouldn't know what to do.

"How much longer until your due date?" Sophie asked,

reading everyone's minds.

"Another six weeks, and, frankly, I don't know how much more I can stand." As it usually did, all conversation turned to pregnancy talk. Growing up in a houseful of women made Evan tough, and he never felt squeamish with these lines of conversations. However, tonight he felt more distracted. He couldn't get CeCe out of his head. Not that it was anything new. She usually filled his thoughts when they weren't together, but tonight especially. Something was up, and it was killing him.

Pulling Evan from his musings, Sophie asked, "Anyone special in your life, Ev?" That was another one of his sisters' favorite topics: his non-existent love life. Evan felt like if he could find a girlfriend, it would take the heat off the job concerns. But he was hardly going to pour his heart out to his bloodthirsty sisters.

Emily patted her belly and sighed. "By your age, I'd already met Zach. Don't let time pass you by," she said in a playful, yet warning, tone.

Mallory scoffed, "Um, hello? I'm older than Evan and I have no prospects." She raised an eyebrow that made Evan squirm in his seat. Mallory was the baby girl, but she was not a doormat. "What about my ovaries? Why are you always busting Evan's balls?"

Sophie scowled and sipped from her wine glass carefully before responding. "We know you're busy with your career, Mal. You still have time."

Mallory wasn't satisfied with their sister's answer. Evan could practically feel Mallory's irritation radiating through the screen. "I wish you both would come down to Buckeye Falls with me. If you saw some of the things Evan was doing, you'd change your tune."

Both Sophie and Emily had the decency to look embarrassed, since Evan had made it clear there was always an open invitation to Buckeye Falls … and the diner … and his life. He was an open book, and even though his family didn't like the genre, it was his book. He owned every chapter.

Just when Evan was about to thank Mallory, she took things a step too far. "Besides, it's not like Evan isn't trying to get a girlfriend. She's not ready yet."

Emily perked up, pointing toward a corner of her screen. "So you do have someone in mind? I knew it! That one time I called you, I heard a woman's voice in the background."

Evan said, "That was Helen. She's in her fifties and happily married. You're way off base." He couldn't fight the grimace at the notion of dating his older coworker.

Mallory was like a dog with a bone. "Ev, come on. You have a major crush on CeCe. No point denying it."

Mallory had been out to the diner several times before. The first day she saw CeCe and Evan together, she'd hounded him for weeks about his obvious feelings. Evan felt the top of his ears turn crimson, but he didn't speak up.

Sophie tapped her lip with a manicured finger. "Is that the girl you took to that Christmas dance?"

Emily and Mallory both chimed in, "Yes."

It wasn't worth pretending any longer.

"Okay, fine. Yes, I have feelings for CeCe. We're friends, and I'm not going to push the issue." That was a bald-faced lie, and everyone knew it. He watched his sisters share looks that could make any grown man shrink into his shoes. Fortunately for Evan, he was a master at dodging their scowls.

"Does she know how you feel?" Sophie asked, shooing Jackson away from the screen.

Emily, always the romantic, practically had hearts in her eyes. "Tell her how you feel, Ev! I'm sure she feels the same way; maybe she's shy?"

Mallory and Evan both laughed at that, knowing CeCe was anything but shy. "That's not the case, trust me." Mallory smirked, wiping a tear from her eye. "Our little brother made it perfectly clear how he feels about her."

Completely caught off guard, Evan rubbed the back of his neck. "I did?" Evan asked, perplexed.

LIBBY KAY

"Oh yeah." Mallory waved him off, a carefree gesture that belied the pounding of Evan's heart. "Every time I see you two together, you're going out of your way to make her life easier. Not to mention, I see the way you two are checking each other out. She's interested, but she doesn't want to be."

Now *that* was news to Evan. CeCe was checking him out? She was interested? Right at that moment, he wished for mind reading powers. Women were complicated, more so than he originally assumed. "I don't think CeCe's into me."

Mallory soldiered on. "It's the age thing. I'm sure of it."

Sophie asked, "Age thing?"

At the same time, Emily gasped. "She's younger?"

Evan reclined in his chair and pulled a second beer from the fridge. He could tell this interrogation wasn't likely to end anytime soon. "No, she's older than me. I'm pretty sure she's your age, Em."

Emily smiled, but Sophie's face fell. "She's thirty? Isn't that a little old?"

Evan leaned forward in his seat, a flash of hurt crossing his features. "Just about thirty, which is not old; it's perfect. I respect CeCe's extra years. She's taught me so much in the kitchen." His twenty-fifth birthday was only a month away, and Evan could not wait to gain a year on CeCe. While it didn't bother him, it was too much for CeCe sometimes.

The two elder sisters exchanged a look of confusion, but Mallory chimed in, "She's the pastry chef at the diner. You should try some of her desserts. They are literally sinful. I really believe she's the reason I'm ten pounds heavier." Mallory nodded sagely, as if that was all the validation CeCe needed.

Deciding he was done falling down the rabbit hole with his sisters, Evan wrapped things up. "Well, this has been stimulating, but I need to get ready for an early day. That fort isn't going to build itself."

Mallory clapped and cheered. "Hooray, I'll be over right

after my shift. I can't wait." Evan smiled at his sister's happy expression. He treasured their times together, knowing she'd eventually follow in Sophie and Emily's footsteps. It wasn't that he didn't keep in touch with his older sisters, but it wasn't the same. He didn't begrudge them their lives; he merely acknowledged they were different from his in a way they couldn't relate to.

Emily waved. "It was great seeing you all. Ev, keep us posted on CeCe."

"Only if you keep us posted on baby updates," Evan countered.

Finally, their video call ended and the sisters sent their love. Before Evan set up his place for Mallory's visit and the movie marathon, he shot CeCe a quick text to check in on her. He hoped she wouldn't mind, but he needed her to know he was there if she needed anything.

After what Mallory had said, Evan spent an hour dissecting moments with CeCe. Stolen glances, brushing past each other, a lingering touch; he was trying to add all of these chance interactions into something real, something he could claim. He had always thought the feelings and attraction were one-sided, but maybe CeCe did see the potential in him as more than a sidekick?

If there was anything Evan knew about CeCe, it was that she wouldn't be rushed to do anything she wasn't ready to do, or wanted to do. He would bide his time, and that wouldn't be a problem. Because CeCe would be worth the wait.

CHAPTER 3

CeCe stood in the diner's kitchen, surrounded by open canisters of flour, sugar, yeast, and salt. This was her element, and yet, in that moment she had no inspiration. Eric's competition gutted her. Usually, she relished any opportunity to bake and show off her skills. That competitive nature only grew when the diner was involved. This place had been her sanctuary. But Eric coming to Ohio, coming close to her safe space, dug under her skin.

Max came out of his office, head down, staring at his phone. He and Ginny's wedding was fast approaching, and he'd been more distracted than normal. "Heading out?" CeCe asked, rearranging the canisters in front of her by size.

Max nodded, not looking up until he reached the door. Finally, he turned and took in the quiet scene in front of him. Tucking his cell phone back in his pocket, he stepped up to the counter and rapped his knuckles on the cool metal surface. "Want to talk about it?" he asked casually.

He could read her like a book. If she was staying late to bake, she'd have the kitchen in a state of chaos by this point. Not that CeCe's baking style was messy, but it was organized chaos. She knew what she was doing, where things needed to be, and when to stop kneading or mixing.

She was a master of her domain, but right now she didn't feel masterful at all. She felt exposed and uncomfortable. Fiddling with the buttons on her chef's tunic, CeCe shrugged. "Not really." She sighed, pushing the cinnamon shaker away. She had no inspiration and forcing the moment would result in subpar baking.

Max rested his elbows on the counter. "We don't need to do this competition—" He let his words cut off, seeming uncertain how to continue.

CeCe forced a smile for Max. He was very important to her, and she wouldn't let her past heartbreak ruin the diner's future. "I've been thinking about it, and maybe we should do it."

Max slowly nodded and looked around the kitchen for a moment before finding his words. His stammer loved to rear its ugly head. Since Ginny came back into his life, his confidence was back, even if sometimes his words faltered. "Y-y-you don't have to do anything for this, CeCe. We don't have to compete, or I can whip something up with Evan. That idiot has no pull over us. Okay? We can pretend the competition isn't even happening. No one would bat an eye."

Rubbing the spot above her heart, CeCe took a deep breath. Her voice caught on her words as she spoke. "I'm going to figure this out. I won't be the reason we don't get to compete. The diner deserves to show off. This is a huge opportunity." She meant what she said, but the words still tasted bitter on her tongue, like when coffee sits on the burner too long.

Max reached forward and covered her shaking hand with his. It was warm and firm, the grasp of a true friend. "You can if you want t-t-to. But do it for you. D-don't do it for us."

Feeling tears welling behind her eyes, CeCe shook her head and went back to her task of reorganizing the canisters. Max patted her arm before stepping outside, leaving her alone with her thoughts. The diner was eerily quiet, which usually calmed her. During open hours, music piping through the dining room speakers, the sound of metal clanging and glasses clinking throughout each meal. Now only the gentle hum of the refrigerator kept her company.

CeCe squared her shoulders and walked toward the far wall, where a small rack held her and Max's favorite cookbooks. Each book was stuffed with scraps of paper, updating or tweaking different recipes. She kept a handful of spiral notebooks, each holding recipes from the different restaurants she'd worked at over her decade-long career. One purple notebook without a title on the cover held a lot of memories, a lot of flavors of her past.

With a shaking hand, CeCe plucked the notebook from the shelf. She flipped it open and already felt her mouth tip up at the corners. Some of her first tart recipes were inside this book, along with a double chocolate mousse and the first iteration of her famous cheesy bites. Lost in the moment, too busy looking at the swirling scrawl over recipes that she'd reworked, she didn't hear the back door open.

"It's nice to see you smiling," a familiar voice said from the doorway.

"Ah!" CeCe shrieked as the notebook tumbled to the floor, a dozen scraps of paper fluttering around her. "Evan, you scared the hell out of me." She splayed her hand over her chest and tried to slow her racing heart.

Evan flushed and held up his hands. "I didn't mean to scare you. I came by to pick up a few things. Max said no one was here, and I didn't think to call out." He knelt in front of her and scooped up the slips of paper. Carefully, he pushed them into a neat stack and handed it to her, who quickly shoved them inside the notebook before thrusting it back onto the shelf.

She'd be lying if she wasn't annoyed with Max. He knew darn well she was there. He had some unusual fascination with them, but most days she shrugged it off. Evan was a nice guy, but that was it. *It had to be it.* She was nearly thirty now; what was the point of drooling over Evan? She was a grown-up with grown-up problems, like an ex she couldn't seem to shake. He was still finding his way in the world. There was no point getting in Evan's way.

Especially now, when she felt lost.

Evan was still talking, but CeCe missed what he'd said. Shaking her head, she asked, "Sorry. What was that?" She watched him disappear into the walk-in fridge and come out with a box tucked under one arm. "You're stealing from the diner now?" She laughed, understanding he'd sooner walk across hot coals than steal anything.

Evan shook his head, a few of his longer curls falling over his forehead. His hair always looked perfectly tousled, like one of the '90s Abercrombie & Fitch advertisements. Not that she spent time thinking about Evan or his hair. Nope, never.

Evan wiggled the box. "It's the leftover soup and some things Max was helping me with. Tonight's the big movie marathon, so I needed to get my provisions."

"Movie marathon?" CeCe asked, her attention on the growing smile on Evan's face. He looked so pure, so happy at that moment. While she felt thrown in a million directions, Evan's attention was solely on her.

"Yeah, I'm hosting a kung fu movie marathon. Happens every year around this time. When I was a kid, my sisters and I would watch our favorite movies in the spring. We'd spend a whole weekend just lying in our pajamas and eating until we puked." He hesitated and chuckled. "Well, I guess I was the only one who puked." He looked down at the box in his arms and grinned. "My plans consist of nothing but eating and watching terribly amazing movies all weekend." He beamed as she forced a matching smile.

CeCe waved him toward the door, wanting to be alone with her rambling thoughts. Evan was too buoyant right now, and she'd sour his mood. "I'll let you get to it." She turned and started pulling spices to put back in the drawers. Creativity wasn't coming, and she didn't want to taint any creations with her current temperament. Her plans now were to go home and hide until she felt human again. *However long that took.*

Evan watched her for a moment. "You're not baking tonight?" He frowned, putting his box down and helping her carry the heavier items. As he slid the flour onto a higher shelf, he stepped back and studied her. CeCe looked tired, but she feared it was worse than she'd thought when she saw Evan's expression. "What's going on?" he asked, crossing his arms over his chest.

Bless him. He worried about her. "Nothing is going on. Just not feeling it tonight." She wiped her hands on her tunic and shrugged it off to hang by their aprons.

Evan picked up his box and held the back door open. "Good, if you're done here you can come with me." He gave her room to walk through the exit before punching in the alarm code and locking the door with his free hand. "I have plenty of food and my sister canceled at the last minute. I can't have kung fu fort time alone. It'll be depressing."

CeCe chuckled. "Do I want to know what kung fu fort time is?" She rubbed her arms in the chill of the March air. Buckeye Falls was not quite ready to give up on winter yet.

Evan gestured toward his car. "Follow me. I'll show you."

Going home with Evan was a bad idea on so many levels. They were friends, and she didn't want to lead him on. Since they went to the Christmas Jubilee together, CeCe felt Evan warming to her even more. She'd be lying if she didn't feel some of the same butterflies, but she wasn't looking for those feelings tonight. Or ever, if she had anything to say about it.

"That's okay. You go and enjoy your martial arts marathon … and whatever a fort is."

Evan's eyes danced with mischief as he stepped closer. He lowered his voice and asked, "You're a little curious, aren't you?"

"Nope," CeCe said, letting the *P* pop. "Go do your fort

thing, and I'll see you tomorrow for the brunch rush." She stepped toward her car but stopped when she heard Evan come up behind her.

"You're totally curious," he teased. "What are you doing tonight?" He held her door open as she slid into the driver's seat.

CeCe fastened her seat belt and looked up into Evan's warm gaze. He was so relaxed, so easy to be around. It would be so simple to follow him home and pretend for a few hours that she could be with him. That she was what he needed, and he was what she needed. But she had a lot of mental baggage to unpack. "I'm busy," she said, trying to pull the door closed.

Evan kept his hand on the door. "Busy with?" he prodded. At first, CeCe didn't respond. She couldn't think of anything that wouldn't sound fake or lame. "I'm guessing you're not baking tonight, since I watched you pack up. There's no wedding planning tonight, so that's out."

CeCe bristled under his knowing gaze. "I have a life outside of the diner and wedding planning, you know."

"I don't doubt it. I just don't think you do *tonight*, meaning you can join me for dinner and the best fort you've ever seen. Come on, CeCe, don't make a guy beg."

Against her will, CeCe's stomach growled, and she covered it with her hand. Evan beamed and wiggled the box again. "Sounds like you're hungry. I have dinner for two right here. Please, CeCe. I can't eat alone in my fort. It'll break my heart."

CeCe gave in, knowing it would be pointless not to. Evan was persistent, and he wouldn't take no for an answer. "Fine." She huffed. "But only for dinner. Then you and your fort will have the night alone."

Evan winked. "You'll stay for at least a couple of movies. The power of the fort is strong." CeCe scoffed, but Evan was undeterred. "Follow me," he said as he gently closed her door.

CeCe watched him bound toward his old SUV and place

the box inside. Maybe she checked him out while he leaned into his car, but she'd never admit it. He wasn't hard on the eyes by any stretch of the imagination. But his heart was open, and she didn't want to break it. He had the whole world at his feet, and she wouldn't pull him into her drama. "I hope you know what you're doing," CeCe said to herself as she followed Evan to his place.

*

Evan vibrated with excitement as he drove to his apartment. The light of CeCe's headlights shone steadily in his rearview mirror, and he couldn't believe his good luck. When Mallory called to cancel, he'd been so disappointed.

Mallory got called into work when there was a major highway accident. Evan didn't fault Mallory for her job, but he was gutted at the prospect of spending the night alone. Despite the canceled plans, Evan really liked his life. He loved working at the diner, especially as his repertoire of recipes grew. Poached eggs, hearty stews, and even basic bread were now old hats to Evan.

He supplemented his diner income with freelance jobs creating websites. He started it as a hobby in college but found he could make a few hundred bucks with every website he developed. In his dreams, he could snag a job with Natalie and Ginny at their event firm, but he was biding his time. He understood they saw him as the young waiter, but he was a man with a plan. No one knew that yet, but they would in time.

Pulling into the parking lot, he said a silent prayer of thanks that he had tidied up his place in preparation for Mallory. Not that he usually lived in filth, but it was definitely cleaner than usual. CeCe parked behind him and hopped out of her car. She took in the modest apartment building, which sat on the east side of Buckeye Falls. Evan rented the upper unit for a steal, and he was gratified to have his own space.

"Follow me," he greeted CeCe as he took the stairs two at a time. Using his elbow, he turned the front doorknob and walked inside.

CeCe obeyed and raised an eyebrow. "You don't lock your doors?"

Evan laughed. "Are you new to Buckeye Falls? What are they going to do, steal my air mattress and cheap beer?"

Letting the door close behind them, Evan headed to the kitchen and let CeCe take in her surroundings. Her jaw dropped when she saw his fort, and Evan nearly burst with pride. "You weren't kidding, this is an actual fort." CeCe toed off her shoes and padded into the living room.

The apartment was open concept, with the dining room and living room being one big space. At the moment, the TV was front and center, and the couch was pushed back into the dining room. An air mattress was inflated and positioned right in front of the TV. There were blankets and nearly a dozen pillows on and around the mattress. The coffee table flanked one side and had a six-pack and a bowl of popcorn.

"Take a seat—I'll bring in dinner. Help yourself to a beer," Evan offered over his shoulder.

CeCe eased onto the edge of the mattress. The far side kicked up under her weight, but she didn't notice. "You normally live like this?" she asked as she tried to move a pillow covered in sequins to the side.

Evan chuckled as he opened his box. He and Max had made a new soup recipe that he brought home in the hopes of impressing Mallory. She understood why Evan wanted to find his own way, even if their other sisters didn't. When he told her he was learning to cook, she was excited to try what he'd learned so far.

Pouring the soup into the waiting pot, Evan turned on the heat and went back to getting everything set for dinner. He carried out napkins and utensils and found CeCe clutching one of the pillows, unsure of where to go.

"This will not do," Evan said as he propelled himself and

gave CeCe a gentle shove to her shoulder. She yelped and fell back on the mattress, which bobbed with her weight.

"Hey!" CeCe's legs kicked up, the pillow bounding across the floor.

Evan stepped around and gingerly flopped on his side of the air mattress. This time CeCe bobbed in a different direction and started laughing, a real laugh that crinkled the corners of her eyes and made Evan feel ten feet tall. "To answer your question," he said, shifting his weight so she fell toward him. "I don't normally live like this. I did this for Mallory. But sitting here alone would have been ridiculous, so thank you for humoring me."

Before CeCe could respond, he stood up, letting her settle back on her elbows. "Good to know," she said, steadying herself.

Evan's steps faltered as he saw her, smiling, relaxed in his home. Clearing his throat, he nearly sprinted away before he said something stupid. The tips of his ears were so hot with nerves, he was surprised there wasn't smoking billowing from his head.

From the kitchen, Evan heard CeCe unmute the TV. He'd cued up another movie before heading out for food. The familiar Chinese narration floated around the apartment, and he was glad to have already turned on the subtitles. After portioning out the soup, he carefully sat on the air mattress and handed CeCe her dinner. "You'll have to let me know what you think."

He trusted CeCe on a lot of issues, but being honest about food was at the top of the list. She dipped her spoon into the bowl and sniffed before taking a bite. Her eyes fluttered closed as she savored. A groan of what Evan hoped was pleasure had him pulling at his collar.

"Evan, this is amazing, truly."

His already flushed cheeks burst into a deep crimson. "Really? You're not just being nice?"

CeCe covered her mouth as she snorted with laughter. "When was the last time I was nice? Especially about food?

I would never let anyone eat, or make, bad food if I can help it." She drew her spoon back through the bowl and helped herself to a greedy bite.

Transfixed, Evan watched CeCe's mouth as she chewed. He always found women's lips captivating, but CeCe took it to a whole new level.

"Thanks," he said as he eased back onto his half of the mattress. He tried not to shift her too much as she ate, but his weight dipped her a few inches closer. Not that he was complaining, and fortunately she didn't seem to mind. He pointed to a plate of bread by her side. "There's some of your sourdough. Max said I could take it home."

Not waiting, CeCe took a slice and dropped it into her bowl. She leaned closer to Evan and stuck a piece in his. She was so close, Evan could smell vanilla on her skin. He never knew if it was her perfume or hours baking every day, but she always smelled like vanilla.

For the rest of dinner, the pair watched the movie in companionable silence. Evan could have recited each line from the subtitles and attempted half the stunts, but he found himself watching CeCe's reactions more. She was drawn in, her eyes darting across the screen as another fight scene began. Her shoulders tensed as the fights grew longer, and he couldn't help but smile when she sighed as the winner stood over the fallen.

"It's addicting, isn't it?" he asked when the first movie wrapped. CeCe's empty bowl sat in her lap and she blinked as Evan took it. "Dessert?" he asked without waiting for a reply. He retrieved a small container of chocolate peanut butter fudge he'd made that morning. It wouldn't be as good as what CeCe made, but when he'd been planning for Mallory, he had known she would love it.

CeCe took the small plate of fudge and rolled when Evan got back onto the air mattress. They both laughed as he took a fallen piece of fudge and held it out for her to eat. It was an intimate gesture he'd thought about doing a million times, but he was surprised by his own boldness.

"Try it." His voice came out hoarse, like it had been run over a cheese grater.

To her credit, CeCe didn't scoff or pull back. Instead, she leaned in and ate the candy right from his fingers. He felt the heat of her breath on his thumb and had to gulp for air. Having her this close, in his kung fu fort no less, was messing with his brain. And, unfortunately, his heart.

CeCe's eyes closed, her head falling back as the confection melted on her tongue. A moment later, she blinked and snagged another candy from the plate. Evan tossed a square in his mouth and was pleased to find the texture smooth and not grainy.

"This is really good. You made this?" she asked.

"Don't sound too surprised." He laughed as he handed her a third piece. CeCe ravenously chewed through the other piece in her mouth.

Covering her lips with her hand, she finished chewing and sighed contentedly. "Seriously, you made this?" she asked, pointing to the now empty plate. "Where did you learn how to boil the sugar like that? There was no graininess, and the texture was smooth and creamy."

Evan reached back to put the plate on the floor before turning onto his side. Resting his head on his hand, he looked at CeCe as she licked her fingers clean. If he died at that moment and went to heaven, he doubted it would be better than what he saw right now.

CeCe fluffed up her pillow and mirrored his pose, facing him only six inches apart. "I mean it, where did you get the recipe?"

"I got it from one of your notebooks, actually. Mallory loves fudge, and Max suggested I check out your recipes."

CeCe's gaze unfocused for a moment, but she recovered quickly. "Which one?" she asked casually, her finger trailing over a pillow.

Evan scratched his chin and tried to remember. It might have been the purple one he rarely saw CeCe use. "I think it was the purple one, with the curled edges." A shadow flitted across her face and was gone in an instant. She didn't say anything at first, and Evan feared he'd overstepped. "I'm sorry. I didn't mean to use your books without asking."

Recovering, CeCe reached out and tucked a fallen curl behind Evan's ear. He felt her touch from his hairline down to his curling toes. There was a strong possibility he would combust. "It's fine," she whispered, letting her hand slowly fall back to her stack of pillows. "You did a great job with it."

The next movie in the cue started automatically, and a loud fight scene jolted them back to the moment. CeCe rolled onto her back, her legs fidgeting. When she couldn't get comfortable, Evan grabbed some pillows and propped them up beneath her head. "Here," he said as he handed her a bright pink pillow covered in glittery hearts.

Holding up the offending object, CeCe laughed. "There has to be a story here," she said through a fit of giggles. "This is the girliest thing I've ever seen."

"You should see the matching bedspread," Evan deadpanned as CeCe dissolved into laughter. She hugged the pillow to her body as she shook the mattress with her teasing.

"You're kidding, right?" she asked, swiping away at a tear on her cheek.

Evan's heart expanded at the sight of her enjoying herself, even if it was at his expense. "Unfortunately, no. My niece, Lucy, gave me the set as a graduation gift from college. I don't have the heart to get rid of them, and I only use them when she visits with my nephew, Jackson."

CeCe held out the pillow and studied it with fresh eyes. Her laughter subsided, but her smile grew. "You really are a nice guy, Evan. Keeping something so silly because it means a lot to your niece."

Evan bristled. For some reason with CeCe, being kind was an ailment to fix. Now was not the time or the place to defend himself, so he simply stepped away. "I'm going to get another beer," he announced to the room as he strode into the kitchen. Usually if CeCe mentioned his nice attitude, a dig at their age gap wasn't far behind.

CeCe followed him, boxing him in by the fridge. "You're mad at me, aren't you?" she asked, clearly perplexed. "You shouldn't have these pillows out if you're going to be sensitive."

Evan spun around, two beers clenched in his hands. Slamming the fridge closed with his elbow, he handed a beer to CeCe. "Before you ask, I'm old enough to buy my own beer," he snapped as he headed back to the couch. He couldn't find a dignified way to crawl onto the mattress when he was this angry.

CeCe joined him and tossed the pillow onto the bed before sitting on the couch. Her frame was so small, she fit on just one of the cushions. She tucked her legs under herself and studied him for a moment before saying, "So you're upset I said you're nice? I don't think I mentioned you being young this time."

"*Younger*," Evan corrected. "You can tease me all you want for my niece's things. I love her and the goofy crap she buys me, but I'm not a child, and I'm not always happy and nice. Damn it, CeCe. I'm nearly twenty-five. We're only a few years apart."

CeCe frowned and took a pull from her beer. Her neck muscles worked as she swallowed, her entire body radiated with nervous energy. "Well, I'm about to turn thirty, so you'll forgive me if I point out the obvious."

Evan was alert and on edge. "And what's so obvious?"

CeCe took another sip and placed her beer on the coffee table. "We're in different stages of life. That's what's obvious."

"Different stages of life? We have similar jobs and live in the same town. How are we in different stages of life?" Evan slammed his beer down, clearly done tiptoeing around the age conversation.

"I'm older," CeCe said, as if that explained everything.

"You're a little older than me, so what? You're hardly on

your way to the nursing home." He scoffed as he rolled his eyes.

CeCe swept one of her arms across the room. "You have a fort in your living room. An actual pillow fort. Evan, I wouldn't do that."

Crossing his arms over his chest, he stared her down. "And that's why you're not having any fun right now. You can't see a world where building the occasional pillow fort is a fun way to spend an evening."

CeCe raised an eyebrow. "How often do you build pillow forts?" she asked, as if it was the most normal question to ask a person.

Without missing a beat, Evan replied, "Twice a year. Now, during kung fu marathon weekend, and once again in the summer when my niece and nephew visit. I think that's a perfectly reasonable timeline of fort building." For a few moments, CeCe didn't answer, just watched Evan as he calmly awaited her reply. "Why does my age bother you so much? Is that the only reason you won't go out with me?"

Evan was impressed with his own boldness, but he was sick of pretending he wasn't interested. He was so tired of seeing CeCe and not being able to touch her, to comfort her while she was clearly going through a tough time. He could be her support … if only she'd let him.

CeCe stiffened and pulled back. "We are not going there now." She sighed, looking for her beer.

"Why not? You never talked about your feelings in a pillow fort before?" he asked. "What a boring life that must be," he mused, looking around at the space he loved and the woman he was crushing on.

CeCe's teeth gritted together and she squared her shoulders. "My life is not boring," she spat. "I have a very exciting life."

"What was the most exciting thing you did recently?"

CeCe looked around, as if the answer was hiding under a stack of blankets. "I don't know, but what about you? What's the most exciting thing you've done recently?"

Not missing a beat, Evan leaned closer and shoved CeCe back. She exhaled into the pillows and sputtered as she got on her knees. Before she could respond, Evan hopped down onto the air mattress, sending her rolling toward the TV. He picked up the pink pillow and playfully tossed it at her, watching her bat it away and laugh in disbelief. She swatted a lock of her hair off her face and blinked at him.

"I had a pillow fight in my fort," he said, lobbing another pillow at her. "That's the most exciting thing I've done recently." He pulled the blanket from under her and watched as she rolled onto the floor.

Now she was laughing and trying to get up on her knees. A look of unadulterated joy crossed her before she grabbed two pillows and jumped, sending Evan back on his elbows. He barked out a laugh as she threw a pillow straight at his head. Dodging the second pillow, he scooped up another and threw it at her. She batted it away and bounced until he lost his balance. As he tried to grab the sequin pillow, she snatched it from his grasp and threw it at him with surprising accuracy.

Feeling the pillow corner hit his eye, he flailed and fell back on the bed. He covered his eyes in mock horror and shouted, "My eye!"

CeCe stopped her celebratory dance long enough to ensure he wasn't permanently blinded, her heart kicking up in concern. "Oh crap, are you okay?" She barely got her question out before Evan grabbed her forearms and turned her onto her back. He positioned her between his legs and walloped her with the softest pillow he had. Her expression shifted again when she realized what he'd done, and she reached out to tickle his sides.

Evan was probably the most ticklish person in the Midwest and quickly tried to get away, but it was no use. CeCe latched onto his bicep and pulled him down onto the floor. The force of his fall caused her to bounce in the air and land on top of him. They were both laughing and catching their breath when he realized she was straddling him.

CeCe's hair fell over her eyes, and Evan reached up to tuck it behind her ear. Their faces were barely two inches apart, and he felt her breath on his lips. Her eyes darkened, and if he lifted his head slightly they would be kissing. Her lips looked satin smooth and would taste like beer and chocolate. Undoubtedly, it would be the best kiss of his life.

But Evan wanted to kiss CeCe when she was ready for him, not when she was clearly going through a tough time. He would be her friend first, like he always had been. "To answer your question, I'm more than okay." Making a show of rapidly blinking his uninjured eye, he held his breath as she inched closer. His body reacted to the feel of her on him, and he prayed she didn't notice. The last thing he wanted was to make her uncomfortable.

CeCe rolled off him and sighed as she tossed one more pillow at him. "So who won?"

Evan propped up on his elbows and took a moment to collect himself. "I'd say it was a tie."

CeCe looked incredulous. "A tie? I clearly had you pinned there." She gestured to his side of the mattress.

"Pinned? Looks like I'm free as a bird, doesn't it?" He flapped his arms in the air and watched her brows draw down. It was the same face she made when she was deep in thought in the kitchen. The look was determined and thoughtful, and right now the hottest thing Evan had ever seen.

Before he could prepare, CeCe lunged at him and threw a pillow at his face. He ducked before it could hit its target and pulled her down underneath him, pinning her with his arms. "Now who's pinned?" he asked, breathless from the feel of her under him again.

"No fair. You cheated." CeCe panted but didn't pull away.

"My fort, my rules," Evan replied with a wink.

Much to Evan's surprise and delight, CeCe lifted her head and planted a soft kiss on his cheek. "Your fort, your rules. I begrudgingly forfeit, but I reserve the right to a rematch."

Evan's face tingled where she'd kissed him, and he contemplated never washing his face again. The kiss print felt like a brand, and he was more than happy to save the evidence of their night together. "When's the rematch?" he asked, steadying her in his arms. The sensation of CeCe was almost too much, and he had to focus on breathing.

CeCe flashed a devilish grin. "Considering you probably have this air mattress up twenty-four-seven, I'm guessing anytime I want." She threw one more pillow for good measure before excusing herself to the bathroom.

Evan laid on his back and listened to CeCe's footfalls disappear down the hallway, and he smiled to himself. There was no way he'd be able to be in this fort without thinking of her. He owed Mallory a thousand dollars for canceling tonight. He also owed his heart an apology. Without a shadow of a doubt, he'd officially fallen for CeCe, and he feared it was bound to end in heartbreak.

CHAPTER 4

CeCe clutched the edge of the sink and stared at her reflection in Evan's bathroom mirror. Her cheeks were flushed and her hair was a haphazard mess, but she didn't look bad. She looked happy, alive. Reaching a trembling hand to her lips, she touched the skin that was just on Evan's stubbled cheek. What had she been thinking? She can't kiss her coworkers like it was nothing. *Right?*

But Evan wasn't merely a coworker; he was a good friend. A friend who clearly wanted more. Standing in his tiny bathroom with the sounds of kung fu fighting coming through the door, CeCe felt a sense of contentment she hadn't felt in years. She trusted Evan fully. He wouldn't do anything she didn't want, but she couldn't abuse that trust. He deserved more than that.

Dabbing a little cold water on her neck, she stepped into the hallway and glanced into his empty bedroom. The linens were navy blue, the walls covered in pictures of family and friends. For a moment, she imagined Evan making the bed in girly pink linens, a sweet gesture for his niece whom he obviously treasured. CeCe had never seen him in a fatherly sense before, and she had to admit it caused her stomach to flip in a not-so-unpleasant manner.

"Everything all right?" Evan asked behind her, reaching out with a glass of water.

CeCe took the water and sipped greedily while she collected her thoughts. Her poker face was hardly legendary. "Yes, thanks for this. I'll need to sober up before I head home."

Evan frowned, but he didn't talk her out of it either. He hitched a thumb over his shoulder toward the living room. "The next movie started. It's a short one. Want to watch it with some popcorn?"

CeCe should say no, but the offer was too sweet, and she wasn't ready to go home to her empty place. "Maybe just the first fight scenes?" she suggested.

Evan turned and walked back to the living room, his head shaking. "No one can resist Bruce Lee in this one. You'll see one scene and want to watch them all."

True to his word, CeCe had been captivated by the entire film, never looking away. She rested her head on a stack of pillows and munched on popcorn for over an hour before the credits rolled, when she realized she was covered in crumbs and half asleep.

"You win. That was amazing." CeCe dusted some crumbs off her chest and reached for her now-empty water glass. Before she could ask, Evan jumped to his feet and returned with a full glass and a couple of beers in his hands.

"At the risk of pushing my luck, the sequel starts next. Care to join me for one more?" he asked, a hopeful expression on his handsome face. It wasn't that she hadn't studied Evan's face before, but never like this. His normal carefree demeanor seemed more relaxed in his home, his cheeks flushed from his drink and the close quarters. A few flecks of golden stubble peppered his jawline, and she fought the urge to reach up and touch him again. *Slow down, CeCe!*

CeCe frowned but took a beer. "What part of sobering up didn't you understand? You're very persuasive, you know."

Evan winked and clinked their bottles together. When the opening credits scrolled across the screen, CeCe knew she did, in fact, want to stay and watch them. Damn Evan and his pillow forts, but this was turning into a wonderful evening.

As the next movie started, she and Evan found themselves sharing a pillow stack, their heads touching as they sprawled on the air mattress. Occasionally, she felt the mattress move with his exhales, the sensation relaxing her more than she expected. At a tense part of the movie, her hand reached out and clutched his, winding their digits together. Ten minutes later, their fingers were still intertwined in a not-so-unpleasant handhold. His skin was surprisingly smooth for someone who worked with his hands all day.

"You'll love this scene," he whispered, bringing goosebumps to her flesh. Leaning closer, she felt the tips of his hair tickle her skin. The feather-light sensation lulled her further into a state of near-hypnosis. Either oblivious or uncaring of her reactions, Evan soldiered on. "That actor was the bad guy in the first one but look how much better his fighting style is now."

CeCe hummed and listened as Evan described not only the actors and their fighting styles, but also the history of certain film franchises. He never lacked enthusiasm at work, but it was fun to hear him discuss something new; something he was clearly passionate about. His voice was steady, almost in tune with her heartbeats, and she found her eyelids getting heavy.

She was no lightweight when she drank, but tonight had been the first time since the announcement of Eric's competition that she was calm and truly happy. Her brain finally stopped overanalyzing her past choices and Eric's past behaviors, even if only temporarily. In this moment, she was simply CeCe LaRue.

Laying there, with Evan's steady, warm presence by her side and her hand held firmly in his, she wondered what life would be like if she gave the guy a chance. Thinking back to their night at the Christmas Jubilee Ball, it had been near perfect. Could everyday have that same feeling if she let herself get serious about Evan?

Thinking of their times at the diner together, CeCe couldn't think of any negative interactions between them. She'd always written him off as another young waiter trying to make a few bucks on the way to his real life. She knew that not everyone working in restaurants wanted to make it a career, so she'd perfected putting up barriers with the wait staff. What was the point of starting a friendship when the other person left after the season? Granted, it occasionally gave her the reputation of a grump, but she wasn't worried about that.

Selfishly, she didn't know if she could leave the diner and Buckeye Falls when things inevitably went south. And they would go south. Women like her weren't built for love. Coming from a broken home, she didn't see herself fitting into a normal family life. Judging from all the family photos and Evan's clear love for his sisters and niece and nephew, he was part of a world she only dreamed of.

But as CeCe felt Evan relax next to her, felt his breathing even out as he drifted to sleep, she pretended for a moment that this was real—that he was hers. That coming home from a long day to pillow forts, home-cooked meals, and sweet kisses was within her grasp. *She could get used to this*, she thought as she felt herself drift away. She could get used to having someone like Evan in her corner, someone who would put her first and do what's best for her. That was a new feeling, and not one that she thought she deserved.

A few hours later, the light of dawn broke through the slats in the blinds, and CeCe pulled a pillow over her eyes to shield herself from the sun. She was still groggy and not ready to start her day. Nestling into her pillow, an arm wrapped around her side and pulled her close to a steady wall. Sighing, she backed into the warmth and smelled the familiar scent of spicy cedar.

Evan.

Her eyes snapped open, and she took in her surroundings. The TV was frozen on the passive-aggressive *Are you still watching?* message. *Don't you judge us, Netflix.* A half-empty bowl of popcorn sat next to her face, and she realized the glitter pillow was under her head, the beading leaving indentations in her skin. Most importantly, Evan was glued to her back, clinging to her like a koala to eucalyptus tree. She wiggled a little to break free, but he only pulled her closer and mumbled something in his sleep.

"Oh no." She groaned as her body reacted and veered closer to him. She needed to get out of this situation immediately, but while her brain clearly wanted to flee, her body wasn't in any hurry.

Carefully lifting his arm away from her body, CeCe reluctantly rolled away. She felt the absence of Evan's warmth immediately and struggled not to cuddle back into his side. As she shifted her weight, the air mattress bobbed and caused him to shift onto his back. The motion jolted him awake, and he looked up to find CeCe tiptoeing toward the doorway, her shoes clutched in her hands.

Holding her breath, she reached for the doorknob, only to hear Evan behind her. "If you give me a minute, I can make you breakfast."

CeCe's shoulders fell and she turned to face him, adorably rumpled from sleep. "Busted?" she asked.

He crossed his arms over his chest and nodded. "You're totally busted." With his chin, he gestured toward the kitchen. "Have a seat, you might as well stay for coffee." He walked past her and pulled down a jar of coffee beans.

CeCe slid her shoes on and looked back and forth between the living room and where Evan stood in the kitchen. The clock on the stove said it was barely six thirty, so she had thirty minutes to get to the diner. Reading her mind, he turned on the coffee maker and opened the fridge. "We don't have to be at work for thirty minutes, at least stay for some eggs."

CeCe stepped closer, hanging her purse on the edge of a chair and joining him at the stove. "Only if I'm making the eggs," she countered.

Evan smirked, one side of his mouth quirking up. "Why do you think I'm asking?" He slid a carton of eggs, a stick of butter, and a bundle of scallions toward her. "I'll be right back," he said as he padded back to the bathroom.

CeCe looked around his tiny kitchen and had to make a decision. She could slip out quickly, pretend they didn't wake up in each other's arms, or she could be the adult she kept saying she was and make breakfast. The rumbling in her stomach was all the sign she needed. Dropping a pat of butter into a frying pan, she got to work on breakfast.

Five minutes later, the eggs were fluffy and perfectly cooked, sprinkled with a handful of scallions. Evan emerged from the bathroom with damp hair and headed straight for the coffee maker. He filled two cups and set the table in the corner of the kitchen. As she eased into a seat, he raised a finger and disappeared. "One thing is missing," he said.

CeCe took a bite of egg. She found Evan holding a plate of familiar pastries. "What's that?" she asked, although she knew the answer.

Evan unwrapped two perfectly formed croissants and handed one to her. "I leave these in the oven overnight, and then they are ready in the morning."

"Did you steal these?" she asked teasingly, not caring at that moment where he got them.

Tearing a piece off and dunking it into his coffee, Evan laughed. "It's not stealing if Max tells me to take it. There have been a few days where we have pastries left over, so instead of tossing them, I freeze them for times like this."

CeCe sipped from her coffee, taking in the scene before her. There was something so intimate, so domestic about sharing breakfast at dawn with Evan. He was just out of the shower and looked so young and fresh, she suddenly felt self-conscious about her own rumpled appearance. As if sensing her discomfort, he gestured toward the hallway.

"I've got clean towels and a diner T-shirt on the bathroom counter. Take a few minutes if you need them," he offered, not looking up from his breakfast. "We don't have to leave for another fifteen minutes."

CeCe scoffed. "And what makes you think I need less than fifteen minutes to get ready?"

Evan met her gaze and his face cracked into a beaming smile. "Because you're low maintenance, CeCe. That's one of the reasons I like you so much."

A small crack formed in her armor at his earnest expression and thoughtful observation. Eric used to criticize her about trying to look more put-together when the press would come to report on the restaurant. She'd hem and haw her way through a shopping trip, always feeling the clothes weren't meant for her short, curvier frame. She was a pastry chef who looked like one. Her body was made from hours in the kitchen, testing her own creations. Her free money went toward pots and pans, not makeup and fancy dresses. Evan saw that about her and liked it, and that did funny things inside her rib cage. *Settle down, CeCe.*

Before she could argue, he cleared their dishes and tapped his watch. "Now we're down to fourteen minutes. Stop overanalyzing the moment and hop in the shower." As he stepped back with their dishes, he stooped down and kissed the top of her head. He was nearly six feet, and it was times like this she didn't mind their height difference. It was a simple, sweet gesture that caused her heart to melt. The kiss made her feel treasured, and she had no idea how to feel about that.

Evan kept his back to her and focused on cleaning up, so she rushed to the bathroom. He was right: they had less than fifteen minutes to get ready for work. Her emotions would have to wait until she was alone and not under his cedar-scented spell.

Of course, CeCe learned the downside of using Evan's shower a moment later when she was covered in the bubbles of his body wash, lost in the familiar scent of him.

The part that shocked her the most was that she was enjoying herself. They'd shared a quiet breakfast and she never felt uncomfortable. In fact, her lack of discomfort was upsetting her, and she choked on her own laughter. She wondered if there was something wrong with her. Why couldn't she just enjoy this moment in time?

Evan met her in the kitchen, holding out a to-go cup of coffee. "For the road," he offered, handing her the extra caffeine she'd need for the day ahead. Sunday brunch was their busiest day.

Taking the coffee, CeCe said, "Thanks for this, and …" She trailed off, looking back at the air mattress that was now tidied up, the pillows lining the head of the bed. "I thought you only used it for kung fu night?" she teased.

Evan shrugged on his jacket, undeterred. "Usually, but I'm keeping it ready. I don't know when you're going to call a rematch." He breezed past her and held the door open, clearly not letting her contradict his plan. She watched him lock up the apartment, then he led the way to her car. He held her door for her again and handed her coffee once she was buckled in. "See you at work." He winked as he closed the door.

CeCe watched Evan follow her to the diner and wondered what Max would say if he heard they'd spent their night. Sure, nothing technically happened between them, but she felt a sense of unease course through her veins. They hadn't kissed, not really, but she felt they crossed over an invisible line of intimacy that she hadn't expected.

What did Evan think about all this? Was he going to say something to Max? Did she want him to?

These, and a million other questions, flew through her mind as she parked next to Max's car. She could smell something savory as she stepped into the morning air and jogged to catch up to Evan, who was holding the door open for her once more. Before she could talk to him about last night, Max greeted them in the doorway, his arms full of ingredients.

"Good morning. I'm glad you're both here." He rattled off a list of their morning to-dos, and Evan stepped right into his routine of peeling potatoes and brewing pots of coffee. She watched him work and realized that he wouldn't say a thing.

True to form, he was letting her call the shots.

For some reason, that made her like him just a little bit more.

*

The morning went by in a blur of dirty dishes, famished customers, and a few stolen glances at CeCe. Evan might be younger, but he wasn't a fool. She would pitch a fit if he mentioned their kung fu fort time, especially at work. Instead, he focused on their workday.

Working at the diner wasn't glamorous, but Evan found it rewarding. He knew all the regulars and had made some friends in Buckeye Falls, thanks to his time on the job. He enjoyed stealing a few moments that morning with Madeline and Otis, while the mayor and his wife ate pancakes in seemingly companionable silence. "So you have to tell me which hand has the sugar packet," Evan told the young girl and her toddler brother.

Madeline stared at Evan's hands, which he held out in clenched fists. "What do I get if I pick the right hand?" she asked, her little face scrunched in concentration. Beside her, Otis picked a piece of egg off his overalls and shoved it into his mouth. While the little boy was pleased with himself, Madeline looked anything but impressed.

"If you pick correctly, you get a cookie." The little girl lit up like a Christmas tree. Her blue eyes darted back and forth before finally settling on his right hand, which she tapped gently with her chubby finger. Madeline jumped for joy when a crumbled sugar packet was presented to her. "You're a smart cookie," he mused, retrieving a pair of cookies from the counter and handing them to her.

Natalie stepped forward and scooped Otis up under her arm. "Now, what do you say to Evan?" she asked, clearly trying to teach her kiddos some manners.

"Thank you," both children chimed in unison.

"You're welcome." He winked at the little girl, who flushed and turned into her mother's legs, embarrassed by her adorable crush.

Natalie tossed a few twenties on the table and took Madeline's hand. "Keep the change, Evan. And thank you for distracting them for a few minutes."

The mayor slid out of the booth and slapped Evan on the back, the motion so jerky it caught him off balance. "You're a nice guy," he said before turning and heading toward the door. Coming from Mayor Snyder, that was a hell of a compliment.

Natalie smiled sheepishly at Evan. "Thanks again— you're a lifesaver."

As the mayor and his family left the diner, Evan focused on clearing the table. Helen came up and took the stack of plates from him, jerking her head toward the entrance and saying, "There's a girl to see you. I've got this." Without letting Evan argue, Helen took the plates and stalked back into the kitchen.

"Ev!" Mallory called from the door, still dressed in her rumpled scrubs from the night before. Her eyes were dark and shadowed, and she looked dead on her feet.

Evan rushed to join her, giving her a quick hug before directing her to an open spot at the counter. "Mal, you look exhausted." He snagged a coffee cup, filling it to the brim.

Mallory scoffed but took the mug and greedily took a swig. "You really need to work on your conversation skills. I think the thing you meant to say was, 'Wow, Mal. You look amazing after a night of saving lives. Let me give you some coffee while you relax.'"

"Waffles or pancakes?" he asked, pulling his notepad out of his jeans pocket.

"Waffles, but add some fruit so I don't feel bad about

myself."

"Be right back," Evan said as he darted into the kitchen.

"Is that your sister? I always forget what she looks like," Helen said as she loaded a stack of dishes into the dishwasher. Evan glanced around to see if CeCe was around, but he didn't see her.

Max wiped a bead of sweat from his brow and beamed. "Mallory's here? Does she want waffles or pancakes?"

Evan handed the slip to Max. "Waffles, and can we add some fruit, please?"

Max tucked the slip above the stove and stirred the bowl of batter. "For Mallory, she can have all the fruit. Why don't you take a break and join her for a few? Judging from how well the mayor's visit went, I think you earned an extra break."

Even though things with the mayor had improved over the last few months, it was no secret there was still a little tension between Mayor Snyder and Max. Those tensions fortunately loosened when Natalie hired Ginny for her events business. Thinking of the business made Evan think about his proposal for their website. Every time Natalie came in, he was so close to mentioning his freelance services, but he kept chickening out. He didn't want Natalie, or anyone, to think he was only nice to the kids so he could get her talking about work.

Lost in his musings, Evan nearly missed the plate Max handed him. "Here you go, and grab one of CeCe's donuts for the road. Mallory will love them."

Evan nodded and walked back to the counter.

Stepping into the dining room, he hopped onto the neighboring stool and slid his sister's breakfast across to her. Mallory's eyes rested on the plate and the donut, and she immediately dove in. "These waffles literally make my day. I'm surprised you don't weigh three hundred pounds with all this good food available."

Evan shrugged and poured himself a cup of coffee. He wasn't hungry, too lost in his rambling thoughts. Between

CeCe and his business proposal, Evan didn't know which end was up.

Mallory devoured half her waffle. "Earth to Ev," she said as she waved her hand in front of his face. "I asked how the movie marathon went last night. I'm sorry I had to leave you high and dry."

For a moment, Evan pictured CeCe at his place, sprawled on the air mattress and laughing without a care in the world. His lips tugged upward, and Mallory didn't miss the shift in his expression. She raised an eyebrow and rested her arm on the counter. "Spill it. Something's up. You never look this happy, even after a kung fu marathon."

Evan glanced around to make sure they were alone, and he whispered, "I had a friend come by. It was nice."

Mallory inched closer. "Was this a lady friend?" she asked, her voice dripping with excitement, her eyes dancing.

There was no point beating around the bush. Mallory could smoke out any detail she wanted within two minutes, even going on zero hours of sleep. "CeCe came over."

Mallory reared back like she was slapped and covered her mouth as she squealed. "CeCe came over? That's amazing!" Evan raised his hands to quiet his sister, but she was on a roll. "Tell me everything. Did you watch movies? Did something happen?" She paused to take in a deep breath and froze. "Wait? Did she see the fort?"

Evan laughed at the look of absolute horror on Mallory's face. "Yes, Mal. She saw the fort. Frankly, if an air mattress pillow fort is enough to scare her away, then she's not the woman for me." He meant the words, even though he'd obsessed over the same thing. Though judging from how the evening turned out, he wasn't worried anymore.

Max walked out and saved Evan from his sister's third degree. Max waved and greeted Mallory like she was his own family, which was one of the many reasons Evan respected him. He was more than Evan's boss; Max was a true friend. "What brings you out today, other than free waffles?" Max winked and Mallory flushed.

"Just came out to see my brother before I head home to crash. It's been a rough week at the hospital." Yawning, Mallory stretched before she exclaimed, "Oh!" Pulling her tote bag up to her lap, she fished around and finally pulled out the newspaper article that had upset CeCe. "This sounds very exciting! Is the diner participating?"

Evan watched Max flinch as he took the paper from Mallory. "Yeah, I'm still working with CeCe on this." He rubbed the back of his neck as the woman herself emerged from the kitchen.

CeCe looked a little tired, but happy overall, as she always did when she was cooking or baking. There was a moment's hesitation as she registered that Mallory was there before giving her a one-armed hug. "Hey, it's nice to see you," CeCe greeted Mallory, and Evan believed her. CeCe was always friendly with people, but she never faked warmth. It's one of the many things he liked about her. She was all bark and no bite.

"I'm here to see when that hot celebrity chef is coming to town," Mallory beamed. "I've watched Eric Watson's show a million times. He's a dish best served hot." Fanning herself with a napkin, Mallory swooned.

Evan rolled his eyes at his sister. "Gross, Mal."

Max chuckled, but CeCe had gone whiter than her chef's tunic. He latched onto her elbow to steady her; she looked like she would faint. "You all right?" he asked as he ushered her to the kitchen.

Mallory went into full nurse mode and followed the trio. Max got a glass of water and pulled out a chair for CeCe. He kept hold of her arm until she took the water and shook her head. "I'm fine, a little tired, I guess. I didn't sleep well."

Evan bit back a retort, having firsthand knowledge that not only did she sleep well, but she snored like a freight train. Mallory didn't seem convinced either, leaning down and checking the pulse on CeCe's wrist. "You sure? You look like you've seen a ghost, and your pulse is a little high." Mallory sat back on her haunches and studied CeCe a moment longer before standing and dusting off her pants. "I think she needs to go home and rest," she told the room.

Max nodded and motioned for Helen. "Helen, can you change the specials board to exclude the quiche today? CeCe isn't feeling well."

Helen gave a thumbs-up and headed toward the dining room. "It's about time you took a day off," she barked over her shoulder.

CeCe gave a nervous laugh and struggled to get on her feet. Evan didn't like the color of her complexion, and fortunately Max read his mind. "Why don't you follow CeCe home, make sure she gets back in one piece?"

Evan nodded and headed toward the wall where CeCe's jacket and purse hung. CeCe sprung forward and waved off their concern. "Everyone relax, I'll be fine. I'm a little tired, that's all."

No one was buying it, but Evan wasn't sure why. Judging from the look Max gave CeCe, he knew something Evan didn't. Mallory looked relieved that CeCe was leaving, but still a little concerned. "Make sure you're drinking enough water, and let Evan follow you back. It will make us all feel better."

Reluctantly, CeCe shrugged on her jacket and forced a smile. "Fine, I'll go home and relax for a bit. But I'm coming in tomorrow." She pointed at Max, who raised his hands in defense.

"Fine, but make sure you rest. Nurse Mallory's orders." Max winked at Mallory again, who officially burst into a shade of crimson that probably needed its own medical attention. Evan would have to remind his dear sister that Max was not only back with his ex-wife, but engaged to remarry in a matter of weeks.

"All right, let's go," Evan said to CeCe, who was a step ahead of him. He had so many questions, but he didn't want to push her. Something was clearly going on, and he had a feeling it had to do with Eric Watson and this food competition. Was CeCe nervous about competing? That seemed completely unfounded. Despite being humble, she was proud of what she'd accomplished in the kitchen.

Then it had to be something else, something bad enough for her to willingly go home for the day. Evan ran a hand through his hair and took a deep breath; he needed to get to the bottom of what was breaking CeCe's heart. Because he couldn't take much more.

CHAPTER 5

CeCe white-knuckled the steering wheel for the entire ten-minute drive back to her place. Evan was a steady presence behind her, never getting more than twenty feet away. Despite the growing tension headache in her temples, she took relief from seeing Evan's silhouette in her rearview mirror. "Focus on one man at a time." She huffed under her breath when she pulled into her driveway.

Evan was out of his car in record time, sprinting to open her door. She let the cool air wash over her, bringing a sense of calm to her brain. It could also have been his strong arm wrapped around her waist that made the tension ease. "There you go," Evan said as CeCe stepped onto her porch.

Dramatically rolling her eyes, she stabbed her key into the lock and shoved her way inside. Not holding the door for Evan, he was forced to drop his arm as he followed. She shrugged off her coat and tossed it on the couch. "I'm fine. You can go back to the diner." She hated how clipped her tone was.

Evan stomped his sneakers on the mat and toed them off, walking in socked feet to join her on the couch. She slid closer as his weight shifted her placement on the cushion. Of course, she could have tried to stay away from his comforting warmth, but her body wouldn't let her. Apparently when Evan was involved, she lost all control.

"You're not fine. You still look pale. Mallory called me to make sure you eat something." Pressing his hands to his legs, he stood and showed himself to CeCe's kitchen.

For a chef, someone going into your personal kitchen was very intimate. It was tantamount to rummaging through someone's closet. CeCe wasn't sure why, but Evan being in her private space didn't bring the same reaction as when others did. As she plodded after him, her cheeks flushed at the sight of him opening her pantry and cabinets. His brow was furrowed as he sniffed an open bottle of hot sauce.

"I can warm something up later. I'm really not hungry," she protested as she propped against the counter. It took every ounce of self-control not to stare at Evan's backside while he crawled into her massive refrigerator. "Really, I've got this."

Finally, Evan stepped back and held out two plastic containers. "Here's some soup and those veggie fritters you made on Monday. Take a seat, and I'll have lunch ready in a few minutes." Without waiting for her input, he turned and started searching for a pot and pan. She couldn't look away as he took control of her kitchen, adding oil to a pan and heating the fritters.

The aroma of cumin and garlic filled the air while he poured out the soup. "I'll get us something to drink," CeCe offered as she strode to the fridge for a pair of water bottles. Evan smiled when he saw her place the second bottle on the counter. "I can't very well have you going hungry, especially since you gave up your shift to play babysitter."

Evan slid a bowl over to her spot. "I wouldn't call this babysitting. You know I want to help." Easing himself onto his stool, he allowed himself a moment to scan over CeCe from her perch beside him. "I'm worried about you. Something is clearly going on."

Squirming on the stool, she turned her attention to the water bottle and twisted the top, fumbling with the cap. It skipped across the tiled floor, where it landed by the stove. Oh well, she'd deal with that later. Right now, all she could focus on was this man, showing more concern and tenderness than she'd seen before. Evan didn't *need* to worry about her, but she couldn't ignore what his concern did to her. Her ribcage could barely contain her heart as it swelled under his scrutiny. While the thought of Eric had her running for antacids, Evan gave her the cozy feeling of having hot cocoa on a winter's morning. This sense of nurturing—of someone taking control—felt foreign but not unwelcome.

"Don't worry about me," she assured him. "I'm probably a little hangry."

Evan looked far from convinced, but he had the patience of a saint and turned his attention to his meal. For all his concern, he was always distracted by food. CeCe had seen him polish off slices of pie after eating half a crock of soup. The guy must have a hollow leg, or the best metabolism in the world. Crunching into a fritter, his eyes fluttered shut as he chewed. "Why don't you make these for the diner? I'm half in love over here." He popped another into his mouth and hummed with delight.

His moans of pleasure sent a shiver down her spine, and she found herself chugging the rest of her water. Maybe she was more out of sorts than she realized. "It's an old recipe I wanted to rework. No big deal."

"No way, these are amazing. This is the type of thing we should enter in that food truck contest," he said confidently. "These are familiar, yet flashy. Plus, fried food is always a winner." Evan's smile dissolved when he saw CeCe's grimace. "What's the matter?" he asked, frowning as she tried to cover her expression with her napkin. "You can tell me what's going on." He crossed his hand over his chest and said, "I'm a vault."

CeCe could have drowned in the bright blue pools of his eyes. That soulful stare almost promised redemption and a fresh start, but she wasn't falling for another set of bright eyes and a sweet demeanor. She was smarter than that, and she wouldn't risk ruining what she'd built here. She hated keeping secrets, but she also couldn't jeopardize her heart.

"Nothing is going on, just not thrilled with the prospect of competing."

Evan tossed his napkin onto his empty plate, his eyebrow raised in protest. "Sorry, but I'm calling BS on that. You are a force in the kitchen, and you know you have what it takes to win. Why not show off a little? If nothing else, it would be great publicity for the diner. We have nothing to lose by competing."

Oh, there was so much to unpack in his statement. So many ways to contradict Evan's enthusiasm and blind hope. She knew better. She knew what being around Eric would do to her. How it would rip her open and expose all her ugly insecurities, the humiliation, all her fears. She had opened her life up to him before, and it nearly ruined her. She would not make that mistake again.

Instead, she took the coward's way out. "Look," she said, lowering her gaze to her empty soup bowl. Perhaps if she told a partial truth, she could get Evan off her back. "I used to work with Eric." Once the words were out, she hazarded a glance to see if he was still paying attention. Before she could chicken out, she continued. "And it ended badly. The thought of seeing him again is not high on my bucket list." There, that was near enough to the truth. Judging from how Evan's expression shifted, it diverted his attention from the cracks in her façade, in her heart.

"Why didn't you tell me?" he asked, his voice lower and his expression sad. "I'm assuming Max already knows." There was a note in Evan's tone that was different from his normal demeanor, and it gave her pause.

"Yes. He knows. Eric's come up in conversation before." And boy, did it. CeCe had poured her guts out at Max's during his reconciliation with Ginny. One too many shots of bourbon had given CeCe a loose tongue, but at least it brought comfort to Max during a tough time.

Evan rose and collected their dishes, his jaw clenched. CeCe sat back as he filled the sink with soapy water and carefully lowered the bowls into the suds. The domestic scene should have looked preposterous, but she found it soothing. He looked like he belonged in her space, made it better. When the dishes were clean and rinsed, he stacked them on the rack to dry. He draped a towel over the dishes and walked past CeCe to the door.

He bent down to put on his shoes, and she felt herself deflate. "You're leaving?" She wasn't sure why she was surprised. Evan had no reason to stay and watch her mope around. He'd already done more than he realized by taking her home. He'd fed her in more ways than one in that short time.

"Are you angry with me?"

He gave up tying his shoes and stood, shoving his hands in his pockets. "I'm sick of no one trusting me with anything. I'm not a kid; I'm a grown-ass man," he spat as he yanked open the door. "You're allowed to confide in me, you know." He stomped down the steps of her porch, his open shoes slapping on the concrete.

If CeCe wasn't so upset at the sight, she would have laughed. "Evan, wait!" she shouted as she followed him to her driveway. He didn't stop, but slid behind the wheel and slammed the door shut. She watched helplessly as he backed onto the street and out of sight. Her toes curled on the cold ground as she realized how empty she felt without him. In the blink of an eye, she'd gone from a comforting cocoon to literally being out in the cold.

CeCe wasn't a fool. It was horrible that she lied to Evan about Eric. From how upset Evan was over hearing the half-truth, she could only imagine how furious he'd be if he knew the whole truth. But she wasn't ready to spill any more details of her past. Maybe Evan was right, and she was trying to protect him. Protect him from her complicated past that she tried to avoid at all costs. But Eric Watson tainted everything, and she needed to keep whatever this was with

Evan intact.

With a long sigh, she stalked back inside. Her home seemed lonely, the image of Evan in her space still in the forefront of her mind. She didn't like to invite many people over, but she didn't even balk when Evan made himself comfortable. That little fact brought her headache back with a vengeance. She felt terrible for upsetting him, and she felt a kernel of despair bloom at the thought that she missed him. Missed having him beside her, supporting her.

CeCe shook her head and fell back onto the couch. Evan was a friend—that's all. There was no use sitting around daydreaming about a future with him. He was too sweet, too wholesome for her. Perhaps he didn't realize it now, but he was better off keeping his heart away from her.

*

Evan drove around for nearly an hour until Mallory called. At first, he hoped he could ignore his sister, until she called for a third time in just as many minutes. Sensing his life would be easier if he answered, he turned on Bluetooth and accepted the call.

"Hey, Mal."

"Don't Mal me." His sister sighed. "Where are you? How's CeCe?"

Hearing CeCe's name made Evan flinch. He stung from the truth that the woman he was half in love with couldn't trust him. Why did everyone insist on treating him like a naïve kid? Pulling into his spot, Evan saw the lights were on in his apartment. "Considering you're in my place, I'll give you the update in person." Stabbing at his phone, he disconnected and stepped into the quickly cooling air.

Mallory waited at the front door, her arms crossed in front of her. He stifled a sigh as he pushed past his sister. "Spill it," she ordered, pointing at her baby brother as he marched into the kitchen.

Glancing at the stove clock, he was pleased to see it was

after six o'clock. A perfectly respectable time to have a beer. Popping the top, he took a swig before turning to face his sister. "CeCe is fine. Turns out she used to work with Eric, and it didn't end on good terms."

Mallory's shoulders dropped at the revelation. "Oh, good, I was hoping it wasn't anything more serious. Did you make her eat something?"

Evan nodded and took another pull from his beer. Mallory gestured to the bottle and he grabbed one for her before propping himself against the counter.

"But that doesn't explain why you look like someone kicked your puppy," Mallory said.

Damn his sister and her ability to see right through him. He couldn't hide much from his sisters, but Mallory had X-ray vision when it came to his thoughts. "CeCe didn't trust me with what was bothering her. Yet again, Max knew, and I was left in the dark. I'm tired of everyone keeping secrets. I can handle the truth. I'm not a baby," he whined into his beer.

Mallory sipped from her drink and studied him from beneath her lashes. "I won't make a reference to giving the baby its bottle," she teased and took Evan's empty bottle away. "However, you need to man up a little more. I'm guessing you ran out of there in a huff, am I right?"

He brushed a pile of crumbs off the counter, not lifting his gaze. "Not exactly."

"That means I'm right, and you acted like a toddler. Did CeCe try to explain? Did she try to stop you from acting like a damn fool?"

Evan grimaced, thinking of CeCe running after him. When she called out, it took every ounce of willpower not to turn around and go back to her. He loved being in her home with her, making her a meal and simply talking. That was why the truth hurt so much, because he felt they were getting past the whole age gap. He felt she saw him as more than a younger coworker; more than the happy-go-lucky guy.

Mallory put her beer down and sighed. "I'm guessing your silence is my answer. What's the big deal? Aren't Max and CeCe friends? It makes sense they'd share things."

Evan cupped his face in his hands and groaned. "It's always like this. I'm the last to know anything."

"Sometimes that can be a good thing," Mallory mused, taking Evan's hand and dragging him into the living room.

The fort was still set up from the morning, and Evan felt his chest tighten at the sight. Waking up with CeCe, cuddling her in his arms, had been a dream. He wanted countless more nights like that. Eating, laughing, snuggling each other. Those are the experiences that Evan wanted to share with her, the everyday, intimate moments that grow into everlasting love.

And then he acted like the kid he was trying not to be, just as CeCe probably expected. "I'm an idiot." He sighed when he landed on a stack of pillows.

The air mattress shifted as Mallory crawled to her spot on the side. "I won't argue with you. Why don't you text her and see if she's okay?"

As if summoning CeCe from the ether, Evan's phone buzzed in his pocket. "It's from her," he breathed, opening the message with a shaking hand.

Sorry about before. Feel terrible. Does your offer of another fort night still stand?

Evan had to read the text twice before her offer sunk in. His face cracked into a crooked grin, and Mallory slapped his arm. "What does it say?"

"She wants to come over."

"No!" Mallory exclaimed, clapping her hands and squealing in delight. "This is awesome. I'm so excited."

Evan took a deep breath and waved his phone. "What should I say?"

Mallory scoffed. "Um, you say come on over." She looked at Evan like he was an imbecile.

He looked down at his phone, then back up at his sister. "This seems too good to be true. I thought I'd have to grovel for a week before she'd even talk to me."

Mallory rolled off the mattress and collected her purse and coat. Walking to the door, she turned to her brother and shrugged. "I won't pretend to know, but I do know that you lucked out big time. You're getting your girl all to yourself for a second night in a row." Raising a finger, she pointed directly at him. "You better not mess this up," she warned before stepping outside.

"Thanks for the words of support and wisdom. I would truly be lost without you." Evan droned behind her. Mallory waved him off as she got to her car.

"Look, be yourself. And when I say that, I mean the best version, where you practice what you preach. Be a man and be honest about how you feel. CeCe obviously likes you enough to invite herself over to your place after you acted like a moron."

Evan splayed his hand over his chest and sighed. "Your trust in me is truly inspiring."

Mallory lowered the window. "Don't mess this up," she urged as she turned on the ignition and drove away. Evan allowed himself a moment before responding to CeCe. Despite him knowing he wanted her at his place, by his side, this was a big step for her.

It was a big step for Evan as well. He wouldn't let this opportunity slip through his fingers; he would be a gentleman and an adult. He would be the man that CeCe deserved. Pulling out his phone, he invited her over and immediately went to work tidying up the apartment again. Fortunately, Mallory had already started dinner. A little bonus that Evan wouldn't squander.

CeCe's response said she'd be there in twenty, which gave Evan enough time to change and shower. He was laying it on pretty thick, but he didn't care. By the time he was combing his hair, he heard a faint knock. Nearly running, he opened the door to CeCe looking like a vision. Her blonde hair was pushed back off her face and her cheeks were rosy from the cold.

"Hey," she said quietly, raising her hand in a small wave. She'd changed from her work clothes into a pair of jeans and a graphic T-shirt from her favorite movie, *First Blood*. Stallone sneered at him, as if he knew Evan had screwed up. In her other hand, she lifted a six-pack of his favorite local beer. "Peace offering?" she said as she stepped inside.

Evan got a whiff of her signature vanilla scent, and it nearly buckled his knees. "Make yourself at home," he said as he took the beer and went in search of a bottle opener. Joining CeCe back in the living room, he was relieved to see she'd already taken up her spot from the night before.

Turning on the TV, she scrolled through streaming services until she found an action movie. "This is one of my favorites," she said, relaxing back on a stack of pillows. Evan gingerly sank onto the air mattress and handed her a beer. "Thanks." CeCe gestured to the TV and smiled. "Since you showed me the wonders of kung fu movies, I thought I'd share my passion for '80s and '90s action stars." She gestured to her shirt and smirked. "You can pick next time."

Next time, meaning this wasn't a fluke. Evan gathered all his strength and kept himself from screaming with delight. If someone asked him what heaven looked like, he would have told them it was this moment. Bliss, pure bliss.

"This is Stallone's best work," Evan said.

"Hands down," CeCe agreed. "I know sequels aren't always better, but there is something about this one." After a moment, she sniffed the air and sat up. "Please tell me that's dinner. I know we only ate a few hours ago, but I'm starving."

Evan placed his beer on the floor and rolled to his feet. "Mallory started a casserole before she left. Your timing is perfect."

CeCe joined him as he plated their meal. "I'm having déjà vu." She laughed. "Weren't we doing this twenty-four hours ago?"

All Evan thought was that he could do this every day. He swallowed past that revelation and focused on food—it was what he did best. "Here we go," he offered her a plate and settled in beside her. Their elbows banged as they settled. Muffled curses and crashing furniture blared through the TV's speakers.

CeCe took a bite of her dinner but kept her eyes on the screen. Since the afternoon, her color had come back and she looked like her normal self. Evan loved to see the peachy hue of her cheeks and the way her eyes flashed when she enjoyed herself. When they were done eating, he took the opportunity to clear the air.

"I want to apologize for how I acted earlier," he started, taking in a lungful of air to bolster himself.

Before he could continue, CeCe placed her hand on his and squeezed it gently. "I need to apologize too. You're a friend, Evan, and I should trust you with things like this." Her voice was low, and Evan had to lean closer to make sure he heard her.

"I'm more than a friend, CeCe." Evan paused to clear his throat. "Or at least I'd like to be." Their legs slid closer; he felt the warmth of her through the denim. The air was thick with anticipation.

CeCe's eyelids lowered as she licked her lips. "I know you would," she whispered, her breath tickling Evan's lips. Putting his weight on one arm, he reached out with his free hand to tuck a lock of hair behind her ear. His thumb slid over her earlobe, and she shivered at the contact but didn't move back. This was his moment, and he took it.

Inching closer still, he asked the most important question of his life. "Can I kiss you?" He lost his self-control, but he would never do anything she didn't want. He needed her fully on board with the situation.

"Yes." CeCe's breath was an exhale as she closed the distance between them.

Evan's senses exploded as their lips met, and he nearly forgot to breathe. Every touch, every thought, was all about CeCe. Her hand went up to cup his cheek and a tiny moan escaped her lips. The sound reverberated through his chest, and he had to stifle his own whimpers. His dream girl was in his arms, sharing the best kiss of his life. Things didn't get any better than this.

Just as Evan was about to deepen the kiss, a scream blasted from the TV and startled them both from the moment. He reluctantly loosened his grip on her. She looked at him, searching his face. "Evan."

Not wanting to frighten her, he traced her cheek with his knuckles before lowering his hand to cover hers. He would not push things further; he would enjoy the moment for what it was. She let him hold her hand for the rest of the movie while she rested her head on his shoulder. As the credits rolled, he felt her stirring. "I should head home. Can't make it a habit of sleeping on your floor," she teased.

"You can sleep on my floor anytime," he said without thinking. Realizing what he said, he covered his face with his hands. *Real smooth.*

CeCe laughed, a sweet sound that took away the sting of embarrassment. "When you make offers like that, it's hard to see why you're still single."

He watched CeCe collect her things and head toward the door, and he couldn't stand to see her go. "Wait," he said, stopping her as she tied her sneakers. She raised an eyebrow. "What are you doing tomorrow?"

"Um, working?" she said, standing back up and meeting his gaze. "You're not proposing another movie marathon, are you? You must really want me to sleep on your floor."

Evan snorted but recovered quickly. "Let me take you out." At his suggestion, CeCe's face fell, but he soldiered on. "Hear me out." He raised his hands up to stop her pending complaints. He adored CeCe, but the woman could tear down the simplest suggestion if she felt cornered. "I'm going to Elm River. There's a karaoke night at one of the local pubs. Come with me."

CeCe didn't say no right away, and he took that as a small step forward. "You want me to sing karaoke?"

Evan raised a shoulder and strived to appear casual. "Or

you can watch me and dozens of other Buckeyes make absolute asses of ourselves. Your choice."

He could tell he had her.

She nibbled on her lip and studied him a moment before chuckling. "You're an interesting guy, Evan Lawson."

"I think you should have figured that out by now, but I'll take the compliment." He gave her his best cheeky grin and watched her fold faster than Superman on laundry day.

"If I say yes," she said, holding up her hand, "then that doesn't mean I'm going to sing."

"I don't care if you sit there scowling the whole time. I think it'll be a blast."

CeCe angled back on her heels, her gaze raking over his living room and the scene of their first kiss. He said a prayer to any deity who would listen that she would give him a chance. They'd had such a wonderful evening, and Evan knew they could be something special—that they *were* something special.

"Fine. But if I'm not having fun, we get to leave."

"You just say the word." Evan closed the distance between them in two strides and gave her a quick hug. He kept it brief so he didn't scare her away with his eagerness. "I'll pick you up at six."

At first she didn't say anything, just blinked and nodded. "Thanks for tonight."

"You're welcome," he said simply, raising his hand in farewell.

He didn't know what that kiss meant for her, but he knew what it meant for him. That kiss was a promise. A promise of a future, one where they were partners. He wasn't naïve; she'd try to push him away. But he had a taste of her now, and he wasn't about to lose her. He'd planned to make their date night count.

CHAPTER 6

"What the hell am I doing?" CeCe asked her reflection for the third time in two minutes. This was madness. Going out on a date with Evan was lunacy. Kissing him had been certifiable, but she couldn't deny how amazing it was. Reaching up to graze her lips with her fingertips, she still felt the impression of his kiss, still felt the heat of the moment.

Pulling her turtleneck sweater over her head and tossing it on the bed, she shrugged on her fourth sweater and felt just as dispassionate. Suddenly she was sixteen and getting ready for her first date, and she hated the sensation. She contemplated calling Natalie, as this was her territory. Natalie could be in the middle of trench warfare in WWI and would still find time to put on eyeliner and straighten her hair. She would know what to do with CeCe in her current state—and what to do with her abysmal wardrobe.

CeCe knew the real reason she wasn't calling her friend, and it had everything to do with the slew of unresolved issues and questions swirling through her. First, there was the fact that Evan was a friend and coworker. Here she was breaking her coworker rule, and she feared it would end badly. "You need to tell him the truth." She huffed as she rummaged through her jewelry box for something to spice up her lackluster outfit.

As she sorted through mangled chains and earrings she'd long forgotten about, Natalie's advice rang through. *You're allowed to be happy.* Thinking back to the last few days, CeCe could admit she had been happy with Evan. He brought a lightness to everything. From the simple task of making her lunch to the silliness of building movie forts, she couldn't deny he made her smile more than she had in ages.

Settling on a pair of simple hoop earrings, CeCe swiped on some blush and studied herself. She looked relatively happy and prepared for a night on the town. These hoops were a gift from an old friend for her twentieth birthday, and she bristled that they were a decade old now. What could Evan see in a woman who was spitting distance to thirty?

But for all her reluctance about turning the big 3-0, she couldn't argue that the age gap issue didn't seem to matter anymore. Evan had proven his youth didn't make him immature, but rather kept him playful, kept him fun. CeCe could certainly do with some fun these days. There was something about her that interested Evan, and she wondered if she should stop second-guessing the moment and roll with it.

Tonight she would push aside her Eric insecurities and would go with the flow. She would live in the moment and enjoy her first date with Evan. She could share more about her past when they weren't out in public. There was always time, right?

A gentle knock at the door stirred her from her musings. Glancing at the clock she saw it was 5:59; Evan was right on time. "Coming!" she shouted, plodding forward with her current outfit and mussed hair. At least she'd added a little sparkle to her ensemble, and hopefully a bit more personality.

Pulling the door open, she found a sight that melted her heart. Evan stood there, illuminated by her porch light, holding a simple bouquet of daisies from the local market. He thrust them forward, keeping his gaze locked on hers. "Hi," he said, his voice huskier than normal. "You look gorgeous."

CeCe felt tongue-tied, taking the flowers before looking down at her jeans and sweater. To say her look was inspired would be a gross understatement. "Thanks. C'mon in. I'll be ready in a sec." She shamelessly took a sniff of his coat as he strode past. Never before had drugstore bodywash been so appealing.

Evan hovered in the hallway a moment before stepping forward and taking the flowers back. "Why don't I put these in water while you finish up?" His gaze went from tip to toes and made CeCe shiver. "Although, I think you look perfect right now."

Handing the daisies back to Evan, CeCe covered the flush on her cheeks and backed away. "Give me, uh, two minutes." She turned on her heel and nearly sprinted back to her bedroom. She pulled her sweater over her head and added it to the pile of casualties on her bed. It was a sad reality that her Target sweater collection left a lot to be desired on date night.

She didn't realize how long she'd been stalling until she heard Evan's footfalls outside her bedroom door. "I'm not rushing you, but karaoke starts in an hour. At this rate we'll need that long for you to decide that you're already gorgeous."

His words melted her resolve, and CeCe pulled a discarded sweater and gave up the fight. He was clearly smitten if a little lip gloss and her favorite sweater were date-worthy. "Okay, I'm coming." She laughed as she walked right into Evan and his broad chest.

Steadying her by the forearms, he smirked as she found her footing. "You look just as lovely in this as you did before. Ready?"

CeCe nodded, but she didn't step back. Evan's grasp was firm, yet gentle, as he held her in place. Her toes curled in her Converse as she imagined him closing the distance, imagined him kissing her again. "I'm ready," she said, her voice barely above a whisper. Ready for what, she still wasn't sure.

Evan leaned down, grazing his lips on her temple in a chaste kiss before releasing her. "I'll drive," he said, clearing his throat.

Thirty minutes later, he pulled his car into the lot of Elm River's only karaoke pub. Elm River was like a sister town to Buckeye Falls. They shared a local highway and both boosted low crime, affordable housing, and Midwestern charm that couldn't be beat. CeCe had been to this pub before, on a trivia night with Max back when she'd first moved to town. He'd been recovering from his divorce, and she was feeling restless from being away from the big city. While the trivia hadn't done much to resolve her homesickness for Chicago, it had fortified her friendship with Max.

"I haven't been here in ages," she mused as Evan held the door for her. She stepped inside and was immediately assaulted by the smell of fried chicken and smoke. "They smoke in here now?" she asked, coughing as they walked through a plume on the way to the staging area.

Evan rested his hand at the small of her back and led the way to their table. "It's the staging smoke," he said through a cough. "It's supposed to create ambiance."

CeCe thought it was more likely to cause lung cancer, but she kept her mouth shut. *For once.*

As soon as they were seated at a table at the corner of the room, CeCe felt herself panic. Everyone around them had a serious expression, some of them even singing in their seats. "Um, is this some type of professional karaoke circuit?" She was being sarcastic, but the look on Evan's face gave her pause.

"Nah, it's just the semi-finals of the annual series."

CeCe gulped. "I'm sorry, what?"

For the first time that night, Evan looked nervous. He

rubbed the back of his neck and said through gritted teeth, "Yeah, it's kind of a thing. I come here every week."

"To sing?" CeCe was incredulous. "Why haven't you mentioned this before?"

"Because I knew you'd make fun of me?" he asked, and she felt bad that he wasn't far from the mark.

CeCe took a moment to collect herself because she really didn't want to embarrass him. "Evan, I know you're into K-Pop, but I had no idea you were into karaoke."

He shrugged and truly didn't seem bothered by her learning the truth of his hobbies. "I live for K-Pop, but I also like music in general. And I think it's fun to watch other people share their passion." Finished with his explanation, he flipped open the drink menu.

Before the waiter arrived for their order, CeCe saw a trio of young women teeter toward their table. The girl in the middle, clearly the ring leader, was in heels better suited for the circus than a night out in central Ohio. They were so high, her legs wobbled like a newborn colt. "Evan," she cooed his name in a tone that would make wild animals howl. "I was hoping we'd see you tonight. You promised me a duet last time."

Evan flashed the girls a smile, and CeCe was pleased to see it wasn't his usual carefree smirk. His normal smile lit up his whole face, causing his eyes to twinkle like he was followed around by his own lighting crew. This one seemed forced, drawing his skin too taut across his jawline.

"Hey, guys," he said as he draped an arm around CeCe's shoulders.

Instinctively, she sunk into his embrace. She wasn't usually one to mark her territory, but she didn't like the predatory glare coming from these girls. "Hi," she said to the trio, her voice dripping with fake warmth. "How do you know Evan?"

The ring leader pulled her shoulders back, clearly ready to stake her claim on the only attractive guy in the bar—and CeCe assumed all of Elm River. "We come here every week to hear Evan sing. He's amazing."

CeCe turned to Evan, who even in the smoky room turned a worrisome shade of purple. His ears practically matched her sweater. "Isn't that sweet?" she asked no one in particular. "I knew he was amazing off stage, but I can't wait to see what he has in store tonight."

Before Evan could reply, or burst into flames, the emcee took the stage and tapped on the mic. "All right, folks," the man said, waving away a cloud of smoke with his free hand. "We'll get started in just a moment. First up tonight are the Ambers."

CeCe knew before she had to ask who the Ambers were. "I'm going to go out on a limb," she started, trying her best to stifle a laughing fit, "that those lovely ladies are the Ambers."

Evan ran a hand down his face, his skin now an unnatural hue. "Please don't hold that against me. I really am here to sing," he protested, and CeCe believed him. Evan didn't play games, and she trusted him. He really was just a guy who liked music and a night on the town. She could hardly fault him for that.

Ten minutes later, the Ambers finished their rendition of a popular Britney Spears song. CeCe hadn't seen that much suggestive gyrating since she'd watched TRL back in middle school. These girls definitely had their sights set on Evan, and thankfully he didn't seem to care. Throughout their performance, his arm stayed firmly around CeCe. During a particularly flat portion of the song, he'd whispered in her ear. "I swear, they're not all this bad." The feeling of his breath on her neck made CeCe shudder, and not in an unpleasant way. She inched closer and rested her head on his shoulder.

To an outside observer, they clearly were on a date. Their sides were plastered together, and she hadn't even reached out to take her drink off the table. When a woman in her fifties took the stage, she said she was going to sing a favorite from Ella Fitzgerald. CeCe inwardly rolled her eyes, fearing the woman would butcher a classic. But much to CeCe's—and everyone's—delight, the woman sang her soul out. Her velvety voice was better suited for a recording studio instead of a smoky pub.

"She's incredible," CeCe said when the song finished.

Evan reluctantly pulled his arm free to clap. "She's my biggest competition."

Before CeCe could ask what Evan was going to sing, the emcee took the mic and announced he was next. Evan pulled himself free and smoothed down the front of his shirt. "Showtime," he said with a wink. Without looking back, he strode to the stage with his shoulders back and his head held high.

There was a confidence to Evan she'd somehow overlooked before the last few days, a way he carried himself that made him stand out in a crowd. She remembered that hopefulness, that sense that the world was at her feet. While incredibly grateful for her life in Buckeye Falls, sometimes, during her darker moments when she felt like Eric had taken her spark, she missed her younger self. She missed that sense of entitled confidence.

Even now, her throat practically burned with the need to tell Evan about Eric, whether from guilt or the smoke machine she wasn't sure. But it was loud, her stomach churning from her drink, and he'd just stepped up to perform—*for her*. Now wasn't the time.

This was cowardly, to shut herself off instead of coming clean. Yet since letting Evan in, soaking in his earnest expression, she felt this connection. She was not ready. Eric, and the way he'd made her feel, still felt like a fresh wound … a wound that needed healing. Healing that needed to happen in private, not in a crowded pub with someone who looked at her like she hung the moon. Selfishly, CeCe wanted to preserve that expression on Evan's handsome face, wanted him to look at her like she had all the assurance she craved. Opening up to Evan, or most people for that matter, was monumental to her because she kept herself protected from scrutiny. She wasn't ready yet to unburden herself, to show Evan that she was an old fool who'd fallen for someone's lies, whose humiliation had nearly cost her the one thing she was always proud of, the one thing she would never sacrifice again—her career.

So instead of having a pity party for her past, CeCe sat back in her seat and studied the scene before her. Evan handled the microphone like a seasoned professional, not a tremble in his hand. Before tonight, she thought she had Evan all figured out. Her easy-going friend was hardly one-dimensional, but much like an onion, Evan had more layers than she expected. Unsure what he was about to sing, or how it would make her feel, she pushed aside her rambling thoughts and stayed in the moment. Little did she know, Evan was about to knock her world off its axis. She was helpless to stop him.

*

Evan took the mic from the emcee and looked out into the audience. Fortunately the smoke machine had died halfway through someone's rendition of *Stairway to Heaven*, so he could find CeCe in the crowd. Never one to shy away from the spotlight, literally, he hadn't thought much about having CeCe here with him for karaoke night. He wasn't nervous per se, but he wanted to make a good impression. He wanted to show her that there was more to him than pillow forts and omelets.

Taking a deep breath, Evan brought the microphone to his mouth and hoped for the best. "Tonight's song is dedicated to the lovely woman over there." CeCe dipped her head, but she didn't frown. That was all the encouragement he needed before the music started. CeCe not scowling was as good as her beaming from ear to ear.

For months, he'd told himself he was going to keep playing it cool. He'd promised himself that he wasn't going to spook CeCe by moving too fast, by asking for too much too soon. Yet after last night's kiss, he'd made a decision. He was going to show his hand. If she didn't like it, then at least he'd know where they stood.

The opening bars of John Legend's *All of Me* started, and he watched CeCe rest a hand over her heart. Granted, he was planning on singing this ballad tonight regardless of who was here, but having her in his space, seemingly enjoying herself, bolstered his resolve.

As the song wound down, Evan made sure to keep his gaze locked on CeCe. She hadn't blinked throughout his performance, and he only hoped that meant she was enjoying herself, meant that she liked what she heard.

"Well, folks," the emcee said, pulling the mic from Evan's sweaty hand, "I'd say that was certainly something special."

Evan didn't wait for the applause to end as he took the steps down two at a time.

Just when he'd reached his table, he felt a tap on the shoulder. He didn't need to turn around to know who it was, as Amber's strong perfume nearly had him gagging. Evan had never noticed before CeCe, but he really didn't like high-maintenance girls. Why spend hundreds of dollars on expensive perfume when you could smell like cinnamon rolls and birthday cakes for free?

"That was like"—Amber let out a long, breathy sigh—"amazing, Evan." She pulled her hand back to wind a lock of red hair around her finger, her lips in a suggestive pout. If this would have been any other time, maybe he'd be interested. But he'd gotten a taste of CeCe, literally, and he'd be damned if he messed that up.

Side-stepping Amber, Evan slid into the booth and placed his hand on CeCe's leg. He squeezed it once before looking back up at the interloper. "Thanks. It's always fun to get up there." He turned his attention to CeCe, who looked like she'd just swallowed her own tongue. He lowered his voice and asked, "Everything okay?" She bobbed her head and reached for her whiskey, which she shot back in one gulp.

Unfortunately, Amber wasn't taking the hints. "My friends and I are about to do another song. You want to join us?" She popped her hip to the side and positioned herself so about a hundred yards of cleavage were on display.

"No, thanks," Evan said, attempting to keep his tone friendly yet firm. "Spending the night with my girl."

For a moment, no one moved. Amber's eyes darted back and forth between CeCe and him before she finally took the hint. "Whatever. Whenever you want to have fun, you know where to find me." She twirled on her stiletto and stalked back to her friends. Evan could only hope that was the end of the Ambers' reign of terror.

"That was something," CeCe huffed when they were finally alone.

"What did you think?" he asked, assuming she was talking about his song choice.

"I think that my breasts have never been that perky," CeCe deadpanned, waving the waiter down for another cocktail.

Evan shook his head, trying to keep up. "What?"

CeCe picked up the straw from her water glass. Without looking up at Evan, she began twisting it in her hands until it resembled a mangled limb. "I'm just saying that if you want to go over with the *Ambers*"—her voice dripped with distain—"I won't cramp your style."

Now it was Evan's turn to be bitter. "You're kidding, right?" CeCe kept her gaze on the tabletop as she twisted the straw until it snapped in half. "CeCe," he said, his tone sharp. "You are kidding, aren't you?"

Finally CeCe looked up, barely able to look at his shoulder. The look of defeat on her face gutted him like fish. "I am sorry. I feel a little dowdy compared to those three." Her eyes drifted around the space, looking anywhere but at him. "My thirtieth birthday is barreling toward me, and I guess I'm self-conscious about it."

Wanting to give the moment the respect and time it

deserved, Evan swallowed past an instant retort. Give the man a blank notebook, and he could fill it with all the things he loved about CeCe. Her age never meant a damn thing to him, but clearly, he'd miss how much it truly bothered her.

"Please pay attention, because I'm only going to say this once."

Just as he got started, the waiter returned with CeCe's whiskey. She greedily reached for the glass, downing half the contents in one gulp. She grimaced at the burn, but didn't interrupt him. "I'm into you, CeCe. Like, really, *really* into you. I pretty much just sang my heart out telling you that fact. Your age doesn't bother me. I'm sorry it's bothering you; I really am. I wish you could see how wonderful you are."

CeCe thrust her hand toward the Ambers, clearly ready for a fight. "They are gorgeous. Can't you see that? They love karaoke and they're age appropriate."

Evan pulled back and raked his hands through his hair. "Do you really think I'm that shallow? That I'm going to take you out, only to dump you at the first sign of another offer? Damnit, CeCe. I like you, and I wanted us to have a real date. I wanted you to share in some of my hobbies, because I hope we can keep doing this." He dropped his hands and motioned between them.

To her credit, CeCe seemed slightly embarrassed by her outburst, but she didn't say anything. Taking his thumb, he gently tilted her chin up until they made eye contact. Her eyes were glassy, from the smoke or unshed tears he wasn't certain. "I want this to be it, CeCe. I want us to date and go out and enjoy ourselves."

CeCe licked her lips and swallowed twice before responding. "And you're sure about the age thing?"

"I hate to break it to you, but it's barely five years. That is nothing."

"It's not nothing to me, Evan. I'm about to turn thirty. I don't sing karaoke, and I don't have breasts up by my earlobes." She was distracting him with humor, but he wouldn't crack a smile.

"I happen to like your breasts, and I don't expect you to sing karaoke. If you're having a horrible time, we'll leave and never speak of this again."

"I'm not having a horrible time," she said, her voice low. "But I don't want to hold you back."

"You're not holding me back. Damnit, can't you see that I want to be with you? With *you*, CeCe. The same CeCe who makes me laugh and puts me in my place. The same CeCe who taught me how to make bread, even though I never let it rise long enough. The same CeCe who loves her job so much it's given me a new passion I didn't realize was missing? What more do I need to do to prove that I'm into you?"

For what felt like an eternity, neither of them breathed. They stared at each other, the only sound between them that of another contestant belting out the wrong lyrics to *Summer Loving*. Perhaps these conversations should have happened outside?

CeCe was the first to move, reaching out for her glass and downing the remains in one go. This time she covered her mouth as she coughed, pulling herself free from the booth and stumbling toward the door. Evan caught up to her in a few paces and carefully snagged her elbow to stop her retreat.

"I can't breathe in here," she mumbled. Evan looped her arm through his and led the way outside. As soon as they were back at his car, he opened the passenger's door and waited for her to step inside.

CeCe studied him, her frown marring her lovely face. He hated that he was responsible for that look of disappointment, and he regretted bringing her here. What was meant to be a light-hearted evening had quickly turned into ammunition on why they weren't suited.

Tossing her purse into the car, CeCe hesitated before getting in. They were so close, he could smell the hint of vanilla at the nape of her neck, could see the scar at the bottom of her ear from where she'd fallen as a kid. She'd told him that story one night when they were closing up together. It was a silly story, but Evan treasured anything she was willing to give him. Right now, he'd give almost anything to hear her voice, for her to say anything that reminded him of who they were—who they could be.

They were friends, friends with a whole lot of potential. Surely this magnetic pull wasn't one-sided?

"I think I could be serious about you," CeCe finally said, the words shaking Evan back to the moment. "And I don't know what to do about that."

Evan felt his heart explode in his chest. "You do?"

CeCe slowly raised her hand until she cupped his cheek, having to stand on tiptoe to make up for their height difference. How easily he forgot her height when they were together. She was such a force, she filled up every space she was in. Her energy, her passion for what she did, radiated around her.

Even now, standing outside with only the din of the pub surrounding them, CeCe was all he could see, feel, and touch. Her thumb swiped around his lips, making him shiver. "I do."

Words escaping him, Evan closed the distance to kiss her. It was slow, tender. They were feeling each other out, finding the angles where they fit best. Cradling her face in his hands, the world around them evaporated. CeCe moaned, and Evan swallowed it, wanting to savor every little thing she gave him. Kissing CeCe felt crucial, like he'd die without her touch, die without having the privilege of her.

As they drove home, Evan held CeCe's hand, trailing over her knuckles with his finger. "Oh no." She gasped and turned to face him. "We didn't stay to see if you won."

He brought her hand back to his mouth and kissed her palm. "I won," he said confidently. He didn't need to see her reaction to know she understood. CeCe was all the prize he needed, and he made himself a promise. No matter how rocky the road got, he was never letting go.

CHAPTER 7

Following her new trend of surprising people, CeCe called off work at the diner. It was one of the few times she'd ever missed a shift with Max, which seemed to floor him. "Is everything all right?" he asked, concern etched into his voice.

CeCe balanced on the edge of her kitchen counter, a mug of coffee in her free hand. "If it's a problem, I'll come in."

"No! Not at all. I'm a little worried to be honest. You've hardly missed a shift in the years we've known each other. I want to make sure you're okay."

Max's compassion and concern for CeCe shouldn't have surprised her, but it did. Despite being partners at the diner, she wasn't used to people caring about her outside the kitchen. Well, that wasn't exactly true. Last night had proved someone else was concerned about her, but she wasn't about to start that conversation with Max. Not now anyway. She was falling for Evan, and that revelation required a lot more thought. It also required a day to herself to pick up the pieces and overanalyze everything. Everything from that kiss to that damn song. A song she's not too proud to admit she'd listen to on repeat for an hour before falling asleep.

Sipping from her coffee, CeCe replied, "I'm fine. Just realized a day to myself is in order. Besides, it'll give me a chance to work on those wedding candies some more. I feel like the vanilla ratio is a little off."

Max chuckled into the phone. "You baking my wedding favors isn't exactly a relaxing day off," he chided. "But I also know you, so I won't push the issue. Take the day and let me know if you need tomorrow. Helen and Evan are here, and Ginny can always help with the dinner rush after work."

"Thanks, Max. I really appreciate it."

CeCe disconnected the call and plodded to her pantry, pulling out the ingredients for candy making. Deep down, she knew the candies were fine as they were. There was a feeling of unease inside her, and the steady process of melting sugar and whipping it into delicate confections calmed her.

Last night with Evan had been a pleasant surprise. She had a good time; she rarely wasn't smiling in Evan's company, but it was something else. She felt safe with him. When those silly girls were fawning over him, she really did trust him. This wasn't like how Eric treated her; she truly believed that Evan only had eyes for her. And while that should have calmed her, it made her uneasy. Yet she couldn't deny she felt cared for with him, like an anchor was holding her still, but not in a confining way.

Then there was the kiss. No kiss had curled her toes like Evan's had. She wasn't sure what his dating history was, but the man could kiss. Man. That's what Evan was, wasn't he? A red-blooded man who had knocked her back on her heels with his patience and respect. God, she'd be a fool to mess this up.

As CeCe poured sugar into a measuring cup, she heard a loud knock at the front door. Tiptoeing to answer it, she saw a familiar silhouette and stifled a groan. Opening the door for her friend, Natalie brushed past CeCe and headed straight for the kitchen. "You don't seem surprised to see me," Natalie said in greeting.

CeCe walked to the coffee pot and poured Natalie a cup while she moved her candy prep work to the side. Easing onto a stool, CeCe settled in for the impending interrogation. "Let me guess. You got to work and Ginny told you I called off today. Am I right?"

Natalie waved a manicured hand in the air. "News travels fast in Buckeye Falls. It's the only downside of living in a small town. The whole place knows your business." She took her coffee and slurped a greedy sip. "So? Spill it, sister. What's going on?"

Knowing Natalie as well as she did, CeCe had two choices. First, play coy and feign exhaustion until Natalie tired of asking questions. Second, go straight for honesty and let the chips fall. Whether it was the extra caffeine or a feeling of contentment, CeCe wasn't sure. What she did know was she wasn't ashamed of her kiss with Evan. Plus, Natalie was like a bloodhound on the hunt. She'd pick up the scent sooner or later and drive CeCe bananas.

"I kissed Evan. Twice. We went out on a proper date last night, but that wasn't the first kiss. He sang John Legend to me, told me he likes my breasts, said the age thing isn't a big deal, and now I'm hiding like a lovesick moron. And I'm thinking about entering the food truck competition." CeCe didn't realize that was how she felt about the competition until the words were out of her mouth. Yet, it seemed to free her, this revelation. She really did want to compete, and she really wanted Evan by her side when she did.

A muscle twitched in Natalie's temple as CeCe's news sunk in. Slowly, Natalie lowered her coffee mug and blinked rapidly. Her false eyelashes fluttered at warp speed, sending a whooshing sound around them. "I'm sorry. What?"

CeCe threw her head back and laughed. "Wow. I was expecting a little more than that."

Natalie shook her head and finally found her words; her brain short-circuited. "You're right. It's just, wow. I'm literally at a loss for words."

At the same time, they both said, "For once."

They laughed and Natalie reached out for CeCe's hand. "Stating the obvious, I like your breasts, too." She snickered as she reached out and poked CeCe in the side, causing her to giggle like the Pillsbury Doughboy. "And if Evan doesn't mind that you're a whopping five years older, then drop it."

"Five years is a big gap," CeCe pressed.

Natalie scoffed. "Yeah, maybe in dog years. Let it go. When I turned thirty I had a big party, cried in the shower afterwards and then recovered. You'll figure it out, trust me."

CeCe shook her head so violently, she feared she slipped a disc. "No, no, no! No parties, I'm serious. Low key, if anything at all."

"Pfft, fine. I won't plan any birthday blowouts, but let the record show you're a spoil sport." CeCe stuck out her tongue, which Natalie promptly ignored. "Now let's get back to the hot gossip. Tell me about the kiss," Natalie ordered as she waited for details. Her necklaces clattered together, a metallic wind chime in the kitchen. "Remember, I'm an old married woman who hasn't seen action in too long. I want all the details."

Natalie's last statement caught CeCe off guard. She assumed her friend's marriage was a happy one. "What are you saying? Is everything okay with you and our fine mayor?"

Natalie rolled her eyes. "We're not here to talk about me. We're here to talk about you. You and the fact that you kissed the hottest guy in town. And I mean that. Have you seen Evan's arms? I feel like he could bench press my minivan without breaking a sweat." She fanned herself with a napkin.

CeCe had to ball her fists so she didn't fan herself. She'd been up close and personal with those muscles on a near daily basis. She agreed wholeheartedly with Natalie; he could probably bench press some serious weight. Clearing her throat, CeCe said, "Yes, Evan's an attractive guy, but that's not news."

"Yeah, the news is the fact that you're finally swapping spit. The poor guy, he's been drooling over you since he started working at the diner. It's pretty much Buckeye Falls' worst kept secret."

"He has not," CeCe argued lamely. "It's a little crush. Totally harmless. And can we please stop with the spit talk? You're killing my appetite."

Natalie wasn't convinced, and frankly neither was CeCe. Evan and she had crossed an invisible line last night, and she needed to figure out what it meant.

"Uh-huh. Then why did you kiss him?" She slurped from her coffee and waited for a reply.

There was no point ignoring her friend's question. "I went over to his place last night to apologize for withholding the truth about Eric and the competition." Just remembering the fact that she still wasn't honest with Evan made her chest tighten. She hated keeping secrets, but she couldn't figure out why she wasn't telling him. He knew a lot about her, but something about Eric felt too sordid to share. The CeCe that dated Eric wasn't the CeCe she was today, but that didn't erase the hurt and embarrassment. She didn't want to taint her potential present with Evan with her past with Eric.

"How did he react when you told him about your ex? That's usually a complicated conversation, to say the least." Natalie tapped on the handle of her mug, eagerly awaiting more gossip.

CeCe busied herself tidying up the sugar canisters on the counter, keeping her gaze away from Natalie's searching stare. But it was no use; the bloodhound had picked up on the scent of deception.

Natalie's nostrils flared. "Wait a minute." She spaced the words out, her eyes laser-focused on CeCe's profile. "You didn't tell him you two dated?" A long stretch of silence filled the kitchen before Natalie finally squealed. "CeCe! Why not?"

CeCe carried the last of her dishes to the pantry and

attempted to keep her cool. She felt a flush of shame creep up her neck at Natalie's accusatory tone. "It didn't feel like the right time, you know? I explained we used to work together and that things ended badly. I figured that was enough to get him off my back about the competition. But then he asked me out on a date, and I thought it would be fun or something."

Natalie muttered into her coffee cup, "Or something indeed."

Throwing her hands in the air, CeCe scoffed. "You told me to be happy! So, technically, it's your fault."

Natalie snorted, an unladylike action she saved for times like these. "My fault?"

"Uh-huh." CeCe nodded. "Go find my happiness, and I guess I'm trying to. And did I mention he sang John Legend? How in the hell can I talk about my complicated dating history when he's literally serenading me?"

Clearing her throat, Natalie frowned. "We'll unpack the singing thing in a minute because I'm not emotionally prepared to think about that hunk crooning for you. But why the sudden desire to compete?"

At first CeCe didn't have an answer. Putting herself, and the diner, out there in competition seemed a long time overdue. They did good work, and her dating history shouldn't dictate their success. "Is this about rubbing your hot boy toy in Eric's face?" Natalie waggled her eyebrows.

Now all the color drained from CeCe's face. She placed her hands on her cheeks and took a deep breath. "Geez. I hope I'm not that shallow."

"No. I don't think you are. Although, it's not a bad idea. You can show up to that competition and kick everyone's butts. Plus, you'll have the sweetest guy in Buckeye Falls on your arm. That seems like a true win-win." Natalie nodded at her own sage advice before draining the rest of her coffee. "Tell me, what are you going to cook for the competition?"

CeCe sat back down on her stool and shrugged. "Not a clue. I was going to take today to rework the wedding candies and brainstorm some ideas."

"Those wedding candies are perfect already. Don't tie yourself down with all that. Start planning your menu for the competition." Natalie checked her phone and groaned when she saw the time. "I gotta run. Ginny and I have a meeting with one of the boutiques on Main Street. They are planning a grand reopening after their renovations, and we offered to help throw a party."

CeCe followed Natalie to the door. "That sounds fun. Let me know if they need help with catering."

Natalie grabbed her purse and hooked it through her arm. "Who do you think is at the top of our catering list?" She winked and pulled CeCe in for a hug. "I'm really happy for you. You deserve to have some fun."

CeCe squeezed a little harder than she needed to, sinking into her friend's embrace. "Thanks, Nat." When they pulled apart, she raised a finger. "Please don't tell Ginny about me kissing Evan. I don't know what it means yet, and I'd rather talk to him first."

Natalie crossed her heart and sighed. "I'll be able to keep this secret for about a week, but then you know I'll fall apart and tell half the town. I'm sorry, but karaoke dates and hot kisses can't stay secret for long."

CeCe rolled her eyes. "That's pretty generous of you. I get a whole week?"

"Tops, but then I'm driving this gossip train straight through Buckeye Falls." Natalie tugged her arm through the air and made a whistling sound. "Toot, toot!"

CeCe waved and watched her friend drive away. When she stepped back inside, she got into work mode, pulling out old notebooks and jotting down ideas that would work in a food truck, but also in a competition setting. Her fritters might work? Evan seemed to be a fan already. Max would have a lot of great ideas, and Evan was coming into his own in the kitchen, but CeCe knew she was the glue that held the team together.

A smile tugged at her lips when she thought of Evan.

His earnest eyes as he focused on learning a new recipe or trying new techniques. There was a lot they needed to figure out between them, and she'd have to come clean about Eric. Especially if they were going to try for something more. Evan deserved to know the whole truth. It was the least she could offer him. It was the least she could offer herself.

*

Going to work at the diner was never a chore for Evan, but today felt especially exciting. He'd replayed the kiss with CeCe so often last night, he was surprised he got any sleep. For once, they finally seemed to be on the same page about the status of their budding relationship. CeCe was into him, and he wanted to do cartwheels down Main Street.

Letting himself in through the back door, Evan hung up his jacket and clapped Max on the back when he entered the kitchen. "Good morning, boss," Evan greeted.

Max chuckled and slid a bowl of eggs across the counter. "Good morning. You're in a great mood."

Helen appeared from the dining room, looking frazzled. Her graying hair was pulled into a low ponytail and two pencils were tucked behind her ears. "The guy's always in a great mood," she scoffed. Despite her gruff tone, she patted Evan's elbow as she walked past. Helen was all bark and no bite.

Evan pulled an apron free and looped it around his waist. He took the bowl of eggs and started cracking them in preparation for breakfast. The two men fell into their familiar morning routine for a few minutes, sharing ideas for the day's omelet special and laughing at Helen's horrible jokes.

When Max told Helen to open the doors, Evan looked at the clock and froze. "Where's CeCe? I didn't realize how late it was."

Max opened another package of bacon and tossed slices onto the grill. Over his shoulder, he said, "She took the day off."

"But she *never* takes a day off," Evan replied. A million horrible visions swam in his mind's eye. Was she sick? Was she hiding from him?

Helen ushered into the kitchen with an empty coffee pot. "Then it's high time she took one." She grunted as she filled the pot with coffee and headed back to the dining room. Before she stepped out again, she barked at Max, "A number four with crispy bacon and a number eight with sausage for table five. I'll be back with the other orders."

Max gave her a thumbs-up and went back to cooking.

Evan fumbled his hands, causing three slices of untoasted bread fell to the floor with a sad thud. Evan couldn't focus on anything other than getting to the bottom of CeCe's absence. "Is she okay?" he asked while tossing the bread in the trash and trying again.

Max turned and smiled at Evan. "She's fine, man. You know I wouldn't be this relaxed if she wasn't all right. I think she truly just needed a day off."

CeCe was too much of a workaholic for that to be the simple answer. There was too much to do at the diner for him to go off in search of answers. Instead, he got to work and tried not to think about all the reasons CeCe wasn't there.

The Kiss? The age discussion? Karaoke? Did he push her too hard?

Fortunately for Evan, he didn't have much free time to obsess about her absence. An hour after the breakfast rush slowed down, Ginny and Natalie came in through the backdoor. "Hello," Ginny called out as she shrugged off her coat. Before she could hang it on a hook, Max was by her side and kissing her senseless.

Natalie sighed at the happy couple and tossed her purse on the edge of the counter. "It's a good thing I like you both, because your PDA is getting worse by the minute."

Helen stomped by with a stack of plates and added her two cents. "You can say that again, Madame First Lady."

Evan couldn't disagree, but the sight of the love birds made him wish for CeCe's company even more. Natalie came up beside him and smirked, and the look in her eyes made him uneasy. Was it possible that CeCe mentioned their kiss? Evan highly doubted it, but why else would Natalie look like she's in on a big secret?

Natalie gave Evan another glance before offering her morning greeting. "Good morning. How are things?" He nearly nicked his thumb with his paring knife. Being under Natalie's focused gaze was terrifying at best. She could likely get even the most seasoned spy to spill their guts in a matter of moments.

"Uh, good morning." He coughed and regained his composure. "What brings you ladies in?"

Ginny came up to her business partner's side and hip-checked her out of the way. "Pay no attention to Natalie. She's excited because we signed a new contract this morning," Ginny beamed at Max, who whooped with excitement.

Picking up his fiancée, Max spun her in a circle and kissed her cheek. Ginny nearly lost a shoe from his display of aerobics. "Gin, that's great news. What services did they buy?"

Natalie answered the question while Ginny was put back on solid ground. "They want the full package. Ginny talked them into everything, including a new website."

Evan's ears perked up at the mention of a website, but he didn't interrupt. *Stay cool.*

Ginny poured a cup of coffee and gestured at Natalie, who shook her head. Sipping from her cup, Ginny continued their news. "The only downside is we haven't hired any web developers yet. The boutique has a tight turnaround time, which makes me a little nervous."

Evan took a breath and finished chopping his vegetables before he interjected. He wanted to look interested, but not overly eager. "What type of site are they looking for? Just created, or supported after creation?"

Natalie stood a little straighter and turned her attention to Evan. "The whole enchilada. They need it built from scratch, but also need someone to post weekly updates and sales. Maintenance included."

Ginny, clearly missing what Natalie was picking up, sighed. "Which is a huge undertaking. We need to get back to the office and start looking for web developers to hire on contract. Damn, I wish I had some of my New York contacts."

When Ginny left her old job in New York, she ruffled a lot of feathers. While some of her old contacts stayed in touch, a lot still showed loyalty to her old boss. Evan didn't know the whole story, but Max had told him enough to know it was a good thing Ginny was out of New York and onto new things.

Max plated the last three orders of the morning and rang the bell for Helen to pick them up. He wiped his hands on his apron and joined the trio at the counter. "Gin, I think you're missing some contacts in Buckeye Falls. We have tech people here," he said.

Natalie's gaze hadn't left Evan, and she tapped his forearm. "I have a feeling our tech people are a lot closer than we think. What did you study at OSU?"

Everyone turned their attention to Evan, who shrunk under their collective gazes. Being the center of attention wasn't his favorite thing. "Business and web development," he said, not able to meet Natalie's eyes.

Ginny gasped and swatted at Max's side. "Why didn't you mention this?" She turned to Evan and her smile grew. "Could you look at the specs and tell us if you could make a site for the boutique? We'd get you on contract, of course."

This was the moment Evan had been waiting for. He was being looked at as an adult, as a professional. "I'd love to see the specs. I can swing by your office after my shift to see their wish list."

Natalie shook her head and started digging through her

LIBBY KAY

massive purse. "No need." She retrieved a file folder and slapped it on the counter. Before she continued, she looked at Max and asked, "Can I steal your employee for a moment?"

Max chuckled, knowing it wasn't really a question. "We're good; Helen just delivered our last order of the morning. I'll go switch the sign and close up before lunch starts." Max stepped over to Evan and cupped his shoulder. "Take my office."

Evan wanted to hug Max. He knew how Evan felt about his web skills and the fact that he couldn't find the right place to use them. This project could grow his portfolio, and it was a big deal. "Thanks, Max."

Natalie wasted no time and strode into Max's office. She gathered up invoices and moved them to the far corner of the cluttered desk. Ginny gave Max another quick peck before following her partner into the office.

Evan poured another round of coffees and took the remaining seat. "Here we go, ladies." He offered their drinks and ran a hand through his hair. Flinching, he smelled cheese and bacon on his skin. He'd envisioned being a little more spruced up before his first pitch meeting. "Let me show you some of my other websites. I have a portfolio I started in school and built during my post-grad internship." He logged into Max's computer and pulled up a website that featured his other projects.

Thirty minutes later, it was obvious his experience and age weren't an issue. The three had agreed on a contract, schedule, and general plan of attack. The boutique would have a new website within a month, with full support and updates on contract through Evan. He had his first long-term client, and he felt weightless.

Ginny clicked away on her iPad and turned the screen to Evan and Natalie. "I'll send the official contract when I'm back at my computer, but does this pay scale look good to you?"

Natalie flashed a thumbs-up and went back to her cup

104

of coffee. Evan had to bite his cheek so he didn't scream with delight. The contract offered more money than he thought possible for a job like this.

Clearing his throat, he nodded. "That looks reasonable. Thanks, Ginny."

"Perfect," Natalie said, glancing at her phone. "I need to swing home real quick and check on the kids. We'll email you the contract to e-sign." She gathered her things and waved over her shoulder as she disappeared into the kitchen.

Ginny collected her things, and Evan held the office door open for her. She reached out to shake his hand. "This is such a pleasant surprise. I'm so glad we get to work together."

Evan shook her hand and couldn't fight the smile anymore. He'd done it—he'd gotten his first contract in Buckeye Falls.

As they walked out of the office, Evan saw the only sight that could make his smile bigger. CeCe stood with Max by the stove, a stack of papers in her hands. Max beamed, nodding like he'd won the lottery. "If you're sure, I'm sure," Max said to CeCe.

"I'm positive," CeCe said.

"What's going on?" Ginny asked.

CeCe saw them and gave Ginny a quick hug. "Well, I have some news to share."

Max elbowed her and laughed. "I think we have some news."

Ginny and Evan exchanged a look, assuming the other knew what was going on.

"We just entered the food truck competition," CeCe said.

Evan searched her face for signs of concern, but all he saw was excitement. "We did?" he asked, looking to Max for his reaction—he seemed content, no worry lines creasing his brow, not a stammer to be heard. "You're sure you want to?"

CeCe waved the papers in the air. "I'm serious as a heart attack. We can win this thing, and I've spent the morning drafting some recipe ideas. Let's do this. Let's kick Eric's ass."

"I'm in!" Max exclaimed.

Evan couldn't wait to kick that jerk's butt. Anyone who messed with CeCe deserved to get knocked down a peg or two. "I'm definitely in."

Ginny clapped and bounced on her feet. "What a morning. I think I need a nap after all the excitement."

Max walked to Ginny's side and wrapped his arm around her waist. "Does this mean your web developer woes have been resolved?" He winked at Evan, who felt like things couldn't get much better.

"They certainly did. Evan is signing the contract today. We found our web developer."

CeCe looked at Evan and asked, "What did I miss?"

A *lot*, Evan thought. He couldn't wait to fill her in on all the details. Without thinking too hard about it, he said, "I'll tell you about it at dinner. Want to come over to my place tonight? We can look at those menus." He gestured to the papers with a steady hand, proud of himself for playing it cool.

CeCe nodded. "Sounds like a plan."

So much had happened in the last twenty-four hours, and things couldn't possibly get better. He'd kissed CeCe, landed a web contract, and now they got to compete in a major food truck competition.

When Ginny and Max excused themselves to Max's office, CeCe came up and proved Evan wrong. She linked her arms around his neck and pulled him in for a quick kiss on the lips. "I'll swing by around seven o'clock. Is that okay?"

Evan's lips tingled from the brief contact. "That's perfect." For the rest of the day, Evan couldn't wipe the sappy smile off his face. He didn't think anything could get better than this.

CHAPTER 8

When CeCe got back to her place, she heard her phone buzz with an incoming text. Hoping to see Evan's number flash on the screen, she was surprised when it was Max. *You're sure about the competition?*

CeCe kicked her shoes off and padded to the couch, where she fell back into the pillows and sighed at the peace of her living room. Her brain ran a million miles an hour, and she liked being back home. She was touched that Max was concerned over the competition, and it threw her past with Eric into sharper contrast. Even during their best times together, he still wouldn't let her arbitrarily call off work. The benefit of hindsight proved how blind she was toward Eric's garbage behavior.

Before she could change her mind, she grabbed her laptop and pulled up the competition's website. With her free hand, she texted Max back to confirm she was, indeed, all right. *Yes, I'm registering us now. We just need to find a food truck.* She included a few emojis to highlight how fine she really was with everything. If she couldn't hide behind a winky face and thumbs-up emoji—what was the point of texting?

A moment later, Max replied with, *I've got a couple contacts.*

I'll email you the details. Want to work on this with Evan?

Naturally she did. Not only did CeCe relish opportunities to work with Evan, she'd started to crave seeing him socially. His charms had burrowed their way past her defenses, and she was done pretending she wasn't enjoying herself. Not even her most productive day in the kitchen could compete with the high she felt laying with him in a pillow fort, or sharing a meal in her home. Eric never made her feel cherished like this, and that drove home the point that she needed to let Evan all the way inside her life.

With a quick reply to Max, *Yep, Evan and I got this,* CeCe got back into work mode. Evan would appreciate the chance to work with her on this, because he was so generous with his time, thoughtful when it came to collaborating. There had been a few times when she wondered what a smart guy like him was doing at the diner, but it wasn't her place to question or judge. She had a whole host of reasons she was in Buckeye Falls. Best to leave people's motives alone.

CeCe scrolled through the registration site for the competition, and her breath hitched at the sight of Eric on the screen. She'd have to face him eventually, but even the pixelated Eric made her uneasy.

Time had been good to him. His dark hair had a few flecks of gray, and there were a few fine lines around his eyes. But he was the same cocksure chef he was years ago. His grin was new, or at least the pearly veneers were, smirking at her through the screen. CeCe remembered a random night together, when Eric confided that he hated his crooked smile. She'd traced his jawline and shook her head, promising him that his teeth were perfect and gave him character. Over their time together, she'd quickly learned if there was something Eric wanted, he never hesitated to go after it. Apparently, that mindset was for more than just people. "Nice Chiclets." CeCe muttered.

Tearing her eyes from Eric, she instead focused on the entry form. Five minutes later, the task was done. There was no backing down. Expecting to feel a zing of apprehension, she was pleasantly surprised when all she felt was excitement over the chance to flex her culinary muscle. Years had gone by since the last time she'd competed in a food competition, and it felt empowering to start again.

There were about two months until the competition. Max and Ginny's wedding was shortly after, and CeCe was glad she'd only have one more event to focus on. Learning about Evan's contract for the boutique's new website was exciting, but she feared he was stretching himself too thin. He was a people pleaser, and she could tell he liked to feel useful and involved.

CeCe closed her laptop and pulled herself to her feet. She had a couple hours until her dinner date with Evan, and she wanted to bring something to his place beyond the recipes to review. Knowing he loved her famous cheesy bites, she rolled up her sleeves and got to work. She fell into the familiar rhythm of grating, measuring, mixing, and baking. During these moments, she let her mind wander. That is, if her foggy brain would allow the time for reflection. From thinking about the diner's upcoming menu to options for Max and Ginny's reception to her budding feelings for Evan, her brain ran a marathon.

CeCe hadn't dated much since she left Eric and Chicago behind. She'd spent some time working at pop-up restaurants on her way to Buckeye Falls, never quite finding the place where she wanted to stay. She had always been a roamer, loving the feeling of not being tied down to anything or anyone. The feeling could have stemmed from her hectic childhood, being ushered back and forth between her parents, but she wasn't sure. Even before her parent's divorce, she had a restless energy at her core.

When she'd met Eric, CeCe felt an unexpected shift in her universe. Her days no longer revolved around recipes and restaurants, but her focus was all on Eric. If he said jump, she would spring into action until he was pleased and she was exhausted.

Need a new menu in time for the big *Chicago Tribune* food review? Ask CeCe.

The waitstaff uniforms were looking dated? Ask CeCe to order new ones.

Don't have time to find a plumber for the leaky prep sink? Ask CeCe.

She had been used to being everything to Eric—until she wasn't.

But the trouble with doing everything for someone was the potential of not getting anything in return. Growing up with '90s rom-coms, she half expected to find her own Freddie Prinze Jr. to sweep her off her dorky feet, someone to dote on her every waking moment. When Eric, one of the hottest chefs in Chicago, started showing interest in her skills outside the restaurant, she fell—hard.

Eric had this ability to make everyone feel singular, feel seen, but especially CeCe. As they closed up each night, he would slide her a plate of a special meal he'd made just for her. He would walk her to the train station, his arm slung over her shoulders, asking about her day and plans for the weekend. As Saturday night turned into Sunday morning, Eric would be at her place making sourdough bread for breakfast before they had to get into work.

On days when CeCe wasn't feeling well, Eric would send a container of his famous chicken soup with a note that made her smile. She probably still had that note lying around in a box somewhere, and she hated herself for keeping it. Certain mementos were better suited for the dumpster.

That was the thing with relationships. When they were good, they were *good*. You wanted to savor all the memories while they were fresh and ripe, much like a summer strawberry. What was the point of falling in love if you didn't have proof of the fall? CeCe still treasured these outdated keepsakes, mostly because very few men had treated her so well before.

Now things felt different. Evan felt different. There was something in his young, hopeful gaze that made her truly feel treasured and cared for. No matter what happened, Evan wouldn't shut her out of his life. He would be there. This notion made her feel better and worse in equal measure.

It was never fair to compare relationships, but it seemed impossible not to. CeCe remembered the day her relationship with Eric fell apart, and it still made her nauseous. Having forgotten something in her locker at the restaurant, she'd doubled back to find Eric in a very delicate situation with a woman CeCe had never seen before. At first, CeCe was speechless. She stood in the doorway with her jaw on the floor and her heart crumbling to dust.

When they broke apart from their embrace, the woman was embarrassed but didn't seem upset. Eric had introduced CeCe as his sous chef, not his girlfriend. He'd introduced Hilary as his wife, and CeCe felt the earth shift under her feet. The next day she told Eric she was giving her two weeks' notice. To say Eric handled the news well would be a gross understatement.

He. Went. Ballistic.

CeCe could still hear the sound of her resignation letter being torn to shreds, could see the strips of paper fluttering around his office as he howled with frustration. "You're not leaving," he'd said as he stomped around like a toddler who didn't get dessert.

"How can you expect me to stay? Do you really have nothing you want to say to me?" Her eyes brimmed with tears, and CeCe hated showing her vulnerability, her pain. *How had she misread the situation that badly?!*

Eric ran his hands through his hair, finally turning to snag her gaze. "You're not leaving," he repeated, as if this time she'd change her mind.

"I can't stay here." She'd meant every variation of the word. The restaurant, Chicago—it had all lost its luster when she'd found out about Hilary. "Can we please be adults about this?" Perhaps she was still numb from the shock of the truth, but CeCe had never truly been afraid of

Eric until that moment.

He'd closed the distance between them in two strides and towered over her in the cramped space. For all the times she'd felt protected by their size difference, then she'd felt cornered like an injured animal. It was a sensation she planned never to repeat again. "We're not done, CeCe."

"Oh, I think we are." She'd been proud that the tremor in her voice was minimal, although she'd run out of space to hide.

Reaching out, Eric held onto her forearms and ground out, "You're not leaving. We're not done. Nothing has to change."

CeCe had been incredulous. "You're married." She spat the word out like it'd burned her tongue. "You can't be serious."

But Eric was serious. He'd been rude and short with her in the kitchen, putting all the staff on edge. CeCe had applied for jobs all over the city, and Eric was quick to get in her way to make terrible references. He'd insulted everything about her, from her time management to her ability to make professional-level patisserie. All in all, he'd been acting like the victim. It had driven CeCe to the brink.

After several months of getting shut down before she even made it to the interviews, CeCe knew she needed to leave Chicago. She'd miss the hustle and bustle, the constant feeling that everything was happening around her. Until she found Buckeye Falls, CeCe didn't think she could live a quieter life. But the town had quickly cast a spell on her that couldn't be ignored.

CeCe was content to avoid relationships in Buckeye Falls. The dating pool was pretty shallow for a small town, so that was her default excuse when Natalie and Max pushed her to date. Only last year did Max even learn about CeCe's past with Eric. Some things were not worth bringing up.

CeCe checked her phone for the time and realized she was going to be late to Evan's if she didn't leave now.

Tossing her cheesy bites into a plastic container, she dashed to the bathroom to run a brush through her hair and swipe a little mascara on her lashes. Nothing major, but enough to show she was trying.

CeCe arrived at Evan's on time filled with a sense of anticipation. This was a big step, and she was eager to start their journey, whatever it may be. As she got out of the car, she saw a familiar face leaving Evan's apartment.

Before she could greet Mallory, CeCe heard her talking to Evan. "You need to come to family dinner this Sunday. I know it's usually a nightmare, but Mom is upset you haven't been in over a month. Please, Ev."

"Hope I'm not interrupting anything," CeCe greeted from the stoop. Mallory looked tired, clad in crumpled nurse's scrubs; her eyes looked darker than her hair. Evan was dressed casually in jeans and a Bruce Lee T-shirt that did funny things to her insides. No man should look that good in cotton.

Evan beamed when he saw CeCe. A girl could get used to that reaction. "Your timing is perfect," he said as he pushed his sister to the side.

Mallory laughed, as only an older sister could, but continued her argument. "You can literally push me down the stairs, but you still have to come this Sunday."

Evan shook his head. "Hard pass. I'm not in the mood for Dad's crap, okay? Mal, you of all people know that."

Mallory chewed on her lip for a moment, taking a moment to change tactics. "It'll probably be the last time you'll see Em before she has the baby," she countered. Watching Evan's facial features shift proved she had won the battle.

Evan ran a hand down his face and sighed with every ounce of energy he had left. "Fine, what time?"

Mallory clapped in delight. "Dinner's at five-thirty, but you know Mom will want you there early so she can pepper you with questions and feed you before dinner even starts. She misses spoiling her baby."

Evan rolled his eyes, his head nearly falling off his shoulders with the gesture. CeCe found this sibling back and forth fascinating. As an only child, she never knew the joy, and frustration, that came from bickering with a sibling. Frankly she was a little jealous of Mallory and Evan's relationship. It would be nice to have someone to pester, and care enough about her.

"If I'm not working, I'll come. Okay?"

CeCe interjected, "But you're off on Sunday. We both are, since Max is off Saturday." Immediately, she was in trouble. Frantically, she looked around as if she could pull the words back, but it was no use.

Both siblings turned to her with opposite expressions. Evan looked betrayed, and Mallory looked thrilled. "Great! Then you can come along, CeCe. I know our sisters would love to meet you."

CeCe arched an eyebrow. "They would?" This notion seemed ridiculous to her. As a child, she rarely bothered bringing friends or later dates to her house. She'd ping-ponged back and forth between her mom and dad's places so much growing up, sometimes it felt like she didn't have a permanent home.

The idea that Evan's parents were together and his sisters talked regularly felt like something from a Norman Rockwell painting—timeless and familiar yet unattainable. CeCe didn't know if she wanted a family of her own, but since the big three-oh was knocking on the door, she'd have to figure that out sooner rather than later. CeCe blinked and saw the siblings were still bickering. Her existential crisis would have to wait.

Evan threw his arm in front of CeCe, as if to protect her from impact. "Absolutely not. CeCe is not going to family dinner. I'd like to see her again."

Now CeCe was intrigued. She'd never seen Evan so worked up before. "What happens if I want to come to family dinner?" she asked, looking at Mallory.

Mallory pulled CeCe into a hug that nearly crushed her

ribs. "You're coming and I can't wait. I'll text directions, in case Chuckles here tries to pull a fast one." Evan tugged on CeCe's hand, trying to pull her into his apartment, but Mallory was determined. "What's your number?" she asked as she retrieved her phone from her handbag.

CeCe gave Mallory her number and watched Evan's face fall. Mallory hugged them both again before sprinting to her car. He shut the door after CeCe walked in and stomped to the kitchen. His shoulders were tense, and she needed to apologize for overstepping. "Look, I'm sorry if I—" but her words were cut off when he turned around and pulled her in for a kiss.

It was a tender kiss, their lips lingering a moment before he pulled back and placed another kiss on her forehead. He cradled her face in his hands, taking his time to kiss her cheeks in slow succession. "You don't have to apologize," he said, not taking his eyes off hers. "Mallory has no boundaries. You can skip the whole thing. She'll understand. I'll definitely understand."

While CeCe was mesmerized by his kiss, she still had questions. "You don't want me to come?" She watched a myriad of emotions flit over Evan's face until he finally smiled and kissed her once more.

"I want you to come. But this isn't how I envisioned it."

"How'd you envision it?" CeCe asked, curious how long Evan had imagined bringing her home to meet his family. She should be put off by that mindset, but since she'd been thinking about Eric so much lately, it seemed like a sweet gesture rather than a confining one.

Evan stepped back and opened the fridge, pulling out two beers and handing one to her. "I wanted to bring you home and introduce you as my girlfriend, and I know we don't know what we are yet. I don't want to muddy the waters this early."

Her mind flashed back to the night before, to serenades and passionate kisses, and CeCe didn't know what she was afraid of anymore. They'd already muddied the waters. Hell, she felt like she was wading through mud puddles when it came to their budding relationship. It wasn't a horrible image, but rather a fun one like when she was a child playing after a storm. If she was really going to join Evan for family dinner, then it might as well be as his girlfriend.

Hearing the word girlfriend on his lips made her heart flutter. How did she feel about this? Was she ready to be a girlfriend again? Looking at Evan now, as he flitted around his kitchen getting their dinner ready, she was ready. Evan was not Eric, and it was time to stop punishing him for the mistakes of her ex.

Sensing CeCe's mood shift, Evan walked to the stove and lifted the lid on a stock pot. "I made some of Max's Thai chicken soup. Hope you're hungry."

Her stomach growled at the news. "I'm starving." And so, she followed Evan to the table, where he served them dinner and they talked menus and ideas for the competition. It was a relaxing evening that made her realize she could really get used to this.

"Let's do this," she finally said when dinner was finished. "Let's give it a shot."

"Which recipe?" he asked, clearly not picking up on the monumental decision at hand.

CeCe took his hand and squeezed. "No, us. Let's do this."

Evan nearly choked on his drink. "You want to be my girlfriend?" He reluctantly took his hand back to swipe at the mess he'd made.

"Yeah," she said with a smile. "I think I do."

And with that, CeCe dove head first into her first relationship in three years. She wasn't going to second guess herself, or Evan. If this was meant to be, then they might as well make it official. Because CeCe knew in her soul this was special, that Evan was special. And judging from the glint in his eyes, the feeling was mutual.

*

CeCe was his girlfriend.
CeCe was his girlfriend.

Evan repeated the mantra in his head for the remainder of their evening. Every few minutes he'd close the distance between them to kiss her senseless, afraid if he didn't take the chance he'd lose it forever. When they'd finished making out like teenagers, Evan led the way into his living room. He'd cleaned up the space and put away the air mattress for the time being.

CeCe frown when she saw the open space. "No forts tonight?"

He shrugged, biting back a smirk at her disappointment. "Nah. I needed to clear some space for my set-up." He gestured to the laptop and stacks of notebooks on the coffee table. Ever since he signed the contract, he was on a mission to draft the website for the boutique. He was still radiating with excitement, and he knew this could be a big break for him and his freelance career.

Despite his excitement over the contract, however, he was even more thrilled about the competition and having CeCe over. She followed him to the couch and sat right next to him as he eased into place. He casually threw his arm over the back of the couch and stifled a groan when she nestled beside him. It all felt so comfortable—warm and fuzzy—like the perfect dream.

Without asking, he turned on the TV to the last streaming service they'd watched. Pulling up an action movie from the '80s, they settled back for a while to watch the big fight scene unfold. When there was a lull in the action, CeCe leaned back to catch his gaze. "Should we look at the last of these menus?"

Evan drew his arm back and cleared the coffee table. "Sure, let me make some room."

CeCe studied him for a moment before pulling a few notebooks from her purse. "You're sure this won't be too much for you?" she asked.

"What's too much?" He raised an eyebrow.

"This." She waved her hands around his workspace. "You just landed a contract, and I don't want to distract you. Girlfriends are a lot of work, you know?" She winked to prove she was teasing.

"You're the best kind of distraction." It was a line cheesier than her famous cheesy bites, but she didn't seem to mind. The flush that crept up her cheeks spoke volumes. "Besides, the whole point of getting freelance work is so I can make my own schedule and keep up at the diner. I really love working there."

"Good. Because we need your help," she said as she splayed her notebooks across the coffee table.

The movie forgotten, the pair combed through dozens of recipes that she had either perfected or wanted to try again. They'd agreed on one savory dish and one sweet dish to try at the diner on Saturday. When she mentioned the fritters, Evan remarked it was a given. After a few yawns, it was clear planning time was over. As he packed up their notes, he got a text from Max.

Evan scrolled through his phone and chuckled. "Well, it's a good thing you are coming to family dinner."

CeCe peered down at his phone. "Why is that?"

"Because Max found us a food truck. And this guy lives ten minutes from my parents. We'll literally drive past his place on the way to their house."

"Then it's meant to be," CeCe said with a firm nod.

Before Evan knew it, family dinner day arrived. With Evan behind the wheel, they drove west to see a man about a food truck. The guy had been in the mobile food scene out in Indianapolis but had had to retire when his wife fell ill. The vehicle was still in great shape; he just didn't have it in him to work anymore.

The seller knocked on the metal door with a sigh. "She's a good old beast." His voice came out sad and low. His expression held years of memories, but also the grief of memories still unmade.

CeCe nodded sagely, her blonde hair blowing in the early spring air. "You're sure you want to sell?" Her voice was light, but Evan didn't miss the tenderness hiding beneath the surface. Apparently, he wasn't the only one affected by the man's predicament.

"I'm sure. Besides"—he exhaled and looked between the pair—"I've got a good feeling about you two. It'd be nice to see the old girl working again." He rubbed the back of his neck and quoted a price that was embarrassingly low.

"Surely it's worth more than that," Evan countered.

"I need to get her out of here." The man hitched his thumb over his shoulder toward his house. "Might as well sell her for a song and know she's in good hands."

With a lift of her shoulder, CeCe agreed. The deal was set. "We'll pick the truck up next week." A couple handshakes and it was done.

CeCe led the way back to the car. "That's a great truck. We really lucked out. Did you see how new that fryer was? We barely need to scour the stainless steel."

Evan tried to relax as he took the last few turns to his parent's house, but it was no use. Not even CeCe's excitement could dull the sense of dread coursing through his veins. He'd spent the last few nights tossing and turning about this family dinner.

First, he had to tell his parents about his web contract. Since it wasn't a traditional job, he assumed his father would hate the notion. Next there was the food truck competition. Would they even understand how exciting it was? And lastly, and most worrisome, was that he was bringing a girl to dinner. Not just any girl, CeCe. Evan was on pins and needles. Family meals never happened without a hefty dose of drama.

As he pulled up to his parent's house, he saw the familiar cars of his sisters and their husbands. He and CeCe were the last to arrive. She reached for the door handle to exit the car when Evan took her elbow. "Wait," he pleaded as he cleared his throat. He felt frantic and needed to calm down.

CeCe pulled back and frowned. She studied him a moment before asking, "Are you okay?"

Was he okay? His pounding heartbeat and sweaty temples were a good sign he was far from okay. He shook his head and tried to collect his thoughts. "This kind of snuck up on me." He gestured toward the house, hoping the movement would convey every rogue thought he was battling. "I mean family dinner. They're going to ask who you are."

CeCe laughed, deliberately misunderstanding his statement. "I'm CeCe LaRue. I'm a chef at the diner with you. I'm twenty-nine years old, a Virgo, and—"

Evan laughed, a tad of the tension melting away. It was hard to be stressed when CeCe shared a genuine smile. CeCe smiles were meant to be treasured, and he wanted the time now to savor it, to tuck it away for safe keeping.

"Thank you," he finally said. "I don't want my family to scare you off."

CeCe got serious for a moment and turned to face him. "I'm not going anywhere. I know we just figured this out"— she flapped her hand between them—"but first and foremost, you've been a good friend, Evan. It's going to take more than a couple nosey sisters to scare me off."

In that moment, he wanted to kiss her senseless, to pull her to him and show her all the things she made him feel. But it was 5:20 p.m. on a Sunday, and he was currently parked in front of his parents' house. This wasn't the time or the place. With a sigh, he opened his car door and took a deep breath. "Let's do this."

Just when their feet hit the sidewalk, the front door burst open as Lucy and Jackson sprinted to the car to meet them. "Uncle Evan!" the kids chorused, each grabbing a leg and squealing as Evan ruffled both of their heads.

"Hey, kiddos. How have you gotten so big?"

Lucy was the first to step back, pleased to hear that she'd

sprouted up since their last visit. She smoothed the pink fabric of her princess costume and nodded toward her little brother. "I'm over four inches taller than Jackson," she declared, holding four fingers in the air triumphantly.

"Yeah, but I'm faster," Jackson countered. In a flash, he'd spun on his sneakered heels and darted back toward the house.

Lucy didn't try to follow her brother. Instead, she turned to face CeCe and dipped in a curtsy. "Hello, I'm Princess Lucy. You must be Uncle Evan's special friend."

CeCe bit back a smile and attempted her own version of a curtsy. "It's a pleasure to meet you, your highness." CeCe winked at the little girl, who giggled in delight.

Lucy took her uncle's hand and pulled him down to her face. "I like her," she stage-whispered. "Time for dinner," she announced and dragged them both toward the house. Evan caught CeCe's eye over Lucy's glittering tiara, and his heart swelled. CeCe was a natural with kids, and he didn't realize until that moment how important that was to him.

"There you kids are," his mother greeted from the doorway. She was still dressed for church in heels with her hair done, a checkered apron over her dress. "We were about to send out a search party." She patted her granddaughter on the head before pulling Evan into a warm embrace. "It's good to see you, dear."

Evan allowed his mother a moment to squeeze the stuffing out of him before he drew back to introduce CeCe. He had no idea how his mother would react, and it terrified him.

From the corner of his eye, he could see CeCe fidgeting with the strap of her purse, her shoulders bunched up to her ears. He'd rarely seen her nervous, and it pulled a little in his chest. "Mom, this is CeCe."

"CeCe, it's so nice to meet you." His mother reached out and gave CeCe a quick hug before pulling back and admiring her son's date. "You're as lovely as Mallory said."

"For once, Mal told the truth," Evan scoffed.

"I heard that," Mallory said in greeting as she joined them in the doorway. She waved at CeCe before playfully punching Evan in the arm.

CeCe reached into her bag and presented his mother with a bag of cheesy bites she made as a bribe. "I made these for you and your husband. Thank you for having me over."

His mom took the bag and smiled, clearly touched that CeCe brought a hostess gift. "Thank you, dear. That is so thoughtful."

Mallory snatched the bag from her mom and moaned. "Are these what I think they are?" she asked, trying to open the bag.

Evan took the parcel from his sister and held it in the air, knowing she'd never be able to reach it. Playing keep-away was one thing from childhood that never got old. "Yes, and she didn't make them for you, Mal."

Before Mallory and he could break into full-blown sibling bickering, Emily joined them. She looked like a tick about to pop, her protruding stomach the size of a beach ball. She rested her hands on her belly and hummed contentedly at them. "You must be the famous CeCe," she said in greeting.

CeCe stepped up and shook his sister's hand, looking down at her baby bump with fondness. "And you must be Emily. Congratulations! When are you due?"

Emily rolled her eyes and patted her bump. "Next month. We thought if we came out for dinner, maybe it would jump-start the whole process."

Sophie came up behind Emily, jaw set, her eyes focused on CeCe. Evan gulped, knowing his eldest sister was the hardest sell. "CeCe, this is my other sister, Sophie."

CeCe reached out to shake Sophie's hand. "It's so nice to finally meet all of you. Mallory and Evan have told me so much about you. I feel like we've already met."

Sophie shared a quick greeting, but didn't let go of CeCe's hand right away. Evan glared until she played nice, and CeCe's hand fell to her side. Snatching her hand before anyone else could, Evan led everyone into the house. He was secretly disappointed that his father hadn't made his way out of the den to greet them, but that was nothing new. His dad worked on his own schedule, and there was no point getting upset about it.

"How can I help with dinner?" CeCe offered as she washed her hands at the sink.

The house smelled like Thanksgiving and Christmas all rolled together, and Evan's mouth watered. Seeing CeCe in his family home, laughing with his sisters, made his mouth water for different reasons. He'd thought about moments like this countless times. Having CeCe involved in all the facets of his life made sense to him, and he was relieved to see her bantering like it was no big deal. Like she really belonged.

But it was a big deal to Evan. CeCe was the first girlfriend he'd brought home since high school, and she meant so much to him. It was crucial that she liked his family and that they liked her. He couldn't imagine anyone not liking CeCe. But when he felt his father's firm hand on his shoulder, Evan knew that if anyone could disappoint, it was him.

CHAPTER 9

"And who do we have here?" a booming male voice asked from the hallway. CeCe spun around, a bottle of mustard clutched in her hands, to see Evan's doppelgänger. Well, doppelgänger wasn't entirely accurate. This man looked like Evan thirty years into the future, and CeCe had to admit she liked what she saw. He and Evan shared the same frame, but his father had a bit more bulk and a dash of pepper in his fair hair. His expression wasn't nearly as warm as his son's, and she assumed the laugh lines bracketing his lips were from scowling other than smiling.

Hoping she didn't look disheveled, she put the mustard down and stepped past Mallory. "Good evening, Mr. Lawson. I'm CeCe. It's nice to meet you." Despite being older than Evan, she suddenly felt sixteen and awkward. It was like when she'd met her high school boyfriend's parents and had spinach stuck in her braces. *Totally mortifying!*

Evan's father took her hand and squeezed, hard. "Please, call me Dale. It's a pleasure to meet you, CeCe."

Evan appeared at his father's side, his jaw tense and his eyes downcast. If she listened closely, she heard Evan grinding his molars to dust. CeCe had never seen Evan so on edge.

Mallory took a towel and swatted at her father's arm. "Dad, either grab a spoon or get out. Dinner's almost ready, and we need all hands on deck."

Dale raised his hands in defeat and took a step back. "You don't need to tell me twice. This is clearly women's work." He winked at CeCe and backed out of the kitchen.

She turned to see Evan, a look of utter defeat in his eyes. Women's work? This guy was surely kidding. No one could be that tone-deaf in this day and age. While her own father wasn't much in the kitchen, he was a hard worker who knew when to roll up his sleeves and dive in. CeCe had to learn how to cook when she spent weekends at her father's apartment, as his usual meal options came in rectangular plastic boxes.

Hoping she misunderstood, CeCe glanced around and saw that Mallory and Emily weren't deterred. Both were focused on their tasks and didn't seem bothered by their father's outdated—and sexist—commentary. Perhaps this was why Evan was horrified to bring CeCe home?

Clearly, there was tension between father and son, and she quickly understood why. Evan was so sweet and tender, open to people regardless of their situation—traits he obviously inherited from his mother. Before she could get too far down the rabbit hole, Mallory tapped CeCe's shoulder and gestured to the pan of gravy. She'd been stirring for a while and the sauce had finally thickened.

"Does this need more mustard? Mom usually has bland gravy, but Em and I were looking online for some gravy pointers. Turns out Dijon does the trick, but I'm afraid we didn't add enough." Mallory handed CeCe a clean tasting spoon.

The gravy had a silky texture and a tangy hit, but it still needed salt and pepper. "A heavy pinch of salt and pepper, and this gravy is perfect." CeCe nodded and tossed the spoon in the sink. It clattered with a satisfying echo. No matter what she was cooking, it wasn't a meal unless she made a little noise.

Emily swept past with a pair of serving platters. "Mind if I jump in to take out the chickens? They should be ready."

CeCe took one look at Emily's swollen belly and shook her head. "I don't think so. You go sit and rest, I'll take care of the heavy lifting." Fortunately, Emily didn't argue. She handed off the platters and left for the dining room, waddling like a penguin.

CeCe placed the platters by the oven and felt a hand at the small of her back. Evan leaned in, his mouth by her ear, and asked, "What do you need?" His touch was soft, yet steady. She didn't know it at the time, but it was what she needed.

"A pair of hot pads would be great. I can take care of getting the birds out to rest."

"To rest?" Mallory asked from her spot by the counter. She'd just finished adding ingredients to the salad and was watching CeCe and her brother intently.

CeCe wiped away a spot of gravy from her arm and nodded. "Oh, yes. You need to let protein rest once it's out of the heat. Otherwise it dries out."

Mallory nodded sagely, clearly impressed by the knowledge she was given. "No way. Is that something you learned in culinary school?"

CeCe thought about it for a moment, but she couldn't remember where she'd learned it. It was one of those things she felt like she'd always known. Just like you slice meat against the grain and never stir a pot of boiling sugar. She was about to say that when Evan cut in, a look of pride on his face. "She probably learned it in Chicago."

Mallory covered her heart with her hand. "I love Chicago." Her voice was light, her eyes staring off into the distance. "I haven't been in years."

CeCe couldn't hold back a matching grin. "It's a great city." Seeing the city through someone else's eyes reminded her how lucky she was to have had those years in Chicago. With the Eric drama whipped back into a frenzy, it was easy to forget how many good times she'd had. Perhaps she was overdue for a trip back? Maybe this time she'd have company for the trip. As if sensing her thoughts, she felt Evan brush past her. His hand trailed down her arm as he went in search of a serving spoon.

"So who are some of the biggest chefs you've worked with?" Mallory rattled off several big-name chefs, counting each off on her fingers. Her enthusiasm was contagious.

CeCe was impressed. Most people outside the restaurant industry wouldn't know half of those names. "Well, when I got started . . ." For five minutes she regaled a rapt Mallory with the stories of the chefs and sous chefs she'd worked with during her tenure in the Windy City. She was careful to omit Eric from the list, and she was relieved when Evan merely nodded as she shared her resume with his sister.

"That is so freaking cool," Mallory observed on a sigh. Her eyes still sparkled as she absorbed CeCe's list of chefs. Just when she was ready to carve the chickens, Mallory shattered the calm. "Wait, and you worked with Eric Watson?"

No, no, no! CeCe wanted to shout in the crowded space. Now was not the time to bring up Eric. Swallowing past a lump in her throat, she kept her head down and studied the chickens as if they were science experiments ready to explode.

CeCe was about to answer, but Evan's mother joined them, her apron removed and her makeup fresh. She looked like she was auditioning to be the next Betty Crocker. "Who is Eric Watson?" she asked, leaning in to taste the gravy. CeCe watched her eyes flutter closed as she hummed her approval. "Girls, this gravy is the best one yet."

Evan reached up into a high cabinet to retrieve a gravy boat, handing it to his mother. "Here you go," he said, steering his mother away from the chaos that was Mallory with an unanswered question. "Why don't you grab a seat? We're bringing in dinner." CeCe appreciated the attempt to change the subject, but it was no use.

"He's only the hottest celebrity chef *ever*," Mallory

swooned. She used one of the hot pads to fan herself.

Sophie entered the kitchen, a child hanging from each arm. "Who's the hottest chef ever?" She shook her arms until Lucy and Jackson let go, both deciding their uncle was the next logical choice to hang from. Evan didn't appear bothered and scooped up Lucy and Jackson in quick succession. Jackson hung from Evan's neck while Lucy perched on his hip. Without another word, Evan took them from the room toward the dining room.

"Eric Watson." Mallory swooned once more for good measure. "He is coming to central Ohio for a competition."

CeCe spooned gravy into the gravy boat and handed it to Evan's mother. Her hands quaked as she listened to Mallory preen. "Here you go, Mrs. Lawson."

Evan's mother shook her head but took the gravy. "Please, call me Pamela. You're in our home. We are all family here." She patted CeCe's arm before disappearing with the gravy into the other room.

Evan returned, *sans* children, and helped his sisters and CeCe plate up the rest of dinner. CeCe was silently impressed when he found a bunch of parsley, which he chopped and sprinkled over the finished chicken.

Also impressed with his technique, Sophie smiled at her brother. "I feel like I'm watching this Watson guy in the flesh. Nice work, Ev."

Evan flushed slightly at the compliment but didn't stop his prep work. "If you guys would take my invitation, you could see me in action at the diner."

Sophie kissed his cheek. "Move closer to Cleveland and you have yourself a deal."

Mallory wasn't satisfied with the Eric-free stream of conversation. "Can we please get back to Eric Watson? What can you tell me about him?"

It was a million-dollar question, that was certain. But now was not the time, nor the place, to air her dirty laundry. And, frankly, she was growing agitated with all the Eric talk. The man seemed to infiltrate most of her interactions since the competition announcement came through.

CeCe took the fastest way to the truth. "I worked for Eric a few years ago when I lived in Chicago. And yes, he's bringing a Midwest food competition to Ohio. Evan and I actually picked out our food truck on the way here."

Evan took the last of the plates from CeCe and let his fingers graze over hers. The touch was welcomed and bolstering. "We're going to kick some butt." He turned to Sophie. "If you can't make it to the diner, you should come out for the competition. You and the kids could stay with me."

Mallory raised a hand. "Or at my place. Any excuse to spoil those kiddos is welcomed in my book."

Sophie shrugged. "We'll figure it out," she offered.

CeCe had a feeling that was Lawson code for *drop it*. She might have to take a page out of their playbook, especially when Eric came up in conversation.

CeCe followed everyone into the dining room and looked for her seat. At the head of the table sat Dale, with two vacant seats to his left. Sophie read CeCe's mind and pointed to the chairs. "You and Ev sit by Dad. I'll go over here with the kids and Luke." Her husband, Luke, waved at CeCe. He was clearly the strong, silent type, but in a crowded room like this, CeCe could understand.

"Yes. Have a seat, CeCe. I'd love to get to know you better."

CeCe sat down and glanced at Evan, who looked like he had sucked a lemon. His eyes were pinched, and a frown etched into his cheeks. The tension between father and son was almost too much to bear, yet Dale seemed oblivious.

Mallory sat next to Emily and her husband, Zach. Pamela sat at the other head of the table and beamed at her family. It wasn't often they were all together, and every mother enjoyed the sensation of the hatchlings coming home to roost. "Everyone, let's say grace."

After a brief prayer, the family dug into their meals. Evan had taken the honors of carving the roasted chickens, which

CeCe thought were moist and flavorful.

As if reading her mind, Mallory chimed in, "This is the best chicken ever. CeCe, you're a miracle worker."

Evan smiled at her, taking a bite of his own meal. "CeCe's a whiz in the kitchen. You should try some of her desserts."

Mallory nodded to the others. "And her stuffed pancakes are the best thing I've ever had. Seriously, they're life-changing." A starry expression crossed her features before she focused on her current meal.

CeCe eagerly absorbed their praise like a sponge, yet she sensed Dale's eyes on her. "So." Just that simple word shifted the group's attention to their patriarch. "Tell me, CeCe. How long do you plan on working at that little diner?" He paused to sip from his wine glass before continuing. "My son seems to think it's a long-term job. Do you feel the same way?"

The sound of cutlery scraping on plates was all that could be heard in the dining room. Even the children were silent, which should have told CeCe all she needed to know about this family dynamic. Evan sat straight beside her, tension radiating off him in waves that should have turned her stomach. Her answer mattered in more ways than one.

"Yes, Dale. I do think it's a long-term job. I have my culinary degree, and working with Max has given me valuable experience. I'm sure you've seen the improvement with Evan's cooking skills over the last year." Using her knife, she pointed to the spread they were all currently savoring. "It's very impressive."

Evan put his fork down and drained the last of his water. There was a slight tremor in his hand, and CeCe was about to ask what was wrong. Fortunately, Dale answered her question before she could ask. "My son doesn't need kitchen skills. He needs to grow up and get a real job."

CeCe knew she was about to open a colossal can of worms, but she couldn't stop herself. "A real job? I take it you don't respect the restaurant industry." It was a statement, not a question. She had come across this type before. A wealthy, white-collared man who thought anyone who didn't have a college degree was stupid, worthless. It was the same type of person who looked down their nose at people who did physical labor. CeCe wasn't a fan of Dale already.

Evan's hand went under the table to squeeze her leg, but she didn't take the hint. "You should be really impressed with all that Evan's doing. He's going to be instrumental in the competition this spring. He's a real talent."

Evan's father was clearly unimpressed. "He's a real talent for wasting a four-year degree. I'm glad Pamela and I invested all that money in his OSU diploma. I'm sure it comes in handy when he's washing the dishes."

Mallory cleared her throat, about to jump to her brother's defense. But Evan was too quick. "You know I do more than wash the dishes, Dad. I've been a prep cook for a couple of months now."

"A job you don't need a degree for. If you wanted to be lazy, you could have decided six years ago. Instead, you're wasting your prime years playing kitchen. It is time to grow up and use that education." Dale rapped his knuckles on the table, punctuating his point. "I can get you a job at the firm in no time."

CeCe sipped from her wine, desperately trying to keep her cool. Who was this guy? And why was he hell-bent on cutting down his own son?

Appetite forgotten, CeCe simply said, "Evan is using his degree. In fact, he signed a contract for web development for one of the boutiques on Main Street. I've seen his portfolio. His work is quite extraordinary." She felt Evan bristle beside her, but she wasn't going to let him be a doormat in his childhood home.

From her side of the table, Pamela chimed in. "I didn't know you were getting freelance work, Evan. That's wonderful news." Her smile seemed genuine, but CeCe could tell Pamela didn't wear the pants in this family. It was

Dale's opinion that mattered most.

"Freelance work? You need to find a firm, get settled in a company that has room for promotion. You think I got to where I am today without hard work at a big firm?" Pausing his lecture, Dale waved a free hand around the room. "These side jobs aren't worth anything if you don't have a team to rely on. You need to think about retirement planning, health care, and life insurance."

Evan stifled a sigh, and CeCe wanted to scream. "Dad, it's not the same as it was when you went to OSU. Freelance work isn't a bad thing. It's experience to add to my portfolio."

Dale was undeterred. "Where will the dishwashing experience go? Is that before or after your part-time side jobs? Son, you need to think about the future." Picking up his glass, he gestured between Evan and CeCe. "You really think CeCe is going to wait for you to grow up? Do you think a woman that age is ready to watch you waste the prime years of your life? What if CeCe wants children? The clock is ticking, and you're throwing it all away."

CeCe felt each statement like a punch to the gut. Suddenly, the chicken was dry and tasteless as a total stranger pointed out all her fears. She was nearly thirty, and she may want children someday. She wanted a partner in life, someone who knew her and would support her through thick and thin.

If CeCe closed her eyes and really thought about it, she saw Evan. A future with him would be filled with love and tenderness, with unwavering support and laughter. There would be pillow forts and cheesy bites, recipe testing and kung fu marathons. Really, what more could a girl ask for?

Suddenly, her skin felt too tight. She looked around the room to find the Lawson clan in various stages of embarrassment, yet no one jumped to her, or Evan's, defense. It was no wonder Evan hesitated to bring her here. "Will you excuse me? I need to use the restroom." She pulled her chair back and stood, her head held high as she strode to freedom.

As her feet hit the carpeted hallway, she heard footsteps behind her. Evan took her hand and stopped her, pulling her into another room. "I'm so sorry," he breathed, closing the door behind them. He covered his face and moaned like a wounded animal. "My father is an asshole. This is exactly what I feared."

CeCe raised her eyebrows in confusion. "You knew this would happen?"

Evan ran a hand through his hair, a rogue blond curl standing on end. "Yes, but I wasn't sure how bad. My dad is a tough customer on a good day, and I could tell when we got here, it wasn't a good day."

CeCe stepped closer to Evan, who had backed himself against the far wall. They were in a guest room, with a frilly bedspread and floral wallpaper surrounding them. She walked around the bed and took one of his hands. "Are *you* okay?"

For a moment, she didn't think he would respond. He looked defeated, drained of his usual spirit. After a beat, he blinked. "Don't worry about me. Are you okay? My father basically called me a useless youth and implied your eggs are drying up. I'm used to this, but I'm petrified you're going to run for the hills. God, he's such an asshat."

"If I run for the hills, I'm taking you with me." Just as CeCe stepped closer, there was a knock on the door as Mallory barged in.

Mallory's eyes were red, like she was holding back tears. "There you guys are. Are you all right, CeCe?"

CeCe laughed. It was humorless. "Don't worry about me. I'm more worried about Evan."

Mallory chewed her bottom lip. It was clear this wasn't a new dynamic, checking in after Dale said his piece. Finally, she offered, "I mean, I'm worried about both of you. Do you need me to fake an emergency so you can leave?"

As far as CeCe was concerned, they were free to leave whenever they liked. "Do we really need an excuse? Can't the excuse be that we're not having a good time?"

Evan and Mallory both turned to face CeCe, and she feared she'd said the wrong thing. Jerk or not, Dale was still their father. That was a sacred relationship, and she should mind her business.

Before she could apologize, Evan took CeCe's hand and stepped back toward the door. "We're leaving," he said without looking back. He pulled them both to the front door with such determination she feared her arm would pop from its socket. Sophie and Emily waited, neither appeared surprised that their guests were leaving before dinner was finished.

"I'm sorry, Ev," Emily said as she hugged her brother. Turning her attention to CeCe, she groaned. "And I'm really sorry, CeCe. Please know that Evan and our father are nothing alike. I promise you that."

"I figured that much out already." CeCe looked for her purse.

Sophie frowned. "Are you sure you can't stay a bit longer? Dad is in a mood, but he'll be better soon. I'm sure."

CeCe looked at each of the sibling's expressions and recognized that was far from the truth. Dale was a bully, plain and simple. Pamela appeared with a plastic box filled with food. "You'll want something to eat for the ride home. I'm sorry we haven't cut the pie yet."

Was this woman for real? CeCe wanted to shake Pamela until she saw sense. Shake her until she saw what horrible things her husband had said to his only son. CeCe couldn't reconcile the Evan she knew with the scene that played out before her.

Evan took the box and opened the front door. "Thanks for having us," he said half-heartedly.

Mallory followed Evan and CeCe onto the stoop, looking like she wanted to cry. "What a mess. This is worse than when I invited Daniel Musgrove over after the senior prom. I'm so sorry, CeCe."

"Don't worry about me," CeCe reassured the younger

woman. "I have thick skin."

While she followed Evan to his car, she feared his skin wasn't thick enough to withstand such negativity from his father. As he pulled the car out onto the road, she watched Evan shut down. He wasn't talking, and his focus was solely on the task at hand. There was no banter, no conversation. Hell, he hadn't even turned on his beloved K-pop to fill the space.

CeCe didn't know how, but she had to help him get out from under his dad's thumb. Evan was working on projects that anyone would be proud to be a part of. He went through every day with blind optimism and enthusiasm for everything he did. It was depressing to think he was suffering in silence, or that he needed his father's approval. As far as she was concerned, Evan was a star.

*

Well, that had gone about as well as Evan had expected. His sisters behaved themselves—for the most part—but his parents had exploded like a 1950s time capsule. His mother, bless her, refused to stand up in defense of any of her children. Even her baby boy, and it nicked away at Evan every time he visited home. Then there was his father. Dale was in rare form, not even waiting until dessert to alienate his son and embarrass his date.

Why, why, why had Evan allowed himself to be bullied into bringing CeCe? He knew better than that. You don't bring a woman home to your parents if you're serious. Any woman worth her salt would run for the hills after that embarrassing and hurtful display.

Unable to look at CeCe and stand the silence another moment, Evan turned on the radio and found his favorite K-pop station. "I'll have you home in less than an hour." He sighed into the steering wheel as he took a turn ten miles over the speed limit. He felt CeCe shift in the seat, but she didn't say anything. Evan couldn't decide if that made things better or worse.

CeCe wasn't known for her ability to bite her tongue. Fortunately for Evan, he didn't have to wait long. When he pulled over at a gas station, she hopped out and met him at the pump. "This is on me," she said, swiping her card and twisting gas cap. He opened his mouth to argue, but she cut him off with a wave of her hand. "Don't get me started. Max will reimburse me for the mileage to the food truck vendor. Now, go inside and get me a Diet Coke and a peanut butter cup. You got me out of there so early, I'll starve to death before we heat up those leftovers." She winked at him and turned to face the pump.

Evan stood there in the fading light and studied CeCe's profile. Her button nose gave her a younger, more childlike appearance in the dim lighting. He was falling hard for her, and he couldn't stand the notion that his parents had ruined a good thing before it started. "I'll be right back," he said over his shoulder, careful to put some space between them.

While he waited in line to pay for his snacks, his cell buzzed with a flurry of texts from his sisters.

Text when you get home, Sophie's said.

OMG, what a mess!, was all Mallory offered.

Emily wasn't much better with a shrugging emoji. *What did you expect from dad?*

"What did I expect?" Evan sighed and pocketed his cell phone. He expected respect and a little interest in his life, notwithstanding years of behavior to the contrary.

He paid for their snacks and headed back into the chilly evening, where CeCe was propped against his car. Despite everything that had transpired that night, Evan felt a tiny kernel of hope in his chest that he hadn't completely blown his chances. Surely, CeCe knew him better than to assume he was a carbon copy of his father.

CeCe met him by the passenger's door, helping herself to a Diet Coke and opening her package of peanut butter cups. "You want one?" she asked, holding the paper tray out to him.

Truth be told, he wasn't hungry. A round of humiliation was bound to ruin a guy's appetite. "Thanks for pumping the gas," he offered lamely.

"Thanks for buying me sugar and caffeinated fake sugar," she quipped, taking a long pull of the Diet Coke.

Evan leaned against the car and crossed his legs at the ankles. Spring had nearly made it to Ohio, and he could smell the changes in the air. His allergies were getting bad, and he could see a fine dusting of green pollen on his car. In a matter of weeks, summer would be knocking on the door, and they would be competing against her old boss. Evan was so relieved they would be part of the competition. Suddenly, he felt he had a lot to prove—and to more people than CeCe's former boss.

Granted, he knew little to nothing about Eric Watson, but Evan still wanted to kick Eric's butt. CeCe was the most dedicated, confident woman Evan had ever met—inside and outside the kitchen. It drove him crazy that this jerk had filled her head with doubt all those years ago. His father's lack of enthusiasm for the competition did nothing to quash the desire to win.

CeCe balled up her candy wrapper and tossed it into the trash. With a sigh, she headed back to the passenger's door and wrenched it open. Evan shuddered at the sound of creaking metal. "You going to drive me home, or are we still moping?"

Evan nearly choked on his soda. "Still moping? Don't you think I have every reason to be horrified? My God, you have every reason to be horrified! This was a freaking nightmare."

CeCe ducked into his car and slammed the door. Evan jogged around to get behind the wheel. When he turned the car on, the radio blasted until she punched the buttons to silence the upbeat pop music. "You have every reason to be horrified, but you don't need to worry about me. I'm more worried about you. You're looking green around the gills." She hesitated for a moment and chuckled. "And thanks for worrying about me, but I'm a tough customer."

Evan turned slowly to face her, and his breath caught in his throat. Her lips quirked up in a lopsided smile, and it charmed him, but not enough to unleash years of disappointment in his father. Instead, Evan offered CeCe the abbreviated truth. "I know you are, and I'll live. But I'd rather not discuss this now."

CeCe gave a quick nod and turned the radio back on. "Fair enough, but you know you can talk to me when you're ready."

As Evan pulled onto the highway, he felt her hand on his knee. Her face remained turned away from him, but she seemed content.

When he took the Buckeye Falls exit, he slowed at the junction to her part of town and his. He wanted her to go back to his place so badly, but he also needed to work on the website before bed. Time was on his side with the contract, but not if he fell behind before he even got started.

As if she read his mind, CeCe said, "You can drop me at my place, if that's okay." Evan nodded and turned left. Squeezing his leg, she let her hand rest for longer than he'd expected. "But this doesn't mean I didn't have a good time. I know you have your website to work on. Plus, we're both exhausted. Okay?"

Evan could only offer a shrug. "Okay."

CeCe opened her door, and Evan took her hand and walked her to her door. "I really did have a good time tonight," CeCe said. Shaking her head, she added, "Well, an interesting time at least." Her tone was light enough, and Evan wanted to believe her.

Rather than dissect his rambling thoughts on her doorstep, he asked, "See you at work tomorrow?"

CeCe stepped forward and traced her fingers down his cheek. Her closeness and feather-light touch sent an electric charge straight down his spine. "Bright and early," she breathed, their faces mere inches away.

Evan licked his lips and closed the distance between

them. She tasted like chocolate, peanut butter, and CeCe—an intoxicating combination he didn't know he needed yet now feared was the only thing keeping him breathing. "Good night," he said, before stepping back and feeling the cool air whoosh between them.

Raising her hand in farewell, she opened her door and stepped inside. He waited until he saw the lights turn on before turning back to his car.

The prospect of going home to his apartment didn't appeal to him, because he needed to talk to someone. While driving down Main Street, he nearly slammed on his brakes at the familiar form of Max leaving the market, chatting with the owner as he flipped the sign to closed. Max's place was near the market, so Evan slowed and rolled down his window.

"Need a lift, boss?" Evan shouted out into the evening.

Max slowed his pace, two paper bags clutched to his chest, and smiled. "Hey, Evan. What brings you out this late on a Sunday?"

"Coming home from food-truck shopping. Did CeCe text you the pics?"

Max shifted his bags and stepped closer to the car, happily accepting the offer. "I'll take that ride if it's no trouble."

Evan reached out to unlatch the trunk and waited for his boss to hop in. Watching Max stow his groceries, Evan turned down the radio. "Your place, I'm assuming?" It was a fair question. While Ginny and Max lived in a cottage off Main Street, they both frequented her father's house.

Harold was a sweetheart, standing by Max even after his divorce from Ginny. Rumor in Buckeye Falls was that Harold was currently playing house with Mona, another one of the nicest people in town. Who knew, wedding bells could be in their future as well. It was like the whole town was in love.

Evan could admit it stung that Max had more support from his ex-father-in-law than Evan did in his own father.

How had Harold kept Max so close, even after the divorce was final and Ginny had moved on? As if reading his mind, Max asked, "How did family dinner go?"

Evan laughed, the sound holding not an ounce of humor. "That obvious, huh?"

Max hesitated a moment before charging on with his line of questioning. "You brought CeCe this time? That was nice."

Evan felt his heart stutter in his chest. He and CeCe hadn't discussed the logistics of their relationship, least of all how they would share it with the people in their lives. "Uh, yeah, since it was so close to the truck. You know, no big deal."

"Makes sense, no point doubling back when you were so close," Max agreed, his lips turning in a Cherise-cat smile. "Was Mallory there?"

Evan squeezed the steering wheel a little too hard. "Yes, actually, all of my sisters were."

Max traced the line of the stitching on his seat, keeping his gaze down. "How was your dad? Did you tell him about the web development contract?"

Evan bit the inside of his mouth to stop from spewing all the awful facts of the night. "Yep."

No one spoke for a moment, until Max finally asked, "And …?"

They had reached the intersection to Max's neighborhood, and Evan took an extra moment at the stop sign to collect his thoughts. He waited until they were in Max's driveway before continuing. "He was an asshole, as usual. Even though he wanted me to get into development, he's disappointed it's not at a firm. There is no pleasing him, and the sooner I realize that, the better." Evan reveled in his bitter tone, savoring the taste on his tongue. Speaking the truth felt almost as nice as his goodnight kiss with CeCe. *Almost.*

Thinking about her brought a flush to Evan's cheeks, but he didn't think Max could tell in the evening light. The sun had set, and now the town was coated in a purple glow. Evan loved the sleepy feeling Buckeye Falls got this time of year, and judging from Max's expression as he looked through the windshield, he loved it too.

"You're a good guy, Evan," Max finally said. He turned to face him and cupped a hand on his shoulder. "I won't go full Hallmark movie on you, but you work hard, treat people right, and make a difference. There's nothing else you need to do, and that includes impressing your father."

A lump formed in Evan's throat, but he tried to swallow it back. The last thing he wanted to do was burst into tears in front of Max. Over the last year, Max had turned from a boss into a friend, a mentor. Evan respected him too much to make a sobbing scene in his driveway.

Whether it was Evan's headlights or the late hour, Ginny opened the front door and walked down the driveway. When Max saw her, his face broke into a mega-watt smile again. Their PDA was over the top, but Evan couldn't help but marvel at how these two souls found their way back together. It was obvious to anyone with a pair of eyes that Max and Ginny were meant to be.

"I'll let you get inside. Your groceries are probably melting."

Ginny opened Max's door and tilted her head in to say hello to Evan. "I was getting ready to panic when I saw your car." Max stepped out and retrieved the bags. Ginny laughed when she saw both of them. "No wonder you're late. I send you out for heavy cream, and you come back with half the market."

Max kissed her cheek and handed the lighter bag to her. "You mind taking this inside, Gin? I'm just finishing up with Evan."

Ginny nodded and took the bag. Before she walked inside, she turned and waved to Evan. "Pick a night and come over for dinner." She didn't wait for his answer, knowing he couldn't pass up the invite.

"Thanks for the ride, and for taking CeCe to look at the

food truck. It's nice to see you two spending more time together."

The pause after that sentence hung heavy between them. Evan wanted to tell Max the truth, but he didn't want to overstep and betray CeCe's confidence either. "Yeah, it's … uh nice to spend time with her outside of work."

Max grinned that cat-with-the-canary smile again and nodded. "Better get this all inside." He held up the bag like a shield. "See you in the morning." He took a step back but didn't close the door. "You know that I only want what's best for you both, right? It's pretty obvious you still have f-f-feelings for CeCe." He hesitated before finding his words. Max only stuttered when he was nervous, and that only made Evan's pulse beat faster. "B-b-but I know you'll treat her right. I can tell she's enjoying your time together."

"You can?" Evan asked, clearly wanting Max to cite his source.

Max grabbed his cell phone from the back pocket of his jeans. "Yeah, she sent this." Handing Evan the phone, Evan saw the picture of the truck. "Scroll through," Max suggested.

The next picture was one of the two of them from earlier in the week, crowded around his kitchen with a stack of notes and menus in front of them.

Evan raised an eyebrow. "What does that mean?"

Max snorted. "You know CeCe as well as I do. Does that woman look like the selfie type?"

Evan opened his mouth to rebuke, but he couldn't find the words. CeCe was usually very open about her opinion on PDA, selfies, and anything that showed other people how you felt. He'd didn't always call her grumpy, but she was hardly a ball of sunshine if the situation didn't warrant it.

"She could have easily sent a text with the menu details, but she wanted to capture the moment." Shifting the bag on his hip, Max took his cell phone back and hitched a thumb over his shoulder. "I should get inside to Ginny, but take that for what it's worth."

"I will. Have a good night," Evan said, his mind still racing back to the picture he just saw. CeCe documented their time together and shared it with Max. But what did it mean?

"Try not to obsess tonight, okay? Your father and CeCe don't need to take over that brain of yours." Hesitating a moment, Max added, "Besides, you need it to create the greatest website of all time."

Evan snorted. "No pressure. See you tomorrow," he said to Max as he backed out onto the street.

For the rest of the night, Evan waffled between frustration over his father to sheer delight over his time with CeCe. She said she wasn't scared of him … or his family. And Evan chose to believe her. After all, she had always been her own woman, doing her own thing. If she didn't want to be with him, she'd make that perfectly clear. He trusted her to always give him the truth.

CHAPTER 10

When CeCe registered for the food truck competition, she had two choices. She could be a coward and leave her name off the registration, or she could suck it up and put down all her fears in black and white. After soul-searching for far too long, she decided to be an adult and sign up with herself as the main contact. As expected, she got a generic confirmation email and didn't expect to hear from anyone at the competition beyond logistics.

Several days had gone by without CeCe thinking much about it. Between the Lawson family dinner and focusing on their burgeoning relationship, she hadn't given the competition a lot of thought. Unfortunately for CeCe, her ignorance was short-lived.

Once she got home from a day with Evan, she pulled on her favorite sweatpants and curled up on the couch with a cookbook and the first action movie she found on TV. While others unwound reading novels, she liked to page through cookbooks and zone out to the rhythmic sounds of people fighting. She was certain if she spent money on a good therapist, there'd be something telling about that.

Maybe it's why she enjoyed Evan's kung fu marathon so much? Or maybe the movies had nothing to do with it.

Perhaps it was the man himself. Yes, Evan's parents were certainly not going to win parents of the year, but CeCe knew Evan was different. He was never disrespectful to her, or his sisters; CeCe was sure of it. She could tell from his behavior at work that he took things seriously and was making his way. It was obvious his father had no idea what his son was capable of, or what he'd already mastered.

CeCe's phone buzzed with a text from a private number. Lost in her thoughts about Evan, her mouth curled into a smile before she even registered what she was reading. Suddenly, her glass of bourbon threatened to come back up.

I knew you couldn't stay away, Pixie.

Her ears rang as she read the message, which practically shouted at her from the screen. With a shaking hand, she turned off the TV and swallowed down the bile. Only one person would text her with that message—or use that damned nickname.

After their break-up, CeCe had blocked Eric's number and assumed that would be that. But of course, he remembered her number; the man remembered everything. Or it could have been the competition registration. Suddenly being brave felt foolish. She'd invited her least favorite person back into her world. The notion made her dizzy.

CeCe mumbled a few choice profanities before standing and pacing around her living room. Should she respond to the text and engage with him? Pretend to be someone else and pull a *new phone, who dis?* She nearly laughed. That would certainly annoy Eric, and there wasn't anything wrong with that. Then she thought back to being an adult. An adult would respond, be blunt, and move on. She'd have to interact with him eventually, and there was no better time than the present.

But as she clutched her cell phone, she knew she wasn't ready to engage with him. Responding to that text would pick at a scab that was barely healed. Instead, she turned the TV back on, poured a shot, and tried to think of anything else. Eventually the alcohol would do its job and make her sleepy. Then she could wait for the clarity that morning always brought.

Because life was never simple, the morning didn't bring more than a headache and a sense of impending doom. She made herself a cup of coffee and got ready for work. Finger-combing her blonde hair, she opted for a no-nonsense headband and a swipe of lip gloss. Even after her caffeine boost, her surly mood loomed over her like a cloud. Even her favorite chef's tunic couldn't cover the chip on her shoulder. With a bolstering breath to face her day, she opened her front door and nearly plowed over Natalie.

"Good morning," Natalie chirped as she pushed past CeCe.

CeCe scoffed. "You know I do have a life, right? You should at least text before you barge in. I'm on my way to work." Holding up her coffee mug and purse, she hoped that was enough to get Natalie out of her house.

No such luck.

Natalie ignored her friend's protests. "I only have two minutes before I take the kids to Anthony's parents and pre-K." Gesturing toward the doorway, CeCe looked out to see Madeline and Otis in the van. Their little mouths were open in dreamless sleep, their tiny heads lulled to each side. "And before you ask, they're fine for a moment while I give you the third-degree."

"What did I do this time?" CeCe sighed. She loved Natalie, but there was always something.

"Aren't we friends? I've been telling myself that we're friends," Natalie deadpanned.

CeCe sipped from her coffee and let Natalie have her moment of drama. "Yes. We're friends. Why? What did you hear? Did someone pass you a note in homeroom that said I have a new BFF? Is this because I didn't wait for you at my locker after chemistry class?"

Natalie pointed an accusing finger, but her tone was light. "I had to learn from Ginny that you went to Evan's family dinner last night. I also heard you got a food truck. How am I supposed to be the First Lady of Buckeye Falls if I'm not up to speed on all the hot gossip?"

CeCe pinched the bridge of her nose. She felt a tension headache growing, and it only had a little to do with Buckeye Falls' gossip mill. Her unanswered text from Eric weighed heavily on her mind, and she didn't think she could handle much else at the moment. "I can assure you, I was planning on telling you today. But I got home late, then I got a text from Eric, and I just—"

Her explanation died on her tongue as Natalie spluttered in front of her. Her eyes grew wide and her mouth opened and closed several times while she struggled to find words. "Eric texted you?" Natalie looked around the house as if he was hiding in plain sight. "What did you do?"

Unsure how to react, CeCe merely shrugged. "Nothing yet. I wasn't sure if I should engage or let him stew."

Natalie stepped closer, reaching out and resting her hands on CeCe's shoulders. "Tell me exactly what the text said." Her serious tone made the hairs on CeCe's neck stand up. This was a big deal, but she didn't realize how big until Natalie's face reflected CeCe's own fears.

"Uh, well. It's going to sound bad."

"How bad?"

CeCe took a steadying breath. "It said, *I knew you couldn't stay away.*" She bit her lip as a slew of expressions crossed over Natalie's pretty face. She was glad she omitted the part about her nickname, as it would have caused her friend to implode like a poorly made soufflé.

"I'm sorry, what? Is this a Lifetime movie or something? This guy sounds like a total creep. Are you sure you want to go through with all this? Should you call the police or something?"

"And say what? 'Hello, I'm reporting a random creepy text from my ex. But I can't prove it was him, so it could be a wrong number or a run-of-the-mill stalker'?"

"And that's a better option?" Natalie was incredulous.

These were all reasonable questions. CeCe nodded, certain she was on the right track. "Look. I appreciate you're worried about me, but it's going to be fine. I like doing food competitions, and this is a great way to get back in the game. Plus, Eric is harmless. He's not going to do anything. He's trying to get a rise out of me. I'm sure of it."

Natalie glanced over CeCe's shoulder to make sure her kids were still sleeping, then she turned back with a look of pure determination. "I think you need to be honest with Max and Evan about this. They need to know what they're up against. What *you're* up against. Promise me you'll take this seriously?"

"Nothing is going to happen. I'll ignore the text and move on. Seriously, I've got this." CeCe sipped from her coffee, hoping the caffeine would wake her from this complicated conundrum.

Natalie didn't look convinced, but she acquiesced. "Fine. I'll drop it. For now. But you should still fill Evan in on your history with Eric. All of it, even the parts that make you uncomfortable. If you're serious about him, you need to."

It's the same sentiment CeCe had been berating herself over, but it didn't make it easier to hear from her friend. Evan deserved to know the truth, but CeCe didn't want to pile on the drama. He had enough with work, the competition, and his new design contract. She would tell him if it came to it, but she didn't see the point in revisiting her past. Not right now anyway. She wanted to be the easy, carefree part of his life.

"I have to get to work. And shouldn't these kids be at school?"

Natalie took her cell phone from her purse and sighed when she saw the time. "Damn, you're right. Madeline is the hall monitor today at pre-K. Have you ever heard of such a thing? A four-year-old telling other four-year-olds to line up? It's ridiculous."

"Good thing she inherited her mother's bossiness." CeCe winked, the jab barely making Natalie wince.

"Poor girl doesn't stand a chance, not with her parents." Natalie breezed past CeCe and stopped at her van. "Back to reality. Call me later, okay? We need to get a proper girls' night on the schedule." Hesitating before stepping into the van, Natalie offered, "Or we could do a double date. Wouldn't that be fun?"

As Natalie drove away, CeCe registered what her friend said. A double date? Sharing a meal with Natalie, Evan, and Anthony seemed outlandish. They'd scar poor Evan for life. CeCe shook her head and got back to the matter at hand; she was late for work.

She drove in a haze, her head racing with conflicting thoughts on what to do about Eric's text. When she arrived at the diner and stepped out of the car, she saw Helen pacing around the back of the lot, a cigarette clenched between her fingers.

"I thought you gave those up," CeCe accused as she sipped from her coffee.

Helen rolled her eyes and took a puff. "I cut back. I didn't quit. Plus, it's an excuse to get away from all the excitement in there." Flicking the cigarette onto the ground, she stomped it out and held the door open for CeCe. "Welcome to food truck central, where nothing exists outside the world of competition. If I hear the phrase 'optimal temperature' again, I'll murder someone or retire early."

CeCe chuckled. "I take it you won't be joining us for competition day?"

Helen shook her head, her jowls following the movement. "Not a chance. I'll be rooting for you all to win, but let's be real ... I'm old, and I don't move fast enough. Competing is a young person's game."

The pair walked into the back of the kitchen, and CeCe froze when she saw the sight in front of her. The rear wall was covered in papers and Post-it Notes. Each sheet of paper covered a different part of the competition, from the logistics of the day to the prep plans. Her eyes practically glazed over with all the details in print. They had a lot of work to do, and suddenly Eric's petty text message was the least of CeCe's cares.

"Good morning." Evan came up behind her and bumped her elbow as he passed with a tray of bacon. Max raised a spatula in greeting from his post by the grill. Helen rolled her eyes at the group and went back out into the dining room, her prep work waiting for her. That was one of the reasons CeCe adored the older woman; she was all bark and no bite when there was work to do.

"Good morning," CeCe replied as she hooked her purse on the wall and washed her hands. "I see we're in full competition mode."

Max barked out a laugh and flipped a row of sausage links. The heavenly sweet, savory aroma made CeCe's mouth water. She really should have eaten breakfast before she left home. "I think we're the cause for Helen picking up smoking again. She said if I mention the word 'logistics' again she'll hand in her notice."

Evan put down his tray and wiped his brow with the back of his hand. "Nah, Helen's all talk. She'll bury us all."

"God willing," Helen chimed in as she walked back into the kitchen for her order pad and apron. "Look alive. We open in five."

CeCe got behind the counter and started lining up plates and bowls. "Sorry I'm late. Natalie came over, and I guess I lost track of time."

Glancing over to see Evan, he winked and gave her a look that made her toes curl. "No worries. Is everything all right?" *Was everything all right?* CeCe wasn't sure, which is why she clamped her mouth shut and merely nodded.

"You two have anything planned after your shifts?" Max asked over his shoulder.

CeCe looked at Evan, who held his hands in the air, a sign of surrender. She realized they needed to tell Max that they were spending time together, that they were dating.

Before she could spiral into madness over the perfect

way to explain the shift in their relationship, Evan answered for them. "I can't speak for CeCe, but I have to work on the boutique website a bit. What's up?"

"If it's not too much trouble, I think we should pick up the food truck tonight or tomorrow. I'll feel better knowing it's taken care of."

CeCe spoke without thinking. "I can pick it up tonight. No problem."

"Can you drive stick?" Max asked, wiping his hands on a towel before tossing it over his shoulder. "I thought you only drove automatic?"

"Why is it a stick shift? What's the world coming to?"

Evan, always the helper, jumped to the rescue. "I can drive stick. If you don't mind me leaving an hour early to write some code, I could be ready to pick it up before dinner."

Max pointed at Evan with his spatula. "Sold. Thanks, man."

"I'll drive us out and follow you back. Otherwise, you'll have to find a ride share, and that sounds expensive."

Evan gave CeCe a thoughtful expression that warmed her heart. He looked at her like she hung the moon. "Thanks. That'd be nice." In moments like these, she realized how genuine Evan was. He lacked the pretense and bravado that made Eric a household name. There was no polish, nothing fake. What you saw with Evan was what you got.

And CeCe liked what she saw.

*

Evan sat in the passenger seat of CeCe's truck, his finger trailing a line of condensation on the window. He'd had a productive afternoon with the framework for the new website, and he reveled in the sense of accomplishment. His work at the diner was fast-paced and relatively simple. One of the best features at the diner was being done with work when they closed. What he got from web design allowed him to flex his creative muscle and delve into something more complicated, something he could control.

Realizing they hadn't spoken in three songs, Evan glanced at CeCe. Her hair was still pinned back from a day at work, but a few blonde tendrils fell loose around her face. In the gleaming afternoon sun, she looked angelic, but he noticed she looked a little tense too. Her jaw was tight, and she seemed too focused on the flat country lane ahead of them.

Reaching out, he tucked a loose strand of hair behind her ear. "You okay?" he asked, his words causing her to jolt in her seat.

"What? Yeah, sorry. Just thinking."

"About what?"

Evan waited her out, knowing she'd tell him what was on her mind in her own time. That's what he loved about her; she didn't speak unless she had something to say. A lot of people found her brash, but Evan liked to think she didn't show her softer side to just anyone. He hoped it meant she was comfortable with him, willing to open up more.

Finally, CeCe cleared her throat and started talking. "The competition and the diner." She paused as she turned onto another road. Evan recognized the familiar turn and saw the truck ahead on the left. He could tell she wanted to talk more, and he hated that they were almost to their destination.

"Are you worried?" he asked as she pulled up behind the truck and turned off the engine. She nibbled on her lip a moment before meeting his gaze. Her eyes looked tired, and he felt his stomach tighten. "Something's wrong. What's going on?"

Just as CeCe opened her mouth, there was a knock on the window that made them both jump. "You two are right on time." The truck's seller waved and stepped back as the pair exited CeCe's truck.

"I'm glad there wasn't any traffic." CeCe laughed.

The drive consisted of open country roads and barely any stoplights. The only traffic they were liable to have was the four-legged variety.

The man nodded and jerked his thumb over his shoulder. "Everything is gassed and ready to roll. I thought we could do a walk-through before you leave."

Evan took charge and inspected the truck. After paying and saying goodbye to the seller, he turned to find CeCe already getting behind the wheel of her truck. She wasn't going to say goodbye?

"CeCe, hold up!" Evan shouted as he ran to the driver's side window. "Where are you going?"

CeCe forced a smile. "Home? I figured we got what we needed."

Unable to argue with her logic, Evan tried another tactic. "But we were talking. Is there anything you want to discuss? You seem distracted, upset even." For a moment, Evan held his breath. Something was definitely up, and he wanted to get to the bottom of it. "You can talk to me. You know that, right?"

"Because we're friends?" Her question pushed Evan back on his heels.

"We established we're more than that," he said, reaching through the window to take her hand. He traced a path over her knuckles and watched her sigh a long exhale. "Aren't we?"

Slowly, CeCe nodded. "We are, I'm sorry. I'm just tired I guess."

"You seem bothered by something. Let me help." Evan watched a flurry of emotions cross her face, but he kept his mouth shut. Growing up with three sisters taught him when to talk and when to keep quiet.

"Do you want to have dinner with Natalie and Anthony?"

The abrupt topic change gave Evan whiplash. "What?"

"Like a double date, you know, four people eating at a

restaurant that we don't work in. We might as well get out there and do couple things." CeCe explained, the words tumbling out of her in quick succession.

"Sure. When?"

CeCe seemed surprised by his quick agreement, frowning for a moment before recovering. "I'm not sure, but she asked this morning, and I forgot to ask you at the diner. Then I thought you might not want to, and then I thought—" Her words trailed off.

Evan was young, but he wasn't stupid. The mayor and his wife wouldn't want to have dinner with him unless CeCe told them about their budding relationship. Evan wasn't sure if this was a test or not, but either way, he was diving in head first. "Let me know when."

Without another word, CeCe turned on her truck and put it in gear. Evan had to step back and drop his arm before she drove off and maimed him. "I'll back up so you can get on the road. Max said we can park that beast behind his cottage for now."

Giving a thumbs-up, Evan walked toward the food truck. He pulled his phone from his pocket and dialed Mallory's number as soon as he hit the road, putting it on speaker.

"Ev, what's up?" Mallory answered. Evan could hear voices in the background and the sound of squeaky shoes.

"Crap. Are you still at work?" he asked, his attention on the country road.

"Yeah, but I'm going on break. You okay?"

Evan explained the situation—from CeCe's distraction to the fumbled date invite. "What do you think it all means?"

Mallory hummed considerately before saying, "I think your girlfriend wants to go out with her friends. Pardon me for stating the obvious, but isn't a double-date good thing? You sound like she's asked you to undergo unnecessary surgery or something."

"But then why is she distracted? Do you think it's

because of family dinner? Do you think Dad scared her?" Leave it to his father to complicate yet another aspect of Evan's life.

Mallory hummed for a moment. "I think if our family scared her, she wouldn't be planning double dates. Or I don't know, Ev. Maybe ask her about it?"

"I did!" he practically shouted, his voice echoing through the truck's cabin. "She said she was thinking about the diner and the competition. She said she wasn't worried about our parents."

Mallory huffed out a laugh. "Maybe she's all hot and bothered about meeting Eric Watson. I know I would be if it were me."

Evan rolled his eyes. "You realize they've already met. She used to work for the guy. Do you think it's just nerves about competing?"

"CeCe doesn't strike me as someone who gets nervous, especially when it comes to food."

Drumming his fingers on the steering wheel, Evan couldn't disagree. "Yeah, you're right. Then it's got to be something else."

Evan heard muffled voices on the line before Mallory came back on. "Shoot, I gotta run. They brought in four people from a bad car crash. Can I call you tomorrow?"

"Of course. Take it easy." Evan disconnected the call and focused on the drive to Max's place. In true Midwestern fashion, the roads weren't winding, but straight as arrows. It was easy to maneuver back to Buckeye Falls. CeCe drove faster than normal, as if she was trying to get through the day as fast as possible.

When they finally arrived at Max's place, Evan was still worked up over what was bothering CeCe. Max greeted them outside with a huge grin on his face. Evan could tell his boss was stoked about this competition, and this was the last logistical piece of the puzzle.

"This beast is amazing," Max gushed, knocking on the side of the truck with his fist.

Evan hopped out and handed over the keys. "Yeah, it's actually not bad to drive either."

CeCe joined them, her face looking a little brighter, her eyes a little clearer. "It's all real now, huh?" She inched closer to Evan and his fingers ached to reach out and touch her.

God, he wanted to stand there and hold her hand and show Max how their relationship had shifted. Because it was growing harder to keep it a secret.

"Certainly is," Max said, his hand tracing the side panel. "Gin found a guy who can paint it for us, but we need to come up with a design."

Evan opened his mouth to volunteer on the designing, when CeCe blurted out, "Evan and I are dating." Her statement killed the conversation. Both men turned to look at her, and she shrugged. "I thought you should know."

Max beamed and pulled them both into a messy group hug. "I knew something was going on. This is great news!" As they pulled back, Max playfully punched Evan on the shoulder. "I'm so happy for you two."

Evan reached out and finally took CeCe's hand, which she took and squeezed. "I don't want to make a thing of it at work," she said, pointing at each of them. "When we're at work, it's work. Got it?"

"Yes, ma'am," Max and Evan said at the same time.

"I feel like I'm missing drill team out here," Ginny said as she joined the trio. Her face was flushed and a towel hung over her shoulder. "You guys staying for dinner? Max made enchiladas."

Evan's stomach rumbled, but he wanted to talk to CeCe alone. While very welcome, her declaration gave him pause.

"Rain check?" CeCe beat him to it. "I have a few things I need to take care of at home. But maybe the four of us can get together over the weekend?"

"The four of us?" Ginny asked, a knowing smile curving her lips.

Before CeCe or Evan could speak, Max exclaimed,

"They're dating! Isn't it wonderful?" Only a man in love could truly understand the rush of emotions coursing through Evan. Watching Max and Ginny find each other again had been wonderful, and Evan cherished the fact that he could be a part of their lives. These people in front of him were more like family than his own sometimes. And while that should depress him, it gave him strength.

Now he wanted to share that strength with CeCe, because he could tell she needed it.

CHAPTER 11

It had been a week since Eric's text. Seven days of CeCe jumping every time she heard her phone ping or buzz. Seven days of lying to Evan, of feeling guilty as sin. This secret weighed heavily in her core, pulling down on her until she felt she couldn't stand up sometimes. But there had been wonderful moments with Evan too, ones she managed to enjoy without the guilt of her past—the guilt of her secrets.

Stolen kisses in the supply closet, meals made together in their home kitchens, and even an impromptu fort at Evan's during a rainy evening. If only she could take her Eric baggage out of the equation, she'd feel like a million bucks. But she still didn't know how to share the full story— the story of her greatest humiliation. She presented herself as a competent chef, a woman who knew her worth. Yet the story of her and Eric was written about another CeCe, a CeCe whom she didn't recognize anymore.

And for all her desire to rewrite history, to write her own story, it was as if Evan had written his own book. The playbook on how to be a perfect boyfriend; attentive, caring, funny, and passionate. All the while she felt like she was writing the counterpart. *How to be the worst girlfriend ever: A Memoir by CeCe LaRue.*

CeCe kept her head down and muscled through the ball of bread dough in front of her. Yet again, sleep evaded her. So, she crept into the diner well before dawn to make bread. While all parts of baking excited her, thrilled her, it was bread baking that was the most therapeutic. No matter her mood, she'd lose herself in the turns and rolling of the dough.

Wiping the flour from her cheek, CeCe was too engrossed in the task at hand to hear the door open behind her. "Someone is up early today," Evan said as he came up to her and looped his hands around her waist. He kissed the nape of her neck until she melted, like one of her famous chocolate lava cakes. When he kissed her like this, savored their closeness, she felt like he was charting out a route on a map. He knew the right places to make her melt.

"I'll have to sneak out early more often if this is the reaction." CeCe dusted the flour from her hands and turned around in Evan's arms. It felt so natural to hold and kiss him in the diner. Having him close, in her favorite space no less, gave her a sense of contentment she didn't realize she was missing. "What time is it anyway?" she asked, reluctantly stepping away to put the bread in the oven.

Evan hung his jacket on the wall and joined her at the prep station. "About six-thirty. Helen should be here any minute. She'll likely bark orders for us to stay away from each other. Who knew someone could be so disgusted by love?"

The use of the L-word should have shocked CeCe, but she was too distracted.

"Love ... I don't mind. It's all the damn canoodling going on around here. I remember when everyone was single and kept their heads down. Now every time I come to work, I have to worry about seeing someone's backside." Helen rolled her eyes as she stalked past the pair, right into the dining room. "Try to keep it in your pants while I'm here, okay?"

As soon as the door closed, CeCe covered her mouth

and burst out laughing. "I'm wondering if she's walked in on Max and Ginny."

Evan flinched but couldn't fight his own smile. "I love them, but I gotta side with Helen. I don't need to see anyone's backside."

CeCe cocked an eyebrow as Evan's eyes dilated and he cupped her face. "Well, except maybe yours." He kissed her gently for a moment before one of the oven timers went off. With a sigh, she walked over and removed another round of bread from the oven.

Evan drooled as he poked one of the loaves with his index finger. "Is this your sweet sourdough?"

"It is. I haven't made it in a while. Takes a little time, so I ..." Her explanation died on her lips as she saw Evan's face sag. "What's wrong?" She reached out and touched his arm. His jaw was tight and his eyes pinched. The lust from a moment ago had faded into his deep blue pools. "Evan?"

Rubbing the back of his neck, he asked, "What's going on?"

CeCe shook her head, clearly not following the discussion. "Nothing. What do you mean?"

"That bread takes nearly four hours to make, and it's not even opening time."

Still missing the point, she tossed her towel over her shoulder. "Yeah, and?"

"And that means you've been here since two in the morning. When I stopped by yesterday, you were half asleep on the couch. Are you not sleeping? Is everything okay?"

Blood rushed to her cheeks as she absorbed Evan's concern. More importantly, what he'd noticed. For years, she didn't have anyone paying close attention to her moods or schedule. Now she had someone in her life that worried about her, wanted to take care of her. Someone who noticed the bags under her eyes and her early hours. This should have made her feel like a million bucks, but it only made her feel worse—much worse.

"It's nothing. Really. I've got a lot going on with the

competition. I know I need to take better care of myself."

Evan reached out, letting his finger trail down her cheek and neck until his hand rested on her shoulder. He gave her a gentle squeeze and waited while she caught her breath. That was the thing about Evan, when he paid attention, he could see clear down to her soul. If he could, he wouldn't like what he saw. He'd find weakness, he'd find a fool.

During moments like these, she felt the difference in their ages, felt the naivety that came with your mid-twenties. Evan hadn't gone through a relationship like she'd had with Eric. Evan looked at her now like a man who'd never had his heart broken. This look lit a fire inside her, making her hot with worry. She held the power to crush his heart in her floured hands, and it took her breath away.

"Talk to me," he pleaded, pulling her to his chest and cradling her cheek against his hand.

It would be so easy for her to unload, to share her concerns over Eric, her fears that she wasn't good enough, the nagging voice in the back of her head that said she was too old for Evan. That she was too complicated. Instead, she went with what needed to be said in the moment, because she wasn't about to pour her heart out before the breakfast rush surrounded by canisters of flour and sugar. "I'm just tired. I don't know if you know this, but I have this new boyfriend. We keep staying up too late, and I need my beauty sleep."

Blinking, CeCe breathed a sigh of relief when he nodded and kissed her cheek. "If I'm keeping you up too late, say the word. I should probably focus on the rest of the website for the boutique anyway. But I can't seem to stay away from you."

Before CeCe could come up with a witty reply, the back door slammed as Max walked in. His dark hair was mussed and his shirt was buttoned incorrectly. She'd hazard a guess that Ginny was in a similar state of frazzled undress.

"Morning," CeCe chirped.

Max waved and looked down, finally realizing he was a

mess. He muttered to himself as he rebuttoned his shirted.

CeCe winked and turned her attention back to the stove, where her last batch of bread was ready to go into the oven.

"Morning, boss." Evan waved back and went to work cracking eggs.

Helen came back into the kitchen in time to see Max buttoning his shirt. She held her hands up in defeat. "So help me, if you all are going to start having orgies back here, I'm calling the health inspector."

Max's eyes bugged out of his head, and Evan barked with laughter. Just as CeCe was about to say something, Natalie materialized in the doorway, clad head to toe in one of her power suits and sky-high heels. "Something tells me I came in at the wrong moment, or maybe the right one. I guess it depends on your point of view." She smirked at Evan, who flushed and turned his back. Helen merely sighed and went back out to the dining room.

"Shouldn't you be at work? And how did you get in here?" Max asked, although there was no venom in his voice. "Gin left fifteen minutes ago."

Natalie shrugged and looped her oversized handbag through her arm. "Back door was open and I needed some caffeine." She turned and stared Max down for a second before continuing. "My officemate was late coming in and forgot the coffee. I have a feeling that's your fault." She gestured toward Max's hair, and he hurriedly ran a hand through it.

Knowing this wasn't going anywhere good, CeCe walked over to the coffee maker and poured her friend a cup. "Here. Your caffeine fix, milady."

Natalie beamed and took the proffered cup. "Thank you. This is why you're such a good friend."

"Because I feed you for free?" CeCe asked, crossing her arms over her chest. She felt Evan's eyes on her, and she tried to keep the blush from creeping up her neck. Standing there now, surrounded by her nosey BFF and her boss, CeCe couldn't believe mere moments ago she had been kissing Evan. He was under her skin, and not in a bad way. Their relationship still felt dreamlike to her. Fragile like a butterfly, but just as beautiful to her.

"No. I mean, yes. Obviously, I want you to feed me, but that's not why I'm here."

"Then what is it?"

"I'm here to feed you. Well, at least later today."

Not that she always knew what Natalie was saying, but CeCe felt especially lost now. "Nat, I don't follow."

Natalie said, "Anthony and I had dinner plans with the Hendersons. You know them, right? They own those three houses by the lake?" She didn't wait for CeCe to reply, just kept plowing forward. "Well, we'd made reservations at the hottest restaurant in Columbus—took us months to get on the list. Now they're out for a sick kiddo, and we're stuck without our dates."

"Couldn't you bring the kids?"

Natalie's head fell back as she laughed. "Goodness, no! This is the hottest steakhouse in the state. As in, no booster seats and coloring books."

"Then can't you make it a date night?" CeCe asked, clearly not seeing the problem.

Natalie pursed her lips. "What? No. I thought it'd be a great opportunity to do that double date we talked about." She spun past CeCe and made eye contact with Evan. "Are you free tonight?" she asked, a glint in her eye.

CeCe stifled a groan. The last thing she needed right now was an hour in the car with Anthony and Evan. While she adored Natalie, sometimes Anthony's people skills left a lot to be desired. The thought of sharing a triple-digit dinner with her own guilt was too much to handle. She opened her mouth to decline, when Evan cut in. "We're free tonight. Is that the new steak house in the Short North?"

Natalie clapped and nearly squealed her response. "It is! It's called Denim. You know, like jeans. Isn't that absurd?" Despite her words, CeCe could see her friend was more delighted at the name than perplexed by it. She could also tell that there was no getting out of this. Evan's grin was so contagious that Max hurried over to join them.

"No way. You have to tell me how it is." Max's expression was dreamy. "I got a reservation for me and Gin after the wedding, but it's supposed to be next level. Are they still doing that cocktail with the dry ice and flames?"

The trio, all aware of Denim's appeal, gossiped like church ladies for nearly five minutes before CeCe finally chimed in.

"Maybe Max could go in my place?" As soon as the suggestion was out of her mouth, the kitchen fell silent. She could even hear the muffled ticking of the oven timer, keeping pace with her own racing heart.

"You don't want to come?" Natalie looked crestfallen. "I thought we were trying to get a date on the calendar?" She looked back and forth between CeCe and Evan.

"I did. I do," CeCe hurried to correct herself, but that seemed like a pretty big night with no notice. In all their years working together, she'd always felt like she and Max could read each other's minds if she flashed him the right look. Turning to her boss now, she could only pray that her face told the full story her lips couldn't.

Unfortunately, Max wasn't doing too hot with mind reading that day. "If you're worried about coverage, it's fine. That new waitress is starting today. She can stay on with me. Go have fun." Max nodded, as if the matter was settled.

Natalie gave a thumbs-up to Max. "Perfect! How about we pick you guys up? About five o'clock? We'll need the time to get to the city in all that traffic."

Evan nodded. "Sounds great. Can you pick us up at CeCe's?"

Natalie agreed and breezed out of the back door, her coffee forgotten and CeCe's brain in ribbons.

For the rest of her shift, CeCe's head was elsewhere, torn between her Eric concerns and her impending dinner plans. Usually she would jump at the chance to try a new restaurant in the city. But none of this felt normal. There were too many similarities to her life with Eric at places like Denim. The snobby chef making rounds, the overpriced drinks and complicated menus; it was all too much for her.

But when she turned around and saw Evan's hopeful expression, she knew she needed to go. She needed to do this for him. Evan had begged CeCe to go out more, to be a couple outside the confines of her kitchen, or his living room forts. If they were really doing this, really being a couple, she needed to up her girlfriend game. And there was no better time to start than tonight.

*

"So what did you do wrong?" Mallory asked Evan from the couch, an open bottle of beer in one hand. A muted cooking show danced on the screen. It was one of Eric Watson's shows. Evan had been secretly watching Eric cook, hoping to absorb his secrets in the kitchen. Evan wanted to win, badly.

But even with all his thoughts about the competition, he knew something was up with CeCe. Despite their nights together, always spent cuddling or cooking, he could see a tension behind her eyes. He'd been working with her for over a year, and since they met, he had become an expert on her moods.

"What makes you think I did something wrong?" he asked, adjusting his tie in front of the hallway mirror.

Mallory took a swig from her beer and scoffed. "Because you're a man, and men are idiots." She looked briefly at her brother as he slicked back his hair and triple-checked his reflection. "Well, not all men. I know you're trying your best. But at the end of the day, you are likely to completely ruin things with CeCe."

"Your faith in me is astounding," Evan deadpanned. He'd given up the hunt for the perfect outfit and settled for dark-wash jeans and a navy button-up shirt that made his eyes pop. CeCe had commented on his eyes before, and he was hoping the shirt would make her smile. Even thinking about her made his lips curve upward.

Mallory finished her beer and padded into the kitchen. She was supposed to be on-call for third shift tonight. But with a coworker offering to work a double, she was now stranded at Evan's place with nothing to do. He'd offered his place for the night, especially since he was meeting Natalie and Anthony at CeCe's. "If you think CeCe is so upset," Mallory continued, "why don't you ask her what's bothering her?"

Evan raked his hand through his hair another time to make sure his cowlick cooperated. "Believe it or not, I tried that. A lot. She said she was fine."

Mallory opened the fridge and rummaged around until she found a bowl of chili. Evan had been saving that for later, but Mallory covered it in cheese and popped it in the microwave. Got to love siblings and their lack of boundaries. Mallory punched some buttons on the microwave, turned, and hopped up on the counter to face her brother.

"Are you sure something is actually wrong? I know you're worried about everything with Mom and Dad and that disaster that was family dinner. Could you be projecting?"

"All right, Dr. Phil." Evan held his hands up in surrender. "I didn't realize you'd be eating my leftovers *and* giving me a therapy session."

Right on time, the microwave dinged and Mallory stuck her tongue out at her brother. "Yeah, yeah. You're just pissed that you're messing up a good thing with CeCe."

"I'm not messing things up with her," Evan insisted. He stalked over to the closet and pulled down his jacket before turning back and meeting his sister's eye. "Am I?"

Mallory sighed and put her chili down before coming over and giving her brother a hug. "First of all, the fact that you're this worried is a good sign. Most men don't even care when they're crapping the bed."

Evan frowned. "You really need to work on your metaphors, Mal."

"Good thing I'm a nurse and not a novelist. Would you pay attention, please?" She put her hands on her hips and gave him a look that would make lesser men whither, but Evan was very familiar with that particular stare. It's the same one that Sophie and Emily perfected, and Mallory was on her way to mastering it herself. "Talk to her, okay? Make sure she knows you actually *want* to know what she's thinking."

"But I told her that, at least a million times."

Mallory stared him down before Evan felt his toes curl in his shoes. Damn, maybe Mallory had mastered the look already. "Just keep talking, Ev. Even if it takes a million and one times. Whenever CeCe is ready to talk, she'll talk." For once, Evan let Mallory have the last word. Besides, the clock on the microwave showed he needed to leave. He hopped in his car and was at CeCe's place in the nick of time.

CeCe sat on her stoop, clad in a sweater dress and navy stockings. "I didn't realize we'd match." She laughed as she kissed his cheek. "You know Nat will think we planned this."

Evan savored the feeling of CeCe in his arms, smelled the warm vanilla scent on her skin.

The sound of crunching gravel alerted them to Anthony and Natalie's arrival. Evan turned and saw the huge white SUV pull to a stop behind his car. Not for the first time, he hoped CeCe didn't see his old car and want something bigger, better. He had plans for himself, and for her. That old car wouldn't be his ride forever.

"Good evening," Anthony greeted from the driver's seat.

Evan thanked his lucky stars he had picked the outfit he did, otherwise he'd look like a goober. He wasn't sure where the mayor shopped for clothes, but he doubted it was the same thrift shops he frequented.

Natalie swiveled in her seat and reached out to take

CeCe's hand. Once she was done greeting her friend, she took Evan's hand and shook it, their elbows bent at awkward angles. "I'm so glad we're finally going out together. I'm so excited."

Evan could tell from Anthony's expression that he was anything but excited, but he managed to keep the conversation going about Buckeye Falls and general sports knowledge until they arrived in Columbus. Evan felt like he was holding his own in the conversation, but as they were seated, Anthony turned the tables. "So tell me, Evan. What do you think of the mess the market is in right now?"

Busy studying the menu, Evan missed the question. His gaze kept snagging on the triple-digit options in front of him. Thank goodness he was a good saver. He'd be damned if CeCe paid for her own $100 steak.

Not sensing Evan's internal calculations, Anthony repeated his question about the market. "Oh, the market?" Evan had to blink and get back in the present. "I think they could stand to expand now that the shop next door closed. If they carried more of the essentials, then no one would need to drive to the big box stores outside of town."

Everyone turned to stare at Evan, who suddenly felt on display. CeCe whispered, "I think Anthony meant the stock market."

Evan officially wanted to curl into a ball and die. "Right, duh." He chuckled, but it sounded lame to his own ears.

Natalie offered one of her carefree laughs, but it didn't make Evan feel any better. "Leave it to Anthony to dive right into MSNBC talk before we've even placed an order."

Fortunately, the waiter came by to take their drink order, giving Evan the opportunity to catch his breath. Being out with Natalie was one thing, but her husband brought things up to a level Evan wasn't used to. "And for you, sir?" the waiter asked, his eyebrow raised and his pen hovering over the order pad. Evan looked down at the menu and decided on a simple cocktail, just something to calm his nerves a little. Although anything carrying a $20 price tag better do more than calm his nerves. When Evan put the menu down, the waiter asked, "ID, please?"

Once again, everyone's eyes were on Evan and he wanted to shrink further into the booth. "Sure," he said as he pulled out his wallet. Showing the waiter his ID, Evan hoped his cheeks weren't turning as crimson as the tablecloth. Thank God he'd switched to a leather wallet after college. The thought of his old Velcro wallet ripping apart at the table made him want to faint.

Sensing his tension, CeCe covered his hand with her own. Out of the corner of his eye, he saw her wink before steering the conversation back to safer terrain. As in, anything not related to Wall Street. "What do you think of that new bar off Main Street?" she asked, closing her menu. He tried to soak up her warmth, hoping it would bolster him through the evening.

An hour later, their empty plates were cleared and Evan felt the night wasn't a total disaster. He and Natalie briefly discussed the project with the boutique, and he had the opportunity to humble brag about his progress on their website. Natalie gushed to Anthony about how Evan had saved the day, and he felt himself inflate slightly at her praise. Every time he caught CeCe's eye, he felt her reassurance that it was going well. Maybe the night wasn't a complete mess after all.

"No way, dude!" a deep voice boomed from two tables away. Shep, one of Evan's friends from OSU, shuffled over to their table, an empty bus bin clutched under his arm. "I thought that was you, man. How the hell are you?" Shep's ruddy face was open and happy while he waited for Evan's reply.

"Who is this?" Anthony asked. It was a simple enough question, but Evan had no idea how to answer. *My old drinking buddy from college* seemed too honest, but *My old study partner from college* wouldn't be bought by anyone at the table. Studying had never been Shep's thing—unless it was studying the female form. That was where Shep had excelled.

When Evan opened his mouth, Shep jumped in. He stuck out his hand toward Anthony. "You must be Ev's dad. I'm Shep. We were frat brothers."

Natalie snorted with laughter as Anthony fumed. "Excuse me?" was all he could muster. Pissing off Anthony wasn't difficult, as Evan had learned before. Yet now was not the time to test the good mayor's patience.

Evan waved frantically, as if trying to stop a highway accident. "No, no, no. Shep, these are my friends and girlfriend. This is Anthony and Natalie and"—turning to CeCe, he draped his arm over her shoulder—"this is my girlfriend, CeCe."

It wasn't lost on Evan that Shep's eyes roamed CeCe's frame, clearly enjoying what he saw. While slightly flattering, he still wanted to gouge his eyes out with his dessert spoon for creeping on his girl. "Damn, Ev. You've really gone up in the world." Shep wiped his hand on his slacks and reached out to take CeCe's hand. In his haste to make a good impression, he swung his bus bin over and whacked Anthony on the shoulder. While Anthony bristled, Natalie was nearly in tears from holding back her laughter.

Natalie's giggles drew Shep's attention, and he reached out for her hand as well. "And you're just as lovely." He hitched a thumb over to Anthony and asked, "You with the old guy, or are you available for drinks tonight?"

"All right," Anthony said in a tone that meant the conversation was over. Bless her heart, Natalie seemed fine with Shep's attention. She offered a slight wave as she pulled herself to standing. CeCe remained silent, lost in the remains of her cocktail glass. Evan wanted to disappear. Immediately, and potentially forever.

Having been lost in CeCe's moods lately, Evan forgot about the one thing that would always be there. The one issue he couldn't fix, no matter how hard he tried. The age gap.

Sure, five years isn't a lot, but it was enough that right

now they were on different planets. Anthony and Natalie had a family and careers, and CeCe had her own house and a string of successful restaurants on her résumé. Evan sat there in his department store jeans with his goofy frat brother, feeling like a child.

And suddenly he understood what was bothering CeCe, because it bothered him too.

CHAPTER 12

CeCe knew Natalie would be on her doorstep as soon as she dropped her kids off the next morning. Instead of fighting the force that was her best friend, CeCe brewed a pot of coffee and started mixing pancake batter before the sun was even up. It wasn't that she minded getting up early, since she hadn't slept a wink. Their trip to Columbus circled through her brain on a loop, taunting her and making her feel like a damn fool.

And why was she feeling like a fool? Let CeCe count the ways ...

First, she should have stood up and shaken Shep's hand to distract everyone from the elephant in the room. Shep hadn't meant to hit Anthony with the bus bin—although she did enjoy the sound it made when it hit his thick skull. Evan was still worried about their ages. She should have confronted it head-on. But rather than making light, she'd stayed silent and played with the olives in her martini glass.

Next, she let Evan leave before they could have a moment to talk. He'd given her a chaste kiss on the cheek and ran for his car before she had a chance to unlock her front door. He'd stayed on his side of the car for the painfully long drive back to Buckeye Falls, never once

173

reaching out for her hand or meeting her gaze from across the back seat.

Lastly, CeCe knew she should have called him or texted or sent a smoke signal. Anything to let him know she was fine—that *they* were fine. The more time they spent together, the more CeCe realized she wanted to—needed to—be with him. She loved the way she was with Evan, carefree and relaxed. She didn't have to pretend with him, playing the part of someone else. She could be dedicated to her job, and he wasn't intimidated. Hell, he encouraged her.

CeCe also loved the way he looked at her, like she'd hung the damn moon. Even when it was the end of a long day, her hair a mess and her face sheened with sweat, Evan always snagged her gaze and held it until she finally blinked. He was clearly into her. Until their disastrous dinner, she'd felt like they could conquer anything, as long as they were together.

"What a mess." CeCe groaned. She pulled out a stool and raked her hands through her bedhead. She needed to talk to Evan, to set the record straight. Having goofy or immature friends didn't matter. Everyone had someone from their past they wanted to forget.

And there was the other elephant in the room. Eric.

CeCe needed to come clean to Evan about her past with Eric. The thought of Evan figuring it out before she told him made her blood run cold. Nope, Evan was too important, and frankly, he deserved nothing but the whole truth.

Sitting in front of her was her cell phone, taunting her with its lack of notifications. Her morning text to Evan was still unanswered, which wasn't really a surprise. She was about to send another text when she heard voices at the front door. Glancing over to the clock on the stove, CeCe saw it was barely seven o'clock. Before she could get to the door, it swung open and two sets of eyes found her.

"That key is for emergencies," CeCe scolded Natalie as she walked into the house and peeled off her coat. Tossing it on the back of the couch, Natalie strode right for the coffee maker.

"Good morning," a sheepish Ginny greeted from the doorway. She at least had the manners to look embarrassed by their friend's gall.

Just as CeCe was going to ask why Ginny was there, Natalie handed Ginny a mug and started her tirade. "Ginny and I have a big client meeting outside of town this morning. I would have left her in the car, but it seemed rude."

Ginny hitched her thumb over her shoulder and offered, "I can wait outside. I have some files to prep anyway."

CeCe stood and grabbed Ginny's arm, dragging the woman to the vacated stool. "Sit and don't be ridiculous. I'll get breakfast started."

Ginny shook off the offer. "As much as I'd love whatever you're making, I already don't fit in my wedding dress." She sighed. "I'm turning into a bit of a mess."

CeCe paused at the counter and gave the bride-to-be a once-over, and she didn't see a problem. When Ginny arrived back in Buckeye Falls the year before, she looked like she belonged on the cover of *Vogue*. She was rail thin with a sharp haircut and sour expression. Now Ginny practically glowed, with a light in her eyes, a constant smile on her lips, and a few extra pounds softening her features. It was clear that she was better with Max than alone, and CeCe breathed a sigh of relief that they'd found each other again.

"Okay, I don't have enough time to tell you how wrong you are. You are gorgeous, Ginny. Max would marry you again if you weighed a million pounds and grew a beard. But I'll compromise, you get a short stack."

Ginny flushed at CeCe's compliment and nodded. "Just a couple of small ones. I really shouldn't be hungry for our meeting."

Natalie slurped from her coffee before finally diving into the matter at hand. "Now that we've agreed we're all eating breakfast, tell me about Evan. Is he totally pissed at Anthony and me? Better yet, are you totally pissed at me for dragging you both to the double date from hell?"

As much as CeCe wanted to rub the disaster in her friend's lovely face, it was pointless. No one would have guessed that Shep would be there, and that Anthony would be a jerk. Well, actually, that last bit was very possible. "I'm not mad at you, Nat. You can rest assured I won't poison your pancakes." CeCe smeared butter on the griddle and inhaled the savory scent. If anything smelled better than melted butter, she didn't want to know about it.

"Then at least tell me that Evan will talk to me again. I could tell he was so embarrassed, and I wanted to cry." When CeCe looked at her friend, she saw the remorse crinkling the corners of her mouth. A frown on Natalie wasn't a normal occurrence, mostly because her Botox wouldn't allow it. "He looked like a sad-eyed puppy that I wanted to adopt and overfeed."

Ginny snorted, but had the manners to look embarrassed. "Sorry," she muttered, "but Evan is adorable."

Unable to disagree on the state of Evan's cuteness, CeCe went back to her frustrations. "If *I* ever get to talk to Evan again, I'll let you know." CeCe ladled batter onto the griddle and waited for the bubbles to pop in the center. The pancakes finally winked at her, promising a carby reprieve from real life in less than a minute. She couldn't think of any scenario that pancakes couldn't fix.

Over her shoulder, she saw Ginny studying her cup, a look of concern etched on her face as well. "I'm sure Evan's busy with the website build for the boutique. We got a call yesterday afternoon that they want to move the launch up, and I'm sure he's swamped."

"Well, at least he can't avoid me at work. I'm planning on snagging him the second I see him." CeCe flipped a dozen pancakes onto a platter and joined her friends at the counter. "Butter is there, and I made a cinnamon honey."

Ginny tucked in immediately. She was a little too intent on her pancakes, slowly buttering them and not lifting her gaze. Natalie was onto her. "You know something," she accused.

Ginny took a second to raise her gaze, and she nodded. "Um," she said, dragging her fork through a puddle of honey. "I overhead Max on the phone before I left. Evan called in sick, something about food poisoning."

Since they had shared meals last night, CeCe knew that was a lie. "He's not coming in?"

"I'm sorry, CeCe. I'm sure he's just really tired." As if remembering her previous statement, she hurriedly added, "Or busy with the website. Very busy." Shoving a forkful in her mouth she repeated, "Busy, busy."

"Smooth." Natalie sighed into her coffee mug. She took a moment to eat a pancake before addressing CeCe. "Look, we're here to help. Should I have Anthony apologize, or maybe we can have you guys over for dinner? Bury the hatchet, or whatever they say." She whirled a manicured hand in front of her, the other holding a fork weighed down with pancakes. She took the world's biggest bite and groaned with delight. "Honestly, I'm going to come over every morning if this is how you eat."

"The International House of CeCe," Ginny teased. For all her concern over her wedding dress, she had polished off three pancakes before her coffee even cooled. The sight of her empty plate made CeCe smile. Every chef wanted to see their meals devoured and enjoyed.

On the other hand, CeCe herself had lost her appetite. The possibility of Evan avoiding her made her feel … a lot of things. Anger over the situation. Fear that this was the end of whatever they were trying to start. Frustration over the fact that he was avoiding her. And in that moment, the frustration won out.

"Why are earth am I sitting here stewing?" she asked, dropping her fork to her plate with a clatter. "I tried reaching out this morning, and he's ghosting me. Over a year of friendship and after one bad night he disappears like that?" CeCe snapped her fingers to punctuate her point.

"He's probably just embarrassed," Ginny supplied. Understanding she was the odd person out, she continued. "Natalie gave me the CliffsNotes version on the way over here." She shrugged and stabbed another pancake from the platter.

"Exactly," Natalie agreed. "I say you stop by on the way to work and have a nice long chat. That always helps when Anthony and I have a fight."

CeCe was dubious at best. "It does?"

Natalie lifted a shoulder, but didn't lift her gaze. "Um, usually. Whatever, we're here for you."

"We'll unpack your baggage later," CeCe promised. "But I think you're right. I need to talk to Evan."

"Let me help with the dishes," Ginny offered with a mouthful of pancake. "It's the least I can do." Before CeCe could pass, both friends were loading the dishwasher and running a rag over the counter. Ten minutes later, CeCe was alone again with a million thoughts and no sense of direction.

Grabbing her keys, CeCe hit the road to Evan's place. They had a lot they needed to discuss, and it was more than last night. She needed to exercise the ghost of Eric, and the sooner the better.

*

"Explain to me why we're up at this ungodly hour?" Emily asked, rubbing her eyes with one hand and cradling her belly with the other. "I could go into labor at any moment." From the pixelated screen, Evan watched his sister stretch and try to get comfortable. He knew nothing about being pregnant, but he knew his sister looked incredibly uncomfortable.

"I don't know why you're complaining. You didn't just get off a double and have exactly ten hours before you have to do another." Mallory grimaced into her screen. She was still clad in her scrubs; her messy ponytail swung as she yawned. "It's pretty early for an emergency Zoom. What did you do, Ev?"

Evan was incredulous. "Why do you think it was me again?" He fell back on a stack of pillows he had propped up on the floor. It was silly, but he craved the feeling of his forts in times of stress. Not having the time to inflate a mattress, a pillow fort would have to suffice.

Sophie gingerly sipped from her coffee cup. Out of the four, she was the most put-together with her hair brushed and a full face of makeup. In the background, Evan heard his niece and nephew running around and screaming. Apparently, no one sleeps in if there are kiddos in the house. "So? Spill it, Ev. I have to get these ruffians ready for the day. Did you and CeCe break up?"

Sophie's question prickled his skin, making Evan feel like a kid in the principal's office. "Why do you assume we broke up? Why can't two people have a rough patch without breaking up?" He peered into three sets of judgmental eyes. Suddenly, Evan feared he wouldn't get support from this trio. He would probably have better luck if he called Shep. Just thinking about his old buddy made Evan frown.

"You must have really screwed up if you're this defensive," Mallory surmised.

Emily nodded, agreeing with her younger sister. "I thought the same thing. But I'm with Sophie—you need to spill the beans. I'll have to pee again in about five minutes, and that's if I don't fart myself into oblivion first."

Evan's eyes bugged out of his skull. "Excuse me, what?" He couldn't imagine his normally prim and proper sister doing anything remotely crass. But after looking at Emily, Evan realized there was even more about pregnancy he didn't understand.

An image flashed through his mind, gone in an instant. CeCe with a rounded belly, her calves propped on his legs while he rubbed her tired feet. She'd hummed contently while her fingers traced an invisible pattern on her baby bump. It was such a domestic sight, so foreign, yet so familiar. Idly, Evan wondered if he and CeCe were headed toward domestic bliss, or a domestic nightmare.

"All right, enough potty talk." Evan interrupted his sisters' bantering about issues he'd sooner pretend didn't exist. Was he in a parallel universe or something? "We went on a double date last night, and it was a disaster."

Finally, his sisters quieted.

"What do you mean disaster?" Emily asked. Her eyes were sharp, assessing the situation as Evan went into the details.

"Wasn't Shep the one that used to get drunk and run around the quad naked?" Mallory asked, clearly missing the point.

Evan sighed and rubbed the back of his neck. "Yes, that was Shep. Look, I'm humiliated. How can CeCe take our relationship seriously if she's reminded at every turn that I'm young?"

"Younger, not young," Emily countered

Sophie hesitated before offering her two cents. "Have you actually talked to her about this?"

Evan looked at his cell phone, mocking him with two unread texts from CeCe. "Not yet."

"I'm guessing she texted, right?" Mallory said, a smirk carving her face in half. She sure knew how to make him suffer.

"Thanks, Mal. That's really helpful."

The kids bellowed in the background and Evan's laptop shook with Sophie's voice. "You two better knock it off while Mommy is on a call!" she shouted over her shoulder.

Silence cut through the screen, and Emily laughed. "Goody. Another forecast of chaos to come."

Everyone chuckled while Evan thought about his lack of communication with CeCe. "Am I a coward? Not wanting to bring up the age difference again, because I'm afraid it'll all end before it even starts?"

Sophie leaned closer and put on her best big-sister voice. "Look, Ev. I've only met CeCe once, but she seems very no-nonsense. Talk it out with her and see where the chips fall. She obviously isn't that worried about the age thing, or she wouldn't be taking you out with her friends."

"I'm with Sophie. You'll never know where you stand if you don't talk to her. I know it's easier said than done, but there you have it." Emily grimaced as she shifted her weight on her seat.

"Communication is key," Mallory said sagely.

"And what makes you an expert on this, oh single sister?" Evan scoffed.

Mallory rolled her eyes as only a bratty sister could. "This might shock you, Ev, but I've had a few boyfriends. Remember that last guy I dated? Paul? He used to—"

Evan shuddered at the thought of Mallory doing anything remotely romantic with a man. Between that image and Emily's flatulence, he was at highwater mark for family time. "All right, I'm going to go. I need to talk to CeCe."

"Good!" all three sisters chimed.

"Keep us posted," Mallory added. "And. Em, I saw on Reddit that the best thing for pregnancy gas is—"

Evan slammed his laptop shut before he heard the end of that sentence.

Pulling himself free of his pillow fort, Evan plodded over to the kitchen to brew a fresh pot of coffee. He needed to get his head together and reach out to CeCe.

But there was also the boutique website to finish, as they had moved the deadline forward. He wasn't too worried about that, but it was still something that required more than one brain cell. Since he chickened out and called off from the diner, he needed to be productive with his time.

Just as Evan finished pouring his second cup of coffee, he heard a soft knock at the door. Knowing Mallory was too far away and Max was busy at the diner, he knew it had to be CeCe. Finger-combing his hair, he padded to the door and opened it to a sight that made his heart hurt.

CeCe was clad in her favorite hoodie, her blonde hair hanging loose to her shoulders. Her eyes looked as bleary as his did, which somehow made him feel better and worse. "Good morning," she said, holding up a covered plate. "I brought some pancakes." She didn't wait for an invitation inside, barreling past him. By the time Evan joined her, she was sipping from his coffee mug and looked angry. "Why aren't you answering my texts? Don't you think we should talk about this?"

Although he hated being called out for his childish behavior, he was touched that she cared enough to come out—and call him out. "Yeah, actually. I do think we should talk about this. I was trying to caffeinate and build up my nerve to face the firing squad that is a pissed off CeCe." His observation brought a small smile to her lips.

"I know you're mad at me, but I want to—" CeCe started.

That declaration brought him up short. "Why would I be mad at *you*? If anything, you should be embarrassed to be seen with a teenager at the best restaurant in Ohio."

"First of all, our diner is the best restaurant in Ohio. And secondly, you're not a teenager." Evan folded his arms over his chest and frowned. "Well, right now you really look like one. What's going on?"

That was the million-dollar question. How could he explain all his roiling emotions and fears over their age gap? After watching how in sync Anthony and Natalie were, how mature and financially stable they seemed, Evan felt he was lacking.

Sensing where his mind was wandering, CeCe stepped closer and reached out, taking his hand in hers. She squeezed it gently, and much like the night before, Evan felt bolstered by the warmth of her touch. "I can see you're having a hell of a conversation up there," she said, gesturing with her free hand toward his forehead. "Care to include me?"

Evan inched closer, loving how she could read him so

well. Their relationship started as friendship, and he felt like it was a solid foundation for something truly special. All he had to do was be honest and take the first step. "I'm afraid you're embarrassed to be seen with me. I'm terrified that after last night, you're going to end things."

"Why would you think that?" CeCe asked, her voice barely a whisper.

"Because you deserve the best, CeCe. You deserve a partner who supports you and wants nothing but the best for you. Not some goof-off trying to get started."

CeCe let go of his hand, raising hers to cup his cheek. She was mere inches away, and Evan felt he might die if they didn't get closer. "You're not a goof-off." He opened his mouth to argue, but she pressed her finger against his lips. "Don't you think you are those things? Supportive? Caring?" she asked.

The question nearly knocked Evan back on his heels. "Maybe? But I'm just getting started, CeCe. I can't afford to take you to those places all the time. I'm working my ass off to get there, but it'll take time." The unasked question Evan really wanted to ask was *What if I'm not worth waiting for?*

CeCe stood on tiptoes and kissed his cheek, lingering a moment longer to savor the feel of his skin. "Do I look like Natalie?" Evan blinked, then slowly shook his head. "Exactly. I love her, don't get me wrong, but she and I want different things from the men in our lives. Completely different things," she added.

"But what if—" Evan started to argue, but CeCe interjected.

"What if nothing. I'm sorry I didn't stand up and introduce myself to Shep. Everyone has a silly friend in their lives, and it makes no difference how old they are."

"I build forts," Evan said before he could stop himself. "I don't see myself stopping that anytime soon. I don't think that makes me a kid, but I'm not in my thirties."

"I knew that before we started any of this," CeCe said. "Evan, I know I used our age as an excuse before, but I really don't think it matters now."

There were countless reasons it mattered, all fighting for real estate on the tip of his tongue. He could practically hear his father's booming voice of doubt reverberating through his head. "I'm not established."

CeCe stepped back and threw her hands in the air. "I don't care about any of that. You are not your father. You are your own person. I happen to like the person standing in front of me. Yes, you build forts in your living room and have frat bro friends. So what? I spend every waking moment watching bad television and stress baking. We all have our issues."

Evan scoffed, "You make it sound so simple. We won't think about the age thing?"

CeCe inched closer, this time reaching out and pulling Evan against her. "Exactly. Let's see where this goes. No more worries about the age gap. And for the love of all things holy, answer my texts. I'm not saying as soon as you get them, but don't ghost me." Her eyes sparkled with unshed tears, and her expression left no room for argument. CeCe was vulnerable, honest. Her lips parted, and she licked her bottom lip. At first, Evan thought she was about to say something else, but her eyes slid toward his mouth and he was a goner.

He closed the distance until their lips brushed in a tender kiss. Evan lingered, enjoying the maple taste of her lips. "I won't ghost you," he promised between kisses. "I really want this. You and me."

CeCe kissed him again before leaning back and grinning. "Me too. Now, let's eat some pancakes."

Evan watched CeCe warm up the pancakes. She moved effortlessly through his tiny kitchen, occasionally stopping to give him a flirty smile. Despite everything that happened yesterday, Evan felt like they were on solid footing. If they could get past the age difference, the two of them could get through anything.

Evan was falling for CeCe. Hell, he was probably in love

with her already. He'd never been with anyone who made him feel valued, someone he could really trust. Evan couldn't imagine any issues bigger than their ages. He was ready to set sail for calm seas with CeCe.

CHAPTER 13

The competition had finally arrived. CeCe had spent the time pre-competition helping Ginny and Max with last-minute wedding prep, crafting a menu for an upcoming business mixer with Natalie, and spending the rest of her time with Evan. Life was good, and she enjoyed the effortlessness that came with being with Evan. They laughed over takeout from their favorite Chinese restaurant, got serious about menu tweaks for the competition, but CeCe's favorite parts were their tender moments together.

Evan passing her in the diner and gently placing a kiss on her cheek when she was baking, or leaving her a note in the pocket of her apron. He found ways to show he was thinking about her, that he was smitten. Everything felt nearly perfect, except for the six-foot secret standing twenty yards away.

"You're sure you're all right?" Max asked, whispering so Evan wouldn't overhear. Despite the stress of the competition and his upcoming wedding, Max was relaxed, damn near blissful. CeCe had to admit that she liked the new Max. She hadn't realized how lovesick he was until Ginny was back in his life. During a few quiet moments on her own, CeCe could draw the parallels to her own connection with Evan. More often than not, she was happier when he was around her, just being himself.

"Yup, perfectly fine," she lied through clenched teeth. "What do I have to worry about?"

Max raised an eyebrow and gestured toward Eric, who was mingling with the other competitors. Everyone was invited to a get-together to get acclimated to the venue and learn the specifics of the competition. Of course, Eric was there. Trailed by a camera crew that caught him swooning over women in their fifties, flirting with women in their twenties, and generally ignoring anyone that wouldn't look good on camera. Some things never changed.

"I can handle the interview. You won't even have to talk to him," Max assured her. He shifted on his feet, trying to block CeCe from view.

"What did I miss?" Evan asked, joining them with an armful of water bottles and event fliers. His blond hair was mussed, evidence he'd been nervously raking his fingers through the tendrils. Even with his competition jitters, Evan brought a sense of calm to CeCe as soon as he reached out and handed her a water.

She took her bottle and nearly downed it in three gulps. Her skin was tender and flaming red, a tell that her lies were cooking her from the inside. Over the last few weeks, she'd had every opportunity to tell Evan that she and Eric had dated. She could have told him one night after work when it was only the two of them in the diner. She could have told him last week when she was over for a sleepover in his pillow fort. They'd spent the night cuddling and watching kung fu movies, and CeCe didn't want to break the spell. Their relationship seemed too close to perfect, something that was foreign to CeCe.

Max stepped between the pair. He licked his lips twice before speaking, struggling not to stutter. CeCe felt white-hot flames of guilt course through because *she* made her friend this uncomfortable. "W-we were just saying, why don't you two go through the checklist for the food truck?

I'll stay here and do the interview with what's-his-face?"

Evan's face fell, and he looked between his boss and his girlfriend. "Did something happen?" Snaking his arm around her waist he added, "are you okay being here?"

His look of utter concern made her stomach sour. Carefully twisting the top back on her empty water bottle, she nodded, her neck so tense she felt the tendons pop with the movement. Her mouth felt dry and grainy, so she yanked Evan's bottle from his hands and took another long pull. When she'd finally collected herself, she felt like a drooling, defective bobblehead.

Before anyone in their group could say anything, a familiar voice boomed behind her. "I thought I saw the unmistakable pixie that is CeCe LaRue."

CeCe stifled a groan as she turned to face her past head-on, literally. "Hello, Eric," she greeted with a tone she hoped sounded natural. She wanted to reach out and slap him for using her old nickname. A nickname she'd never really liked, as she was conscious of her height.

Eric looked just like his TV show, overly polished and shiny. There was at least a quarter inch of stage makeup on his face, and his hair was slicked back with so much product, she feared it was a fire hazard. *Everyone, keep your propane tanks away from our fearless host!*

Eric snapped to his cameraman, who lowered the camera and took a dramatic step back. In a low tone only she could hear, he said, "I've been looking for you all day. Why haven't you returned my texts?"

CeCe stood to her full five-foot-two inches and asked, "How's your wife?"

The question hit its mark and had its intended effect. Eric blanched, adjusting his collar and finally acknowledging they weren't alone. "Gentlemen, nice to meet you. I'm Eric Watson."

Evan looked back and forth between Eric and CeCe before extending his hand for a shake. "Nice to meet you. I'm Evan Lawson."

Before the other man could reply, Max leaned in and introduced himself. "And I'm Max Sanchez. We're looking forward to getting started tomorrow. Thanks for putting this on here in central Ohio. We don't always get the big events and competitions."

Eric snapped again, bringing the cameras and lights back on. "Well, it's nice to meet you all. Coming to Ohio seemed like a great way to showcase other midwestern chefs. I guess the culinary world exists outside of Chicago," he said with a laugh that grated on CeCe. The assistants and cameraman laughed at the terrible joke. "Looking forward to seeing what you've got," Eric said, his gaze latching onto CeCe.

When Eric and his entourage finally walked away, CeCe felt herself deflate as the tension eased from her muscles. Who knew seeing your heartless, cheating ex could be so exhausting?

Max handed her his unopened water bottle, and CeCe drained it as she collected her thoughts. Next to her, she felt Evan tense as Eric laughed at something another contestant said. It was clear he wasn't a fan of the man. "Are you sure you're okay? You look a little …"—Evan studied her face and finally offered—"red."

CeCe's cheeks burned under Evan's attentive stare, and she couldn't hide her nerves any longer. "Nervous about tomorrow, I guess."

Evan's eyes traced the lines of her face, inventorying her expression before responding. "What did he say to you? You look like you saw a ghost."

CeCe spluttered. "A ghost? I hardly think seeing your ex …" she faltered and hastily added, "boss. Ex-boss. Seeing a former boss can be stressful. Especially since we didn't end things on great terms."

Before Evan could respond, Max stepped closer and took their empty water bottles. "There's a gap now before the orientation. You guys want to find some lunch? I need to find Gin."

As if on cue, Evan's stomach rumbled and the mood

lightened. "You want to try that Korean place we passed on the way into town?"

CeCe smiled, knowing how much Evan loved all things Korean. While Buckeye Falls was growing and offering a wider variety of restaurants and shops, it still lacked anything Korean. "That sounds great. I'll hop over to the restroom and meet you guys out by the truck."

Max clicked away on his cell phone, alerting Ginny to their plans. She had taken over the diner's promotion of not only the competition, but the general marketing as well. Max would have been happy with just the locals knowing about the competition by word-of-mouth, but Ginny wouldn't let it go. CeCe was glad Ginny was tenacious, as the exposure could really take the diner places. Granted, she never wanted the diner to be like Eric's restaurant in Chicago, but there was definitely room to grow.

"Gin will be here in twenty. She's mingling with some vendors." Max tucked his phone into his pocket and looked at his staff. She could tell he was nervous. She needed to set the record straight, but it wouldn't do well to upset their flow before the competition. "I'll meet you guys later on. Enjoy lunch."

Evan took her elbow and turned CeCe toward the exits where the restrooms were. "I can meet you over there. Does that work?" CeCe merely nodded as she stared into Evan's honest eyes. They were so clear, so open to her. While his blind trust should have made her feel invincible, it made her stomach sour.

CeCe bolstered herself. Maybe they could get through the competition without Eric being a problem? Heck, maybe she wouldn't have to tell him ever. Then Evan would always look at her like that, with an affection that made her feel six feet tall. "Sure," she managed to say, despite her dry throat.

Evan kissed her cheek and promised, "See you in a minute." CeCe shivered at his touch, and not in a bad way. She stood in place and watched Max and Evan disappear into the crowd. She sighed and turned in search of the restrooms and a few moments of peace.

As soon as she started walking, she hit a wall. A familiar wall that smelled like expensive cologne and a hint of spice. "Finally got you alone." Eric's voice was a low rumble.

CeCe pulled free of Eric's grasp and put a foot of space between them, but it wasn't enough. Sharing the same oxygen as him seemed too much, too intimate. After Evan's kiss a moment ago, she wondered how she ever fell prey to Eric's charms. Not knowing what to say, CeCe simply asked, "What do you want?"

Eric smirked, and it made CeCe's stomach lurch. "I want you," he said.

Her eyes rolled without her permission. "That's a pretty cheesy line for such a famous chef. I'm sure Hilary loves it when you flirt with everyone you meet."

Eric scoffed, his smirk fading. "I don't flirt with everyone. I'm here to see you."

CeCe crossed her arms over her chest and squared her shoulders. "Well, you can follow me and my team tomorrow when the games begin."

Breaking eye contact, Eric looked over his shoulder to ensure they were alone. "What's the deal with those guys? Was that kid kissing you?" A flush crept up Eric's neck, and CeCe got a cheap thrill from upsetting him.

"That's my boyfriend, Evan. And he's not a kid, so don't be rude." Standing there defending her life choices with the man who nearly broke her felt absurd, and she had already had enough. "You know what? Why am I standing here defending my choices to *you*? I don't owe you anything, and if you can't judge us fairly, then that's your problem."

Eric stepped closer and CeCe tried to back away, but she'd run out of real estate. Her shoes kicked against a wall and she felt like she could suffocate being this close to him again. "I'm a professional, pixie. I'm a little disappointed you don't remember that."

CeCe remembered a lot of things. None of which she

wanted to revisit in that moment, especially with Eric so close. She chastised herself for separating from Evan and Max, as they provided the buffer she needed. It was like those nature shows when one wildebeest breaks free of the herd and falls victim to a pride of lions. The look on Eric's face now was dark, brimming with false pride of his own. If she wasn't careful, he'd devour her whole right here in the exhibit hall.

"Well, I should go. My boyfriend and I are grabbing lunch. I'm glad it's a blind competition, otherwise I would pack up and leave right now."

Eric raised a shoulder in a shrug. "You really don't think I can be a professional?" he asked, his voice dangerously low.

"I don't think you can be a lot of things," CeCe snapped back, surprising herself with the venom in her tone. "Goodbye, Eric. I can honestly say I hope I never see you again." Without waiting for a response, she pushed through the crowds on the way to freedom.

She was strong because it took everything she had to stand up to Eric. And she was strong enough to win this competition. Frankly, working with Evan and Max made her feel indomitable. But even all the planning and sharp words couldn't protect her from her secret coming out. Sooner or later, Evan would learn the truth. She just hoped it wouldn't break them.

*

Not for the first time, Evan felt like something was up with CeCe. She was overly cheerful at lunch, her voice unnaturally high and her laughter false. She stuck her chopsticks into her noodles and twirled them for a moment too long, causing the bite to untangle and flop back into the bowl.

CeCe finally gave up and tossed them onto the table, retrieving a fork and stabbing her lunch until she realized

Evan was watching her. "So, are we going to talk about this?" Evan asked, gesturing with his chopsticks to the macerated mess in front of her.

"Not that good with chopsticks, I guess," CeCe said, shrugging and averting her gaze. "You know me."

Evan studied her for a moment. Ever since they'd seen Eric, CeCe was acting like her clothes were put on backward. Even now, she fidgeted under his appraisal. "You're the most dexterous person I know. I've seen you balance a pot of boiling sugar while whisking egg whites and yelling at Helen. You can literally do anything. What is going on?"

Evan's words had hit their mark, as CeCe flushed and offered him a weak smile. "That's really nice," she said, her voice finally down to normal tone and volume. "You seem to see everything."

"Only when it comes to you," he replied, reaching out and taking one of her hands in his, squeezing it before letting go and taking a sip of water. He didn't want to make her uncomfortable, but he needed to know how to help her. "Is working with Eric going to be a problem?"

Caught off guard, CeCe nearly choked on a bite of noodles. Covering her mouth, she coughed a few times before asking, "Why would you think that?"

Evan laughed. It was hollow and sounded forced to his own ears. "You're a nervous wreck, and I mean that from a place of concern. This guy seems to mess with your confidence, and I'm not here for it. I'll pull us out of this competition right now if it's too much. Nothing is worth watching you get this—" He was lost for words. He raked his gaze over CeCe. Her hair was a little mussed, like she'd run her hands through it one-too-many times. Dark smudges under her eyes had taken away from her usually rosy cheeks. "Frazzled. Nervous."

An expression crossed CeCe's face that he'd never seen before. Her eyes misted over and her bottom lip trembled. One hand balled in and out of a fist, her knuckles cracking with effort. It was as if she was afraid to make any sudden movements, was afraid to let something go. Cursing under his breath, Evan realized he'd brought her close to tears. "God, CeCe. I'm sorry, I didn't mean to—"

Before he could finish, she stood and rounded their table, kneeling so they were at eye level. "Don't you dare apologize," she warned, poking his chest with her index finger. He flinched at the contact. "That might be the nicest thing anyone has said to me. I mean it." Her voice hitched at the end, and Evan pulled her to him, kissing the top of her head while he cradled her against himself. Her hair smelled faintly of vanilla, all warm and comforting.

Even during times of distress, he loved holding her. He loved when she opened up to him like this, loved when she allowed herself to be vulnerable. This was a CeCe not everyone got to see, and Evan treasured the notion that he was worthy of her true self.

If Evan had the guts, he'd tell her right now that he was in love with her. But pouring his heart out when she was upset wasn't romantic; it was selfish. What she needed now was his support, plain and simple. So he swallowed his declaration and saved it for another time, for when they were alone and celebrating their victory against this asshole. Because whether she'd admit it or not, Eric was trouble with a capital *T*.

"Let's get out of here, get some air." CeCe nodded, and Evan kissed her temple before they broke apart. Tossing a handful of bills on the table, he led the way out into the sun.

The competition was held close enough to Buckeye Falls that everyone could have commuted, but instead they got hotels. Their hotel was only a five-minute walk, so Evan took CeCe's elbow and directed her onto the sidewalk. They walked in silence for a moment, watching locals and other competitors walk the streets. Every few paces, they were stopped by someone who recognized CeCe.

"Oh my gosh, CeCe!" a woman with purple spikey hair shouted from a few feet away. She practically ran over an old woman with a cane to get to the pair. "I thought that was you." Without waiting for CeCe to reply, the woman crushed her to her chest in a brutal hug. "Girl, you look great. Getting out of Chicago was the best thing you ever did."

Beside him, Evan felt CeCe tense before offering the woman a smile. This wasn't a genuine CeCe smirk, but rather a grimace. "Roxie, it's good to see you. Are you still at Blue?"

The two women chatted for a moment before Roxie turned to Evan and gave him a slow head-to-toe appraisal. "And who do we have here?"

CeCe shook her head and motioned to Evan. "Sorry, duh." She giggled nervously. "This is my boyfriend, Evan."

Evan shook Roxie's hand, and the woman whistled in approval. "You two are adorable, if you don't mind me saying."

"Thanks, I have to agree," Evan quipped. He reached out, snagging CeCe's hand. It wasn't much, but he hoped the gesture calmed her. "It's nice to meet you, Roxie. I take it you're competing too?"

Roxie nodded. "Yes. I'm here with a pair of my sous chefs. I should have known CeCe would be here. We don't stand a snowball's chance in hell now. It's nice of you to come out and support your gal, though."

"Oh, no. I'm competing with CeCe. We work at the same restaurant."

Roxie's eyes sparkled as she turned back to CeCe. "Girl, I see you're breaking your own rules. Good for you." Roxie swatted Evan's arm before taking a step back. "Go have some fun. I have to meet my team, but I'll see you around." With a wave over her shoulder, Roxie disappeared and CeCe's pinched face gave Evan pause.

"She seems nice," Evan said, watching CeCe as they continued their walk to the hotel. Evan realized there was a lot about her time before Buckeye Falls he didn't know about. Suddenly he was starving for details, hungry for morsels of her past that she hadn't been willing to share. "So how do you know all these people?" he asked, reaching down and taking her hand in his. Unlike a moment ago, her palm was slick with sweat and nearly slid from his grasp. Giving a gentle squeeze, he prayed the movement conveyed his support as well as his curiosity.

CeCe tucked a lock of hair behind her ear. "Roxie and I used to wait tables out of school, then we started in some of the same kitchens in Chicago. Some are old coworkers, others I've just met through my travels. This may surprise you, but I can be pretty bossy if I visit a kitchen I like." She winked at him, and Evan laughed, recalling how she got her job at the diner years before. Max was quick to share the story whenever anyone asked, and CeCe didn't shy away from defending her early criticism of the diner's desserts.

Before Evan realized where they were, CeCe stopped in front of their hotel. "You mind if I head in and rest for a bit?"

"Sure. Can I walk you up?" he asked, hoping she'd allow him to join her for at least a moment of peace in the elevator. He wasn't ready to give up this one-on-one time with his girl yet.

And because his sister had the worst timing in the world, that is when he heard her voice coming from the hotel lobby. "There you guys are," Mallory said as she bounded over to them. She was dressed in her favorite non-work outfit of yoga pants and a Bruce Lee T-shirt. It was the same version as his favorite, a gift from Sophie several Christmases prior. "I was about to check in. How are things going?"

Mallory and CeCe exchanged a quick hug before CeCe took another step back toward the elevator. "We're good, but I'm glad you're here. You can keep your brother company while I snag a quick nap." CeCe leaned in and kissed Evan on the cheek before darting away like a skittish wild animal.

Evan frowned. Ever the observant sister, Mallory

sighed. "What did you do?"

"I can safely say this time it wasn't me, but that doesn't mean I know what's going on." Cupping the back of his neck, he exhaled until his shoulders slumped.

Mallory looked concerned. "Is CeCe okay? She looked a little tired."

"I hope so, but something's up. She's been acting cagey since we got here. Plus, we bumped into an old friend who made a comment that seemed to rile her up." Evan raked a hand through his hair, unable to stay still. "I wish she'd talk to me."

Mallory took her brother's arm and yanked him toward the door. "I just drove two hours on I-70. Let's dissect your relationship over food. Have you had lunch yet?"

Thinking back to his half-empty noodle bowl, Evan shook his head. "Let's eat."

Evan hoped Mallory could help him get to the bottom of CeCe's withdrawn state, because it was driving him crazy. He was in love with her, and he wanted to make her life as bright as she had made his.

CHAPTER 14

CeCe had never been much for girl talk before she met Evan. But now, mere hours away from the competition, she needed a second opinion on things.

"You're telling me you haven't told Evan about your past with Eric yet?" Natalie's voice screeched through CeCe's cell phone. Through the line, she could hear the clacking of her friend's heels as she stalked around. Natalie was a world-class pacer.

CeCe flopped back on her hotel bed and covered her face with her free hand, the other clutching the phone until the plastic case creaked under pressure. "Yes, I know. Okay? I'm not calling for you to tell me I'm in the right. I'm calling because I need to know how to bring this up to Evan *now*. It's been nearly two months that I've kept this secret. I feel terrible." Natalie was quiet for a long pause, and CeCe pulled the phone back to make sure she was still on the line. "Either I've offended you or you hung up on me."

"Sorry. I'm trying to figure this out. I'm not exactly the queen of honesty and open communication." Natalie's tone was too truthful, too heavy to be mocking.

"You're not?" CeCe asked, practically scandalized. While Anthony wasn't her chosen partner, she assumed Natalie was happy in her marriage. Why else would she stick around with everyone's favorite surly mayor?

Natalie practically snorted into the line. "CeCe, come on. You've seen Anthony and me in action. I would hardly call the PDA police on us. Marriage is tricky sometimes. Let's just say there are times I don't speak my piece."

CeCe bolted upright, sending a stack of pillows cascading onto the floor. "You're telling me you don't tell Anthony how you feel? Nat, you tell me every thought you have. I know what you ate for breakfast and how much you spent on those new shoes you got in Cincinnati. How is this possible?"

Sighing, Natalie continued. "Marriage makes it different. Hell, love makes it different. Anthony and I used to be crazy about each other. Of course we still love each other, but it's not the same. We've let too much time go by with certain things unsaid. Throw in two kids under five, and it's a whole other kettle of fish."

"But Evan and I are just getting started," CeCe urged. "We shouldn't have anything left unsaid." Waiting a beat, she added, "And we don't even have a house plant, let alone kids."

Natalie snorted. "Then take your own advice and start talking. Evan is clearly crazy about you. He's probably noticing something is up anyway. Give the poor kid some credit."

CeCe rolled her eyes. "Stop calling him a kid, okay? He's a man."

Natalie laughed. "I'm well aware he's a man. Remember that time with the tinsel last Christmas? I'm pretty sure seeing him shirtless burned off one of my ovaries."

CeCe didn't need a reminder of Evan and his looks. She was certainly attracted to him physically, but it was the other side of him that had really drawn her in. He was funny and attentive, always asking her how she was or what she needed. And Natalie was right; he knew something was up after CeCe bumped into Roxie. It was eating her alive not to be honest with him. He deserved the best. She just hoped she was good enough for him.

"I need to tell him now." She sighed.

"You do," Natalie agreed. "Sorry I don't have anything more helpful to say."

Even though Natalie couldn't see her, CeCe nodded. "No, this was helpful. I needed to be reminded of the truth."

"Evan is a good guy, CeCe. He'll understand. Just be honest. Tell him why this has been so hard for you. Everyone handles breakups differently."

"I will. And you be honest with me too, okay? I want to be here for you if you need to talk. About Anthony or anything."

Natalie was quiet for a moment, as if choosing her words. "I will. Thank you, CeCe. You're a good friend."

"Ha! I learn from the best. I'll text you later after the first round."

"You better. I downloaded the app so I can watch the results live. Me and all of Buckeye Falls are rooting for you."

CeCe knew she had friends back in town, but it calmed her to hear it. Never had she felt so connected to a place. When she lived in Chicago, she made friends and felt a connection to her work. But in Buckeye Falls, it was different. Max, Natalie, Evan, Helen, and even Ginny had become her family. She couldn't picture her life without them in it.

CeCe hung up and decided to take that nap she mentioned. Her body felt heavy with both mental and physical fatigue. As she drifted off, she allowed herself a moment to imagine a proper future with Evan. A future where she told him everything, no matter how much it hurt or how embarrassed she felt. Natalie was right, Evan was a good guy. He would understand.

The sun had set by the time CeCe stirred, and she flung her legs over the bed. She didn't have much time to get ready before their double date with Max and Ginny. She knew it wouldn't be a carbon copy of their date with Natalie and Anthony, but she still didn't want to be late.

Gathering her purse, CeCe flung open her hotel door and bumped right into Max and Ginny. They held hands as they walked toward the elevator, Ginny's head resting on Max's shoulder. They fit together like two puzzle pieces, and it was easy to see why they belonged together.

"Perfect timing," Max said when he saw CeCe.

Ginny hugged CeCe. "It's good to see you. How are you feeling about tomorrow?" From the expression Ginny wore, CeCe could tell Max had spilled the beans about her past with Eric. Proving, yet again, that Evan really needed to hear the truth from her.

"I'm feeling good. Excited to get started." CeCe pushed the button for the elevator and the door opened. Evan stood there in slacks and a button-up shirt, looking like he was ready for a night out on the town.

"Hey," he greeted, tugging CeCe into the elevator first and kissing her cheek. "You look amazing, as usual," he said under his breath before detaching and reaching out to shake Max's hand and wave to Ginny. "You guys look adorable."

Ginny flushed at his words and melted into Max's side. "Evan, you're too sweet. We were talking about tomorrow. Are you feeling ready?"

Evan nodded, draping his arm over CeCe's shoulder and tucking her against his side. She drew strength from his closeness. Being near him was the best place to be, her own safe haven from life's chaos.

When they arrived in the lobby, it was packed with other competitors. CeCe recognized some people from earlier in the day, but she kept her eyes down and focused on Evan and her friends. The foursome walked down the street to try a fusion restaurant that boasted the best Brazilian Thai food.

"This reminds me of a place I used to go to in New York," Ginny said as she scanned through the menu. "Everything sounded wild in print, but it was heaven on the plate."

Max reached over, snatching his fiancée's hand and kissing it before picking up his own menu. The sight bolstered CeCe's resolve to tell Evan the truth, because she wanted a future like that. Thinking back to her conversation with Natalie, she wanted that for her friend too. CeCe made a mental note to follow up with Natalie as soon as they were back in Buckeye Falls. She'd selfishly missed her friend's own hiccups with relationships, and that didn't sit right with her.

The group ordered their meals and delved into conversation about the competition and their jobs. Ginny sipped from her wine and nodded to Evan. "How is your website for the boutique coming along? I hope Natalie and I aren't overworking you."

Evan beamed. "No. I'm happy to have the contract. I have the framework up and the graphics selected. I'm waiting for the shop owner to send over some pricing guides and inventory lists. I should have it done before next week. I wanted it out of the way before the wedding."

Max winked. "Which cannot come soon enough." Either oblivious to their audience or simply not caring, Max cupped Ginny's face and kissed her as their waiter arrived with their meals. The waiter cleared his throat and started placing their plates on the table.

CeCe's chest nearly exploded with the need for that type of connection. She'd known Max for years, all before his and Ginny's reconciliation. While she'd never considered Max anything but happy before, he was practically ecstatic with everything he did these days. She'd caught him whistling the wedding march while taking out the trash last week, like he was walking down the aisle instead of out to a dumpster.

Evan speared a dumpling from her plate with his fork. "Trade you a dumpling for a steak egg roll?"

Laughing, CeCe reached over and took an egg roll from his plate. Not waiting for a reply, she took a huge bite and laughed when the sauce spurted out onto table. "I guess I'm a little overzealous." Evan smiled, reaching out to swipe a blob of sauce from the corner of her lip. Without blinking, he licked the sauce off his thumb and winked.

Yeah, someone needed to turn the AC up in this place. CeCe blinked and reached for her iced tea, eager to slow her pulse and racing thoughts. He did things inside her ribcage that likely warranted the help of an esteemed cardiologist.

"Want to split a dessert?" Max asked, pulling the dessert menu from the center of the table. "I heard they have these mango tapioca thingies that are to die for."

Ginny wiped her mouth and shook her head. "Oh no," she lamented. "I barely fit into my dress when I went in for a fitting last week. I need to cut back."

Clearly not having it, Max raised an eyebrow and shook his head. "You realize you're marrying a chef again, right? Food is never not going to be around."

Ginny laughed and inched closer, lowering her voice. "And you realize you'll have a naked bride if she can't zip up her dress."

"I fail to see the problem," Max cooed.

"Okay," Evan said, his voice full of laughter. "I'm usually not bothered by PDA, but you guys are so sweet you're giving me diabetes. We might as well skip dessert."

CeCe reached out and took his hand under the table, squeezing it before she agreed. "I'm with Evan on this one. Yeesh."

Before Max and Ginny could reply, a familiar squeal erupted from the entrance to the restaurant. Turning around, CeCe paled when she saw Eric walk in, surrounded by a slew of women. One of those swooning women was Mallory, practically fanning herself as she followed Eric and his harem inside.

Evan pulled back and rubbed the back of his neck. "This will not be good." He ground the words through his teeth. "What is Mal doing?"

"Fangirling?" Ginny suggested.

"Fan what-ing?" Max asked, clearly not up-to-speed on slang.

"It means she's making an ass of herself," Evan said, pulling himself to standing and marching to his sister.

Taking the opportunity, Max lowered his voice and asked, "Is everything okay? I heard Eric found you at the exhibit hall."

CeCe took one more careful look over her shoulder and sighed. "Yeah. It's fine. Frankly, I'm more worried that Evan doesn't know about us. I'm terrified he's going to learn it from someone else."

Max swallowed, his Adam's apple bobbing in time to the cheers from the entrance. "Y-y-you need to tell him, CeCe. Now."

CeCe paled at the appearance of Max's stammer. It reared its ugly head when he was worked up. "I will. Tonight. I was planning on it before everyone's favorite asshat showed up." She hitched a thumb over her shoulder and slunk down in her seat. During times like this, she was grateful for her shorter frame.

Ginny took action, pulling her wallet out and waving down their waiter. "I'll get this covered. You guys save Mallory from herself. I'll meet you outside."

Max and CeCe nodded. He led the way, shielding CeCe from Eric's line of sight. When they walked past, she reached for Evan's hand and gently tugged. Their eyes met for a moment, and he nodded. She couldn't wait to get back to the hotel and open up to him. She was ready to share the burden of her past. All the reasons she'd stayed quiet fell away, because she didn't care anymore. Eric was the past, and she was looking at her future.

It didn't matter how she'd acted before, didn't matter how she'd reacted to Eric's behavior. She was herself, the best version of herself, now that she'd found her confidence. Eric's decisions, and reactions to her leaving, had no bearing on her life. Of course Evan had a lot to do with that change, but she'd found what made her happy on her own. Clutching his hand now, she could only pray he could feel her love through their intertwined fingers.

Yet all her bluster and resolve crumbled at the sound of Eric's voice. "Is that my favorite pixie, CeCe?" Eric's voice cut through the din of the crowded restaurant. There was a slight slur in his words, as if he'd started happy hour early.

CeCe stumbled and walked into Max's back while Ginny gasped behind them. Evan's hand grew slick with sweat in hers, sensing the tension. "What's going on?" he asked no one in particular. His eyes darted back and forth between Eric and CeCe. Evan practically snarled at Eric, and she was momentarily touched. Then reality came crashing in and she had to focus on breathing.

Never one to miss an opportunity to upset her, Eric stepped closer but kept his voice loud. "So how is my favorite ex doing?"

Evan's hand slipped from CeCe's grasp and she felt like collapsing to the floor in a boneless heap. Her fingers flexed, desperate to feel the solid support of Evan's grasp. But when she reached out, all she felt was cold, empty air.

CHAPTER 15

Evan's ears rang so loudly, it was as if a fire station had been erected in his skull. Of all people, it was Mallory who broke the silence first. Her wide eyes darting back and forth between her celebrity crush du jour and her brother. "What did you say?" she asked, her voice dangerously low.

Eric leaned closer still and practically sneered at CeCe. "I asked how my favorite ex is doing. We didn't get a chance to properly catch up earlier." Despite the rising tensions in their group, a few of the groupies grew bored and sauntered out of the restaurant.

Sensing he'd need her, Mallory stepped closer to Evan. "What is he talking about?" she whispered in his ear.

Evan shook his head and tried to slow his heart. Beside him, CeCe stood ramrod straight, her hands balled into fists at her side. Her eyes shone with fury. She stared Eric down for a moment before finally breaking the silence. "You're drunk. Go back to your room and sleep it off."

Eric reached out to CeCe, but she jumped back and wedged herself between Evan and Max. "You always did know how to read me, my little pixie." Eric's expression was soft, but the look in his eyes made Evan's stomach churn. There was a high probability he was about to lose his egg

207

rolls all over the floor.

He turned to CeCe now, blocking Eric's face from her vision. "CeCe, what is going on?" For a moment, she didn't speak. Her mouth opened and closed a few times while her eyes scurried between Evan and Eric. "Talk to me," Evan pleaded. He hated the weakness in his voice, but he'd never seen her look like this—like a stranger.

Suddenly, Eric started clapping and barked with laughter. "I love this." He hiccupped. "My CeCe keeping secrets." He turned and looked Evan right in the eye. "I'm guessing she didn't tell her little boy toy about us, hmm? That we were together. For a year." That last little detail felt like a punch to the solar plexus, and his knees buckled.

Heat crept up the back of his neck as Eric's words sunk in. "You guys used to date?" In the far recesses of his mind, Evan searched for the tiniest hint that CeCe had mentioned this before. He wouldn't forget a detail like this, surely. He never would have pushed to be in the competition if it was all about showing off to her ex. Her celebrity ex, who was standing in front of Evan with a smirk he wanted to wipe off his face.

CeCe took Evan's arm. He felt the pressure of her grip through his sleeve, but it wasn't enough to break the spell Eric had on him. "Poor kid," Eric scoffed.

Us.

Two little letters strung together to have maximum impact on Evan's heart. He felt the word cut through him in waves, a lump forming in the back of his throat. No, CeCe definitely hadn't mentioned their romantic past. Evan wasn't naïve, he knew she'd dated before him, but this felt like more. This felt like he was a fool. A kid who didn't know the difference between reality and make-believe.

From behind, Evan was vaguely aware of CeCe and Max talking. Whether it was to him or to Eric, he wasn't sure, and he didn't really care. Stepping back until he reached the door, Evan burst out of the restaurant and into the cooling evening air. Without paying attention to where he was going, he stumbled onto the sidewalk and started walking.

The look on Eric's face, the lack of anything from CeCe, it was too much to bear. Evan shoved his hands in his pockets and stomped forward, hoping he could walk until he found a hole to bury himself in. He felt like a damn idiot.

"Evan!" Footsteps pounded behind him. "Evan, wait!"

Evan kept pace until a hand fell on his shoulder.

"Ev, stop," Mallory breathed. Stepping in front of her brother, she gave his chest a shove. "Where do you think you're going?" she asked, anger rising in her voice.

"I don't know, and frankly I don't care." His tongue was like sandpaper in his mouth. He was shocked he could formulate words. How is it possible that five minutes ago he was having a wonderful evening with his girl and his friends? Now he felt hollow and alone—and immensely foolish.

"You need to go back and talk to CeCe," Mallory ordered, pointing back the way they came. "You need to go—" but Mallory stopped talking when Evan's eyes filled with tears.

"I need to be left alone, Mal. I need to think and have some space." He looked at his sister and hoped she could feel his pain enough to back away. For once, to stop being the annoying big sister. "Please." His voice cracked as a tear fell, dissecting his cheek. Angrily, he swiped it away.

"Oh, Ev," Mallory said as she pulled him in for a hug. "It's going to be fine, you'll see."

Evan wiped his face on his sleeve. Add crying in public to his list of things he never wanted to do. "Mal, I gotta go." He spun on his heel and didn't stop when she kept calling his name.

He wasn't sure how he'd even gotten home, but Evan lay on his couch with his arm draped over his face. All his stuff was still in the hotel, but that was the least of his concerns right now. Thanking his not-so-lucky stars, he was glad he only had to drive an hour in his zombie-like state. It probably wasn't safe to drive, but it wasn't safe to sit around a strange town and piece together what had transpired at the fusion restaurant. All the way home, his cell rang so much, he'd turned it off. As soon as he entered his place, he buried the infernal device in a kitchen drawer before collapsing onto the couch. He wasn't sure if it was CeCe, Max, or Mallory calling. Frankly, he didn't care either way.

CeCe had kept a secret from him, an important secret from her past. What did this mean? They were supposed to be partners, equals. Partners don't keep secrets like this from each other. Did she not trust him to handle the news? Evan bristled a little, seeing as how he'd turned tail and run all the way back home.

But there was something else Evan couldn't get past—the fact that CeCe never ran after him. If the situation were reversed, he would have followed her anywhere. He would scream and cry and try to let her see his side. But CeCe had remained stoic, unmoving, and seemingly unfeeling toward his pain.

After another hour of wallowing in self-pity, he pulled himself up and went to the fridge for a beer. He hated the cliché of drowning his sorrows, but he didn't see a way past his clogged emotions at the moment. Popping the top, he plodded back to his bedroom and flopped on the bed.

As he turned over, a puff of CeCe's scent came from the pillow. She'd spent the night earlier in the week, and he could smell the cinnamon and vanilla that always clung to her skin. She didn't need perfume, her baking had infused her with warm, welcoming aromas. Tears welled in his eyes as he slugged from his beer and tried to forget that the woman he loved had lied to him.

And boy did he love her. He'd swallowed the declaration a dozen times, but it was pointless to deny it now. Planning on tell her at the competition, he felt like a fool now. Lying in the dark, the beer blurring the corners of his vision, he was eternally grateful he'd chickened out on sharing how he felt. He couldn't imagine how much worse it would be if he'd made his grand declaration. As it was, he was drowning over his feelings for CeCe. He was head over heels for this woman. If he were honest, he had been since the first day they met.

How different things seemed now, with over a year's hindsight and the sting of betrayal. After a year of flitting from one dead-end job to the next, Evan finally found the diner and a sense of community. College provided the security and comradery he craved, but after leaving his father's internship, he felt listless. Max, CeCe, and even Helen, had shown him what he was capable of without making him feel small. He couldn't imagine not having them in his life, which made this new revelation sting even more.

Evan trusted easily, and his stomach churned knowing he'd been humiliated in front of his friends—in front of his girlfriend. The fact that CeCe was the reason for this gnawing sense of loneliness made his eyes burn and he couldn't stand it. Things with CeCe had never felt this complicated. If he wanted to have a difficult relationship that made him feel small, Evan could call his father.

And that made Evan even angrier, his relationship with his father. If they were like other fathers and sons, he could call him now. He could drive to his childhood home and pour his heart out. He could ask for advice on how to fix this mess. But no, Evan knew that was impossible. Asking his father for love advice would be tantamount to suicide. Not only would he get an earful of judgment over his career path, he'd be ridiculed for not seeing this coming.

Evan finished his beer and realized it was dark outside. The day had certainly not ended the way he wanted it to. He'd planned to spend the night with CeCe. Tonight he wanted to tell her he loved her, that she was the woman for him. Age difference be damned, he knew what he wanted. He wanted CeCe.

The trouble was, he didn't know if that meant a hill of beans at the moment.

*

CeCe stood in the restaurant, feeling numb and hollow. She heard Evan's rushed footsteps as he fled the scene, and she feared she'd lost him. Every fiber in her told her to turn and run, to find him and apologize until there were no more words left to say. He deserved better than this blindsiding moment—this humiliation. In her haste to save herself from the embarrassment of sharing her past, she'd steamrolled him instead. The pain she wanted to avoid was now squarely on Evan, and she nearly doubled over with the frustration over her own stupidity.

It was all different now. She wanted to end the chaos, end the pain. She was tired of having Eric as a shadow she couldn't outrun. This ended now. *It had to.*

Squaring her shoulders, CeCe checked to make sure she wasn't alone. Max and Ginny stood frozen beside her, wearing matching expressions of disbelief. Sensing CeCe needed the support, Max reached out and cupped her shoulder. "We have your back," he whispered. There wasn't even a tremor in his voice, and it bolstered her.

"Now that we're alone," Eric slurred and stepped closer. The smoky smell of whiskey hit her nostrils, and she fought the urge to gag.

CeCe stepped to him and stabbed him in the chest with her index finger. The quick motion stung her, and she could tell from Eric's expression that he was surprised.

"What was that for?" he asked, rubbing the sore spot.

"That's for being a first-rate asshole," CeCe spat. "And this," she said as she raised her hand and slapped him across the face, "is for being a total heartless creep who likes to stalk his exes. You stay the hell away from me and my friends. You understand me?"

Eric's face turned beet red. "Don't you ever—" A worrisome shade of purple crawled up his neck all the way to the top of his ears.

CeCe flinched as his tone, hating herself for appearing weak in front of Max and Ginny. She'd had more than enough time away from Eric—to not let him scare her—to not let him get under her skin. Her relationship with Eric had turned into the equivalent of checking for bad eggs. If you missed one, it ruined the whole dish and made you sick as hell.

"You don't get to tell me what to do anymore," CeCe finally found her words. She sucked in a breath, feeling her resolve strengthen. Eric was over a foot taller than her, and she had to crane her neck to meet his eyes. The effort was worth it, though, as she watched the muscles in his neck tense.

"I get to do whatever I want, and I'll—" Eric's words hitched when he saw their audience was back. Two girls in their late teens had their phones out, one of his groupies had her phone trained on him. His own vanity won out over revenge. "Sorry, folks, nothing to see here." He flashed his signature grin and backed away from CeCe. "Misunderstanding with an old friend. Enjoy your meals." The grin on his face was so forced, his molars creaked.

CeCe glanced around the dining room, noticing that more than one person had their phones out. She had a thought, a thought that would rip off the scab and end this pain once and for all. It meant exposing more of herself than she liked, but CeCe knew it was time. No matter what happened with Evan, she needed to do this. *For herself.*

"Old friend?" she asked, her voice steadier than she felt. "That's pretty rich," she spat.

Eric's eyes blazed and color flushed up his neck into his hairline. Despite being drunk, his rage seemed to sober him. "Not here," he warned, his voice not quite low enough. The muscles on his neck flexed as he tried to take back control of the situation.

"Not here?" she repeated, feeling Max and Ginny behind her. "But you were willing to air my dirty laundry a moment ago. Right here, in front of these nice people." CeCe swept her arm across the room as more diners tuned into the free show.

Eric took a step toward the exit, but CeCe side-stepped to block him. "Let me go," he warned.

CeCe shook her head, her blonde hair bobbing around her face. "I don't think so. You were so keen to talk about our past, so let's talk." Holding up her hand, she ticked off all the things she wanted to discuss—all the areas of their past that required closure. "Do you want to talk about how you lied to me?" She stuck out her pointer finger. "Strung me along for a year while you were *married*?" CeCe paused long enough to hear a few muffled gasps from their audience, but it didn't slow her down. She extended her middle finger, and not in the way that she would have liked. "Then, as if that wasn't painful enough, you decide to start calling and texting nonstop. When I felt like I would suffocate under you, you had the audacity to blacklist me in all of Chicago. I couldn't even get a job at a deep-dish pizza chain by the time you were done dragging my name through the mud." CeCe exhaled, preparing herself for the coup de grace. "No, Eric. Not only are you going to stand here and listen to me, you're going to apologize for ruining my career in Chicago, my evening with friends, and upsetting my boyfriend."

Eric blinked, his expression slack, as if he couldn't believe what just transpired. It wasn't every day Mr. Hollywood got dressed down in public. "I can't believe you're acting this way," was all he said as he blinked at her.

"Did you not hear a word I said?" CeCe asked, her voice hitching. "You tried to ruin my life, Eric. And I let you, for a time. But then I got on my feet and found a restaurant that respects me and lets me be me. No strings, no lies, no bullshit." She banged her fist on her chest at her words, the feel of her spiked heart rate oddly comforting.

Suddenly, the dining room erupted in chants and whoops for CeCe. She heard a few *You go, girl!* And *You tell him!* before she backed toward the exit herself. "You're going to pay for this," Eric warned.

"No, I don't think she will," Ginny spoke up next to

CeCe. She gestured to their audience, phones still trained on their group. "You're about to go viral, so I think you should go while you have any dignity left."

Max slung his arm around Ginny's waist and tugged her closer. "I'd do as she says. She's in PR and knows what she's talking about."

CeCe reached out and took Ginny's proffered hand, squeezing it with all she had. Eric took one more look at her before storming out of the restaurant to a chorus of boos. One customer threw their chopsticks at his retreating back, another a balled-up napkin. For someone who was used to an audience and endless praise, she knew that would hurt him. *And she didn't care.*

The nightmare was finally over, or at least, the first part. Now she had to find Evan.

A few onlookers came over and hugged CeCe, thanking her for standing up to a creep like Eric. She thanked them, but struggled to get outside. It had been too long since she'd seen Evan, and she needed to make this right.

Max pushed them outside, with Ginny bringing up the rear. "Let's take a seat over there," she said, gesturing to a bench. "You look like you're going to collapse."

CeCe couldn't argue. Her body felt heavy and exhausted, like when she used to run half marathons. Stumbling to her seat, she reared back and groaned as the realization of what just happened hit home. "Oh my gosh." She screeched. "That was horrible."

"I'd say it was incredible," Max offered. "You stood up to that bully and gave him a dose of his own medicine."

Ginny nodded next to Max, her face breaking into a smile. "I would say that's the best personal PR I've ever seen. You did a number on him, CeCe. And it sounds like he had it coming."

"Too little, too late, I'm afraid," CeCe said. She kept looking around her, certain that Evan would pop out from behind a shrub and come to her aid. It felt wrong to be this raw and not have him by her side. Her hands itched with the need to pull him close, bury her face in his neck and inhale his spicy scent. She let out a breath and shook herself back to the moment. "Did anyone see where Evan went?"

Max and Ginny both shook their heads. CeCe turned to look for Mallory, but didn't see her either. This was bad.

"Let me walk you back to the hotel. I'm sure Evan's just in his room cooling off." Max's words were reassuring, but they rang hollow. Evan was angry and embarrassed, two emotions she could have avoided with the truth.

Why, why, why didn't she tell him the truth?

The sound of panting announced Mallory's arrival. "Hey," she breathed heavily. "I'm glad I found you guys." She doubled over and rested her hands on her knees as she struggled to catch her breath.

Max asked, "Where's Evan?"

Mallory shook her head and frowned. "He's gone."

"Gone?" CeCe felt herself blanch at the notion he wasn't sticking around for her. Wasn't bothering to hear her side of the story.

Mallory bit her lip, clearly torn about how much to share. "He's really upset, CeCe. I've never seen him so worked up. He said he wanted to be alone. I'm guessing he went back to Buckeye Falls."

Max pulled his cell phone out of his pocket and dialed Evan's number. He waited a moment before saying, "It goes straight to voicemail."

Ginny reached out and took CeCe's hand, tucking it into her elbow and pulling her to standing. "We're going to go back to the hotel and regroup. I am sure he didn't go far."

CeCe was touched by Ginny's concern, especially since their friendship was in its early stages. But of course Max would love a woman like that, who selflessly gave her time to friends. He would expect nothing less.

"Thanks," CeCe said as she was ushered back to their hotel. Her legs felt heavy. The effort of lifting each foot was monumental.

Once alone in her room, CeCe tried calling Evan a dozen

times. Her texts went unanswered, and she felt bile rising in her throat. Had she blown it? Evan was so easygoing; she couldn't imagine him not wanting to hear her out. But then she thought back to their trip to his parent's house. How adamant he was that he wanted a partner, someone he could trust. And here she sat, a liar who withheld the full story.

A quiet knock sounded, and CeCe bolted to answer it. Standing on the other side was Max, his features tired. "C-c-can I come in?" he asked.

CeCe looked over his shoulder, hoping against hope that he wasn't alone. He was. "Sure." She sighed, holding the door open for Max to join her.

"Sorry, it's just me. I know I'm probably the last person you want to see." Realizing what he said, Max laughed. "Well, maybe not the *last* person."

CeCe sat on the corner of her bed and gestured for Max to join her on the other side. He eased himself down and grimaced, an expression filled with bad news. "Have you heard from him?" she asked, fearing the answer.

"I can't get a hold of Evan, but I asked Helen to swing by his place. His car is out front, but he's not answering the door. Frankly, I'm relieved we know where he is."

CeCe couldn't disagree. "No, you're right. I'm glad he's home safe." Not able to sit a minute longer, she stood and began pacing the room. "Do you think I should go see him?"

Max chewed his bottom lip, trying to figure out the best solution. "Honestly, I don't know. Evan's pride was hurt, and he's probably upset you didn't tell him yourself. But he's crazy about you. I say give him the night to sleep it off. I'm sure he'll be back tomorrow in time for the competition."

The competition.

The whole reason she was in this mess. "Oh God, the competition." CeCe groaned. "Can we do it without Evan? Hell, should we do it without Evan?" CeCe remembered all the cell phone videos of her confrontation with Eric and she paused. "Do you think my tirade made it online? Is it possible they might cancel the competition?"

Max rubbed the back of his neck, taking a moment to think. "You know, that's a possibility. We'll have to see in the morning when the video goes viral."

"I guess. Who knows?" CeCe wasn't sure if she wanted to do it at all. She had nothing to prove to Eric, and she didn't know if she could be in the same zip code as him anymore. All of the reasons she fled Chicago were still valid.

"That's the other reason I'm here. CeCe, we don't have to do this. We can hop in the food truck and drive it back to Buckeye Falls."

"But you paid for that truck for this competition. What's the point if we're not going to use it?"

Max didn't seem concerned. "How easily you forget. Do you know how many summer festivals we could use that truck for? The competition might be why we got the truck now, but that doesn't mean it's the only reason. Right now, I'm more worried about you and Evan. Screw Eric and this competition. It's your call."

CeCe paced a little more, wracking her brain for the right decision. Should they compete and show Eric what she could do without him? Or should she pack up and go after the man she loved?

Yep, that's right. CeCe knew from the pit in her stomach that she was in love with Evan. She knew he was more important than anything else in this scenario. The trouble was, how was she going to tell him now?

CHAPTER 16

Evan woke to the sound of pounding on his front door. Easing himself up to sitting, he felt his hangover sharply. Groaning, he slowly padded to the front and peered through the peephole. Fearing it was Helen again, he was relieved it was Mallory.

"I can see you through the peephole, dummy. Let me in," she barked from the other side of the door.

Knowing he really didn't have a choice, Evan unlatched the lock and stepped back while his favorite sister barged in. She carried two coffees and had a paper bag wedged under her arm. Heading straight for the couch, Mallory deposited her goods on the coffee table. "Why do you smell like a frat house? Is Shep here or something?"

The mention of his frat brother brought too many negative thoughts to mind. Instead of engaging in his sister's questions, Evan shot her the bird and took one of the coffees. "Not that I'm complaining about the caffeine and pastries, but why are you here?"

Mallory rolled her eyes. "Geez, I wonder." She made a show of looking around the apartment. "Could it be because you're hours away from competition and you're here? Or could it be because you had your heart broken and I'm making sure you're alive?" She stared down her brother and sighed. "Drink your coffee and let's talk."

"I don't think we have anything to talk about. CeCe lied to me, made a fool of me, and I'm not going to the competition."

"I see we're getting right to the big stuff." She huffed. Opening the paper bag, she handed her brother a cherry Danish. "Eat up, then we gotta go."

"I'm not going," Evan said, taking the pastry and eating half in one bite. He was hungrier than he realized. Mallory sipped her coffee for a moment and didn't reply. Evan knew that meant she really had something to say. Her eyes slowly moved around the room, cataloging every detail. She did this when she was thinking, and the longer she stared the worse it got. "Spill it," he ordered, finishing his breakfast and dusting crumbs from his hands.

Mallory put her coffee down and turned to face her brother. "Mom and Dad are coming to the competition."

Jerking back as if he'd been slapped, Evan could not have been more surprised. "What?"

"Mom texted this morning that she got Dad to take the day off. They're headed there now."

Evan ran a hand down his face and felt the pastry turn in his stomach. He was in no mood to cook today, let alone see CeCe and Max. He was embarrassed, raw, and angry. It wasn't a good mix to cook award-winning food. If he didn't go though, his father would never let him forget it. Evan would prove he wasn't even committed to the job he said he loved.

As if reading his mind, Mallory chimed in. "I know you have a lot you need to figure out with CeCe, but think about what would happen if you didn't show up. Think about Dad, just for a second." She held up her hand and pinched her fingers together.

Mumbling a few choice profanities, Evan stood and paced the length of the living room. Mallory's eyes ping-ponged back and forth, tracking his progress. "I need to go, don't I?" he asked after another moment of stomping around.

Mallory nodded and let out a long breath. "I really think you do." She gave him an expression he couldn't read, and Evan felt the hairs on his neck stand up.

"There's more, isn't there?"

Mallory tried to smile, but it didn't reach her eyes. "When it rains, it pours," she mused. "I'm guessing you haven't looked online today." Evan shook his head and felt his knees grow weak. "You better sit back down for this one," Mallory said, patting the empty couch cushion beside her.

Evan sat back down and watched Mallory pull out her cell phone. After a few swipes, she handed the device to him. Evan saw CeCe on the screen, standing right in the fusion restaurant. His heart rate spiked and his mouth went dry. "What is this?" he asked, fearing it was what he saw yesterday. Eric throwing CeCe's past in Evan's face. "I don't think I can watch this," he warned.

"You need to. It's not what you think it is." Giving his sister a quizzical glance. "Ev, I'm serious."

Evan gave up and pressed play.

The video started, and he heard CeCe's voice, angry yet strong. He watched her knock Eric down word by word, his confidence crumbling as the scene unfolded. Just as Evan was about to ask more questions, Mallory swatted his arm. "Shhh, you need to see the whole thing."

Evan listened to CeCe's words, absorbed their meaning. He was so pleased to see Max and Ginny beside her, offering the support she needed to confront her ex. *Her ex.* Evan still couldn't believe CeCe lied to him, but at the moment, he wasn't too worried about it. He trusted the words coming out of CeCe's mouth, and it pained him to hear about her painful past with Eric. Evan hated that she hadn't trusted him enough with that burden, because he wanted to carry that for her. He wanted to wipe that sour, hurt expression from her face and never let her feel that way again.

When the video concluded, Evan handed Mallory her phone with a shaking hand. "I need to go see CeCe," he declared.

As he tried to stand, Mallory reached out and held Evan's shoulder. "Hold on, there's more."

"How can there possibly be more?" he scoffed, his brain short-circuiting at all that he'd witnessed.

Tapping away on her phone, Mallory handed it back with a new page pulled up. "Eric is out of the competition as judge and host. They pulled in some producer from the *Food Network*. There's even a statement that Eric's new show is canceled. Look." Mallory pointed to the article.

Evan scanned through it, picking up on how CeCe's confrontation and the viral video started a firestorm against the celebrity chef. As soon as the video was posted, several women came forward to share similar experiences about Eric's behavior on the job and in his personal life.

At the end of the article, Evan saw mention of Eric's wife, Hilary. "Looks like his wife is already making a statement that she's filing for divorce."

Mallory grimaced, like she'd drunk a glass of spoiled milk. "Yep. The guy is a scumbag of the highest order. And thanks to CeCe, the whole world knows it." She shuddered. "I can't believe I used to fangirl over that guy. Ugh, he's disgusting."

"No argument there." Evan stood and marched back to his bedroom. "I need two minutes to change."

Mallory collected their breakfast trash and went to the kitchen. "You're too wound up to drive. I'm taking us in."

When Evan emerged from his room in fresh clothes, he frowned at his sister. "What the hell am I going to say to CeCe? I need to—"

"You need to do a lot of groveling. But you also need to say your piece as well. We can discuss that in the car." Mallory held up her keys and jangled them in his face. "Let's roll."

*

"He's not coming," CeCe said for the twentieth time that morning. "I should have gone after him. I'm an idiot."

She and Max were already in the food truck, the fryer splattering away and the oven making the cramped space a million degrees. Not looking up from her fritter batter, CeCe whisked it with abandon. "I'm an idiot," she repeated, her elbow cramping as she overworked the batter. It would be tougher than silly putty at this rate.

Max plucked the whisk from her hands. "For the last time, stop taking out your stress on our fritter batter. They'll be as heavy as paperweights if you keep this up." Max slid the bowl away from CeCe and gestured to a stack of onions that needed chopped. "Can you do some knife work, or is that a dangerous request right now?" He winked at CeCe, but she grimaced.

"I can cut an onion," she said defensively. What CeCe wasn't saying was that cutting the onions, and a lot of other things, were supposed to be Evan's job. He was supposed to be there, shoved into this oversized tin can prepping for the competition. He was supposed to be by her side, literally and figuratively.

Max handed her a fresh bottle of water. "Drink this. You're dehydrated and I need you on your A-game."

"Ha! Fat chance of that." She huffed as she peeled an onion. "My A-game flew out the window yesterday in a blaze of glory."

Thinking back on the last twenty-four hours, CeCe couldn't believe this was her life. After the showdown with Eric, she received dozens of texts and calls from friends and former coworkers.

You're a badass! He deserves to go viral. You go, girl! Roxie declared.

You're my hero! replied another former sous chef. This woman had also been one of the whistleblowers to come out in the morning with a similar story from the year before CeCe moved to Chicago. It somehow made her feel better and worse that Eric had acted this way with other women.

CeCe knew she'd done the right thing confronting Eric so publicly. He deserved more than what she dished up, and she couldn't believe the tides had turned so quickly. As if reading her mind, Max asked, "Is this what cancel culture is? Is Eric canceled?"

From the doorway, Ginny laughed and stepped into the hot space. "You get cuter every day. You know that?" She handed her fiancé a cup of coffee before giving CeCe a caffeine boost of her own. "Yes, Eric is canceled. In more ways than one. Did you hear they have another judge for the competition?"

CeCe had heard, but it still brought a smile to her face that she got to hear the news again. "Yes. And I'd be lying if I didn't say it made me happier than a pig in shit."

Everyone chuckled, but the atmosphere was still tense. Lowering her voice, Ginny asked, "Any word from Evan?"

Max shook his head but stayed focused on the bacon he was frying. "He'll be here," he said. His voice held so much certainty that CeCe clung to his words like a life raft in stormy seas.

Ginny nodded, seeming satisfied with their progress. "Mind if I snap some action shots for the diner's social media pages? When you win, I have a whole montage planned." Not waiting for anyone to respond, Ginny took out her phone and started snapping.

Before she stepped outside, she handed her phone to CeCe. "This text came through from Natalie. She said she hasn't been able to reach you this morning."

Tell CeCe I know she'll kick ass today because that's what she does.

CeCe wiped her hands on her apron and took the phone. "It's because I haven't been looking for anything on my phone except word from Evan."

"He'll be here. I'm sure he needed some time to clear his

224

head," Ginny assured her. CeCe wanted to hug Ginny for her optimism, but she couldn't move beyond Max in the tiny space. Besides, hugs led to tears, and she'd had enough of that this morning.

Last night had been the longest night of CeCe's life. A jumble of emotions kept her from sleeping, but she was surprisingly alert right now. A weight she didn't realize she was carrying had lifted after she told off Eric. Even before she realized her scolding went viral, she felt finished with him like she never had been before.

Unfortunately she also felt finished with Evan. The notion tugged at her chest, and she had to rub over her collarbone to keep from crying. She had betrayed Evan, even after months of promising herself she wouldn't. Actions spoke louder than words, and her actions muddied the waters in their relationship.

"Do you have the onions ready?" Max asked, reaching out with an empty bowl.

CeCe blinked and looked down at the cutting board that was covered in misshapen onion pieces. "Gosh, if I diced this badly in culinary school, I would have flunked out." She grabbed a handful of onions and tossed them in the trash. "We're not going to win if I dice like that."

"Then let me do it," Evan said from the door of the truck. CeCe had to blink several times to make sure she wasn't hallucinating him into existence.

"Evan?" she asked, daring to make eye contact. He looked as wrung out as she felt, and that somehow seemed promising.

Without uttering a greeting, Evan stepped inside and shrugged out of his jacket. "The plan is for me to dice and prep the veggies, right?"

His blue gaze didn't reach her own, but CeCe didn't care in that moment. What mattered more was that Evan was here. She didn't know what it meant, but she needed to do a lot of groveling. It had to be a good sign, right? Showing up meant he cared—even if it was just about the diner. Evan was a thoughtful, loving person. Maybe she hadn't ruined things after all?

CHAPTER 17

CeCe nearly nicked her finger on her paring knife as she sliced apples for their dessert. Max and Evan spoke animatedly about plating for the judges. "I think we need to keep it simple," Max insisted as he chopped cilantro for the fritters.

Evan grimaced and held up an intricate radish he'd carved. "And I think we need to catch their attention before they take a bite. We will win on flavors, but we can't look forgettable."

Max studied the vegetables and finally nodded. "You're right. Let's give it a try. We're here to impress them, not just kick ass."

Evan chuckled, the first relatively happy sound he'd made since coming back. CeCe tried to focus and not worry about all the words left unsaid between them, but it was impossible.

Ginny stuck her head in the truck. The opening in the door let in a heavenly whoosh of fresh air, and CeCe nearly fainted at the sensation. "Anything I can help with?" Ginny asked, her phone poised to take another picture. When the guys weren't looking, she snagged a shot of them leaning over their plates. The picture was drool-worthy for a lot of reasons. Evan's blond curls framed his face as he placed a radish in the center of the plate. Max's scruff made his jawline look as square as Henry Cavill's. Judging from Ginny's flushed cheeks, she wasn't complaining about her photography skills—or the man she got to go home with.

CeCe tried not to gawk as Evan angled himself so Ginny could take another shot. The muscles on his forearms flexed as he adjusted the plate. "The judges will love it," Ginny assured everyone as she clicked away. "I'll get out of your hair and post these." Her smile was so genuine and giddy, she looked like a kid on Christmas.

Mentioning the judges brought their current situation back into sharp focus. Eric was gone, and someone else was in his place. She didn't have to impress him, and that felt freeing. What felt more freeing was that she didn't *want* to impress him. Although it hadn't happened the way she'd liked, CeCe had gotten control over Eric and that situation. And control felt damn good.

Control. It was what she wanted right now with Evan. While she was thrilled to have him by her side competing, they were a long way from pillow forts and stolen kisses. She needed to make good—and fast.

"That's the last of the fritters. I have the honey garlic aioli ready over there," Evan said as he gestured to a bowl of the sauce.

Max nodded, adding a sprinkle of parsley. "I'm ready too. CeCe, how are those stuffed donuts going?"

CeCe pulled out her tray of decorated donuts from the warming oven and gave a thumbs-up. "Ready. I was waiting to plate until the very last second."

Max took the tray from her and helped with arranging the sweet portion of their entry. They'd gone with a fried theme, similar to what people would find at a Midwestern state fair. But instead of funnel cakes and corn dogs, they went with elevated, fancier carnival fare.

"Evan, can you take our entries to the judges' tent? CeCe and I can clean up and meet you over there for the results."

Without looking at CeCe, Evan brushed past and took the trays from Max. "You got it, boss. See you over there." He left the truck without a backward glance, and CeCe felt as hollow as one of her unstuffed donuts.

When the door finally slammed shut, CeCe let out a sigh and propped herself on the counter. She felt raw with exhaustion from cooking and a myriad of unsaid words to Evan. Sensing she was on edge, Max pulled a small bottle from one of the cabinets. "No matter what happens with the judges, we made some damn fine food today." He splashed a shot of the amber liquid into two plastic cups and handed one to CeCe. "I have a bottle of champagne saved for when we win, but we could both use something right now."

CeCe took the proffered cup and sipped it greedily, knowing the whiskey would go straight to her head. "Thanks. I appreciate you thinking we're going to win."

"We will win," Max said with certainty. "There's no way anyone has more creative, yet comforting dishes on their plates."

CeCe knew he was right, but today didn't feel the same. "Don't you think we've sort of ... lost our mojo?" She twirled one hand in the air and sipped her whiskey from the other.

Max sipped and thought for a moment. CeCe watched his throat bob as he collected his words. "Th-there were a lot of emotions these last few days. But sometimes that leads to magic in the kitchen." He watched CeCe's expression turn skeptical. "Hear me out," he offered, placing his empty cup on the counter. "Evan and you clearly need to work through some things, but at the end of the day, he showed up to help us out. All three of us did our best, and that's all we could have asked for." Letting his gaze sweep across the food truck, he added, "Frankly, this was amazing. I feel like I won already."

CeCe couldn't argue with that logic. While Evan didn't show up specifically for her today, she was touched he showed up for Max and the diner. "Good point." She sighed.

The pair busied themselves with tidying up the food truck. No one would want to come back to a mess after the results. If they won, they'd want to celebrate. If they lost, they'd want to go home and sulk. While CeCe scoured the grill, she heard a familiar voice outside the truck.

"This has to be it, Pamela. It has Buckeye Falls on the logo."

CeCe peered out the window to see Mr. and Mrs. Lawson stumbling along the grounds. Neither one of them wore appropriate shoes for an outdoors event, and it didn't surprise her. CeCe whispered to Max, "It's Evan's parents."

Max blanched faster than the vegetables they had just cooked. "You're kidding. His dad is here?"

CeCe nodded and raked her fingers through her mussed hair. Having foregone any makeup for practicality, she pinkened her already flushed cheeks. "What should we do?"

Before either could answer, there was a firm knock at the food truck's door. "Hello?" Pamela's voice echoed from outside.

Max took off his apron and shrugged. "Looks like we're letting them in." Without hesitating, Max flung the door open and welcomed the Lawsons inside. "Good to see you both. Please, come on in. CeCe and I just finished cleaning up."

Pamela stepped inside first, her designer purse clutched to her chest like a shield. She tried not to touch anything as she slid past Max toward CeCe.

Dale was not nearly as dainty about it. He stomped up the stairs and hovered in the doorway. "It's so small," he grumbled. Looking past Max's shoulder, he frowned. "Where's Evan?"

CeCe jumped in right away. "You just missed him. He went to bring our entries to the judges."

"That's nice," Pamela said, although her tone didn't sound like it was. "We were hoping to see Evan, you know."

She shrugged and looked uncomfortable. "In action, I guess."

"Glad we drove all the way out here for nothing," Dale said under his breath.

Max jumped in, retrieving a covered dish that had some of their samples. "I happen to have a little bit of everything we submitted right here." He pulled off the lid and handed a small plate to Pamela.

Turning to give one to Dale, Max's hand faltered when the older man stepped back onto the steps. "None for me. I'm not hungry."

Pamela looked dismayed as she bit into one of her fritters. "Please, Dale, just a taste?"

Practically sneering at his wife, Dale finally took the plate from Max. He sniffed it like it might be poisonous before finally taking a bite from the fried enchilada ball Evan made. Despite Dale's expression, CeCe didn't miss the glint in his eye as he chewed. Whether he wanted to admit it or not, he liked what he was eating.

"These are all delicious," Pamela swooned at her now-empty plate. "Did you three really make everything in here?" For the first time since stepping into the truck, Pamela looked around the space with appreciation.

"Yes, ma'am," Max replied, his voice dripping with pride. "That rectangle right there was Evan's own creation. He took my usual enchilada recipe and found a way to make it portable."

Pamela grinned. "He did? That was my favorite part." Finally, a look of pride washed over her face. CeCe's heart swelled at the sight, but quickly deflated when she remembered Evan wasn't here to see it.

Handing Max back his nearly untouched plate, Dale turned and walked outside. Pamela hesitated, but followed her husband. CeCe had seen enough for her liking, and she couldn't hold her tongue another second. Regardless of what happened—or didn't happen—with Evan in the future, she knew he deserved a hell of a lot better than this.

Following the couple onto the grounds, she asked, "You're not sticking around to hear the results?" That couldn't possibly be true. Why spend the time coming out if they weren't going to wait and see Evan?

"We should be getting back," Dale said without turning to face CeCe.

"Thank you for having us," Pamela offered lamely. For once, she seemed embarrassed by her husband's behavior. Her feet marched in place as her husband strode ahead.

CeCe wouldn't stand for this. She didn't know if it was still the adrenalin from her interaction with Eric, the heartbreak over not speaking with Evan, or simply her dislike of the man standing in front of her, but she snapped. "This is ridiculous!" she shouted, stopping the pair in their tracks.

Dale turned slowly to face CeCe. "I'm sorry?" he asked, his tone hard and cool like the edge of a razor.

Squaring her shoulders, CeCe said again, "This is ridiculous. You need to stay and see your son and hear the results. You've come all this way."

"We don't need to do anything. And you can't tell me how to raise my son."

"You already did raise him," CeCe began. "And, frankly, you managed to do a tremendous job. Although I think a lot of that credit needs to go to Evan. You raised a man who is creative, respectful, loving, and so giving. He would give you the shirt off his back if he thought it would help. He would do anything to make you proud of him." She gasped for breath and realized that, for a second time in as many days, she'd drawn an audience.

Dale's face had turned a worrisome shade of red as he found his words. "Young lady, you think you have the right to speak to me that way, but I'll have you know—"

CeCe wasn't having it. "I can speak to you any way I like. If memory serves, you had no qualms telling me my business. I was a stranger, and you gave me an earful on my choices in life. Well, here is a choice I've made. I love your son. And I won't stand by while you dismiss his work, his passion."

Pamela dabbed at her eyes with a tissue and cleared her throat. "Evan is very lucky to have you in his life," she said. "It's nice to see him supported by someone who cares."

"Pamela, get in the car. We're leaving," Dale barked.

Surprising everyone around them, Pamela shook her head. "No. We're not leaving. CeCe is right. This is important to Evan."

"What should be important to Evan is getting a real job, being a man. He needs to grow up." Dale's jowls shook as he spoke, looking like a balloon about to pop.

"He is grown up! Have you seen what he's done with his website projects? He's so talented and dedicated. He'll work a double at the diner, go home to work on his website development, and still find time to make me dinner. Every day he shows how much of a man he is, and I'm lucky enough to be a part of his life. If you'd only pay attention, you'd see he's given you a million reasons to be proud of him." CeCe's voice hitched, and she realized she was crying. Max reached out and handed her a towel, which she shook off. The sensation of her tears made CeCe feel alive, made her feel things for the first time in a while.

Dale stepped closer to CeCe, his eyes dark and filled with unchecked rage. "How dare you stand here and talk to me like that?"

"Enough." Pamela pulled him back to her side. "Stop acting like this. CeCe is right. I'm only sorry it took me this long to see it." Turning to CeCe, Pamela took one of her hands and squeezed. "Thank you for loving our son so fiercely. He deserves nothing less."

CeCe didn't have the heart to tell Pamela that Evan deserved a hell of a lot more than her. She merely squeezed her hand back and nodded.

She watched the couple walk toward the exhibit hall and let out a lungful of air. She felt drained and needed to find a place to sit. Before she could step away, she was pulled into the fiercest hug of her life. "Ooof," she exhaled as Mallory pinned her. The other woman was not that much taller, but her embrace made CeCe feel like a rag doll.

"That was the coolest freaking thing I've ever seen," she said as she released CeCe.

"What? I just barked at your father, in public."

"And it was about twenty years in the making. Well done." Mallory gave CeCe a thumbs-up and finally stepped back. "If I would have been quicker with my phone, I would have recorded it."

CeCe's shoulders slumped. "I think I've had enough viral videos for one week."

"I don't know. I think this one would have been bigger," Evan said as he stepped past his sister.

CeCe couldn't fight the goofy grin that crossed her face. "You saw that?"

"Sure did." He inched forward and stepped between CeCe and his sister.

For once in her life, Mallory knew when to step away. She giggled and followed Max as they went toward the exhibit hall.

"Can we talk?" CeCe asked, feeling the whiskey churn through her. She had said so much to Dale, but now she wanted to—needed to—say it to Evan.

*

Evan thought he might rip in half at all the battling emotions rushing through him. On his way back from submitting their entries, he had a feeling of hopelessness he couldn't shake. He wasn't sure how CeCe felt about him, and he was stressed about seeing his dad at the competition. He wasn't even sure he believed Mallory that their parents were coming, so stumbling upon CeCe dressing down his father—in public no less—was simply incredible.

Never before had Dale Lawson been told what to do, let alone how to act. CeCe cut him down faster than a sack of potatoes before the brunch rush. Yet for all her words, and there were a lot of them, the part that stuck out was that she loved him. CeCe told his parents—and half the attendees—that she loved him. His heart felt like it tripled in size, but he still had so many things he needed to say as well.

"There's a bench over at the entrance. You mind if we talk for a minute? They won't announce the winners for a little while." Evan reached out his hand, and CeCe snatched it up, pulling him closer to her. He smelled her familiar vanilla scent, and felt his heart stutter. Being angry with CeCe didn't sit right with Evan. The sensation was awkward and uncomfortable, like a threadbare hand-me-down sweater. Hopefully after they talked, he wouldn't feel that way ever again.

When they reached the bench, Evan gestured for CeCe to sit down. She slowly sat, but stayed perched on the edge, ready to jump up at any moment. "Evan, can I just—"

Shaking his head, Evan frowned. "I need to say a few things first. Okay?"

CeCe bit her lip and nodded.

Evan paced back and forth in front of her. He wished he wore a pedometer so he could have tracked all the pacing he'd done in the last day. His hair was mussed and his cheeks were flushed from hours working in the hot food truck. He feared he looked awful.

"So let me get this straight," he bit out, trying to slow his pulse. "You and Eric used to date?" CeCe barely raised her head in the affirmative before Evan soldiered on. "I think I understand. You didn't think I could handle the truth. Right?"

"That's not the whole picture."

"Can you please paint the whole picture for me, please? Because where I'm standing, you've been keeping a pretty big secret from your past. I want us to be honest with each other, CeCe."

Finally, CeCe stood and stepped closer. Evan wasn't ready to touch her yet, so he took a step back. CeCe licked her lips before speaking. "I'm sorry. It sounds lame now, but I am. I should have realized you could handle the truth. And we've talked about this. I don't see you as some kid. You're so much more, and I should have trusted you with the truth. I should have trusted you with the pain of it all."

Banging a hand on his chest, he continued. "But do you see how this made me look? How this made me feel? Damn it, CeCe. I'm in love with you! I want to tell you everything, share everything. I feel like I'm out here on a ledge alone sometimes. If you're in pain, no matter from what, I want to know. I want to help."

CeCe covered her heart with her hands, her voice shaking as she spoke. "You're not alone. I know it's cold comfort now, but keeping this secret has been eating me up for weeks. I wanted to tell you, really, I did. I just didn't want to bring Eric and all of that drama into what we have. I was afraid it would taint what we've built together, and I couldn't stand that. I'm not saying I was still in love with Eric, but I was still carrying around a lot of the guilt and hurt from that breakup."

Evan rubbed the back of his neck, keeping his eyes down. "But I want to help carry your burdens. I want to be your partner."

"I want that too. I meant every word I said to your parents and to Eric."

"Eric's a creep!" Evan exclaimed. "He's an abuser who deserves a lot more than he's getting now. Losing his career is only the beginning of what he deserves." Evan balled his fist, flexing his fingers until he shoved his hands in his pockets. "You shouldn't be afraid to share pain like that. It's why I'm here. I want to help."

"You do help, more than you know. Evan, these last few months have been the best of my life. I didn't realize I could be with someone without giving up a piece of myself. Please, you have to forgive me for lying. I know now that I wasn't protecting you. I was hurting you."

After another long exhale, Evan finally looked up to

meet CeCe's gaze. He inventoried every detail on her face, from the sparkle of tears in her big eyes to the way her blonde locks shone in the sunlight. He loved this woman with a fierceness that scared him, and he wasn't willing to let her go.

"You haven't had to rely on people for a while, but do you think you could lean on me? CeCe, I want to be with you."

A single tear slid down her cheek as she crept closer to Evan. "You do?"

Sniffling, Evan fought back his own tears. "Well, duh." He laughed through the tightening of his throat. "I'm sorry I ran away without letting you explain. I realize that was a childish thing to do, and I hate myself for it."

CeCe reached out her hand and traced a line along Evan's wrist. He shivered with the contact and watched her eyes dilate. "Your reaction made perfect sense, given the situation. Don't apologize for that." She hesitated before asking. "Does this mean you'll give me another chance?"

Evan sighed, feeling his nerves on edge. "CeCe, I'll give you a thousand chances. I love you, and I want to be with you through everything."

"I love you too," she whispered, sliding her fingers down and taking his hand in hers. "I've loved you for a while."

A smile tugged at Evan's lips. "You have?"

"Yeah, but I was a little too proud to admit it." She winked at him and Evan couldn't wait another minute. He closed the distance between them, drawing her lips to his. He kissed her with everything he had, hoping to convey all his emotions, apologies, and hopes.

Evan kissed CeCe like a drowning man, coming up for gulps of air to keep himself afloat. "I love you, CeCe. I won't embarrass you by saying how long." They both chuckled as he cupped her face in his hands. "But I'll say I love you a little more after watching you with my parents. That took a lot of guts, and I don't think anyone has ever stood up for me like that."

"I know they're your parents, but I had to say something. You're a good man, Evan. It was high time someone gave you the credit you deserve."

CeCe's words pushed Evan over the edge, and he felt a fresh stream of tears. Not knowing what to say, he pulled CeCe back to him and kissed her forehead. They stood in silence for a moment until the sound of applause filtered out behind them.

"We should probably get inside and see if we won this damn thing," he offered, even though he didn't want to break apart.

CeCe kissed him again and nodded. "You're right. I want to be there for the results, especially since Max is certain we're going to win."

Evan looped CeCe's arm in his and steered her toward the exhibit hall. "Frankly, I don't care if we win or lose. I feel like I've already won."

"That's a pretty cheesy line, even for you." She winked.

"Get ready, because I've got more where that came from."

As they walked toward their competition fate, Evan knew it really didn't matter what happened. He had his dream girl on his arm and he'd proven to himself that he could craft recipes worthy of competition. Evan learned all he needed to know that day. He was simply ready to see what came next.

EPILOGUE

Three weeks later

The bride looked lovely in her ivory tulle gown—which zipped up without issue, all her worries and snacking be damned. Rumor had it the dress was flown in from New York, but she wasn't giving away details. The groom cried while she walked down the aisle, but he wasn't the only one. The wedding march barely drowned out the sounds of Buckeye Falls' happy tears.

"Ginny looks gorgeous," Natalie mused from her place in line with the other attendants. Ginny's father, Harold, served as best man, with Evan standing behind him as a groomsman. Natalie had wanted to be matron of honor, but Harold's girlfriend, Mona, had taken that honor. Natalie was making the most of it, despite teasing Ginny for weeks that they'd been friends since high school. She smoothed the skirt of her pink silk dress and dabbed at the corner of her eye. Mascara wasn't allowed to run today.

"Ginny always looks gorgeous," CeCe replied, who didn't wear her formal wear with the same grace as Natalie. She tugged at the halter top of her dress, snagging Evan's eye as she adjusted the fabric. For all of CeCe's rumblings over dressing up, Evan looked like he was made for that tuxedo; a grin big enough to rival Max's smattered across his face. There was a time in the not-so-distant past that CeCe didn't see herself standing up here on Max's big day. She'd protected herself from so many of her favorite people because of one bad relationship. But those days were thankfully over.

The truth was, CeCe hadn't been this happy in, well—ever. Since the competition, she and Evan were practically inseparable. Their time outside the diner was spent in pillow forts, cooking in each other's kitchens, and laughing with their friends. It was effortless; it felt right; it felt real.

The best part of their reconciliation was their communication. CeCe made it a point to share her thoughts with Evan about everything, and he did the same. Sure, they still were human and something would inevitably come up, but they were both playing on a level field this time around. No more secrets. No more games.

CeCe found another way to spend her time outside the diner. She started seeing a therapist who was helping her work through her unresolved issues with Eric. Even after she and Evan talked it out, she realized there were more demons that needed to be addressed. It was the best decision she'd made all year.

Evan had found his own ways to improve, although CeCe didn't think he needed too much work. He found two more clients after the boutique's website was a success. Steadily, he was making his way on his own terms, and it was exactly what he needed. He'd also made headway with his parents, standing firm with his father on his career plans. If he wanted to cook at the diner and work freelance, that was good enough for him. Evan no longer needed their approval.

Interrupted from her musings, CeCe jumped when applause erupted as the happy couple kissed. Natalie sniffed a little and CeCe had to elbow her in the side. "Your mascara will run if you keep this up."

Natalie rolled her wet eyes. "Please, that stuff costs more than most people's daily salaries. I should be able to run through Niagara Falls without it running." Dabbing one more time at her eyes, Natalie sighed contentedly. "I'm not usually so emotional at weddings. I thought I'd be able to keep it together, but they're just so happy."

Glancing out into the crowd, CeCe saw Anthony staring at his wife with a surprisingly sweet expression. He was clad in a tailored suit and seemed reasonably happy to be in attendance. While he didn't share his wife's watery attitude, he did clap when the bride and groom walked past. CeCe thought that was a start.

As Max and Ginny made their exit, Evan tugged on CeCe's hand. "Shouldn't we get to the reception and make sure the caterers are set up?"

CeCe smiled and shook her head. "Already taken care of. I called them when I was helping Ginny with her dress. Nat swears they're the best, but I felt better checking."

Evan chuckled and pulled her hand to his lips, kissing the inside of her palm. "You always think of everything. It's one of the things I love about you."

CeCe stood on tiptoe and whispered in Evan's ear, "What else do you love about me?"

Before Evan could answer, Madeline joined them. The little girl was clad in her puffy flower girl dress, her chubby hands clutching the basket with the focus of a woman on a mission. "Why are you kissing?" she demanded, her big eyes roaming between them.

Evan laughed, leaning closer to the little girl. "Because we're in love and that's what people in love do."

Madeline frowned, looking over to her parents, who were ushering Otis back into his tiny suit jacket. "But Mommy and Daddy don't kiss."

"Of course they do. They just don't want you to see."

"Why?" the girl asked, clearly intrigued by the potential for mystery in her parents' lives.

"Because kissing is for grown-ups." Evan offered, and

CeCe could tell he was biting back a smile of his own.

Madeline pondered this another moment before reaching into her basket and handing Evan and CeCe each a flower petal. "Mommy said I needed to put these on the floor, but I wanted to share them." She lowered her voice and stage-whispered, "Don't tell." Scurrying away, she disappeared into the crowd where Mona scooped her up.

"Did I hear my daughter rat me and Anthony out for not kissing?" Natalie asked, Otis hanging from her hip. "So much for mystery in Buckeye Falls."

"Evan came to your rescue. He said kissing is for grown-ups." CeCe reached out and tugged on Otis's arm until the boy giggled.

Anthony joined them, kissing Otis on the top of the head. "Thanks for buying us a couple years before Maddie goes boy crazy."

The five of them walked out of the venue and got ready for the reception. Otis babbled the whole way to their cars, and CeCe could only imagine it was a fascinating story. Just as they got to Evan's SUV, they were stopped by Helen. "There you two are. I wanted to give you this. When I went to the diner this morning, it was wedged in the mailbox." She handed a padded envelope to them and headed toward her car. "See you at the reception."

"What is it?" CeCe asked, handing it to Evan to open. "If I try to pry that open with my manicure, Nat will kill me."

Evan didn't wait before tearing it open and pulling out a silver plaque. *2022 Midwestern Food Truck Champions* it read across the top, with all three of their names scrawled below. "I was wondering when this would arrive," Evan said, a look of pure wonder on his face. "I still can't believe we won."

CeCe playfully shoved his shoulder. "Watch it, mister. We worked really hard for that plaque." Evan slid the plaque back in the envelope and tucked it under his arm. From the other side of his jacket, he retrieved a small envelope. "Since we're suddenly handing out envelopes." He laughed.

"What's that?" she asked, her skin prickling in anticipation.

"Open it and find out," he said, an adorable grin creasing his face.

Raising an eyebrow, she did as she was told. The envelope held a birthday card with a few balloons printed on the front. Inside it simply read *Happy Birthday. I cannot wait to celebrate the birth of my favorite person.* A ticket to Buckeye Falls' only spa was inside.

"My birthday isn't for a couple days," she remarked, looking back at his eager expression with tears in her eyes.

"I know. I also know you're still not looking forward to it, so I figured I'd share my well-wishes now, when you're least expecting it. And this way, you can have a little pampering while you come to terms with being fabulous."

CeCe pressed the card to her chest, careful not to wrinkle the paper. "Thank you, Evan. This is exactly what I wanted."

"Do you know how easy it is to shop for a girlfriend who literally doesn't want anything for her birthday?"

"I aim to please," she retorted.

Reaching out, he took CeCe's hand and drew her close. After all they went through, he still marveled at his reality with CeCe. No other plus-ones for the wedding; no more hiding his feelings and biding his time. He'd gotten the girl, *his* girl. No pretense, no barriers, just the two of them.

"Having such a low-maintenance girlfriend is great," he teased. "It's only one of the reasons I love you."

CeCe giggled, actually giggled like little Otis. Even after all these months with Evan, it still felt surreal to be this happy with a man. She wasn't about to complain though and fell into Evan's embrace, kissing him senseless. "I love you too, more than I thought possible."

"I'll never get tired of hearing that," Evan beamed.

"And I'll never get tired of saying it." CeCe sighed, content with everything around her. It took her a while to find her happily ever after, but CeCe knew Evan was worth the wait. She'd fallen hard, and she was so pleased he'd caught her.

The End

ACKNOWLEDGEMENTS

Let me start by thanking the team at Inkspell Publishing—specifically Melissa, Yeza, and Shel. This book, and its predecessors, would not be possible without your support and guidance. You make the post-writing process a delight. Thank you!

To the team at BH Writing Services—specifically Jessica and Judy—thank you for getting this book polished and presentable.

To my writing friends in Ohio and Indiana. Thank you for being sounding boards and celebrating (and sometimes commiserating) about this wonderful craft of writing.

Time for some inside jokes...

To Thelma—thank you for being a friend—and a rock. Your support and undying sense of humor truly keep me sane.

To Ernie—our friendship is one of my favorite things. Thank you for being not only a friend, but a writing buddy as I started my publishing journey.

To the Jets—we're more than a gang, we're a support system I could not live without. Your laughter, memes, and encouragement truly keep me going. When's our next girl's weekend?!

To my parents, thank you for being my cheerleaders and seeing my potential.

To my sister, who puts the Fiesta in Mexico. I will always appreciate your support, laughter and snark.

Finally, to my husband. This book would not be possible without your support and sacrifice. I love you from the bottom of my heart. Thank you.

Happy reading, everyone!

HERE'S A SNEAK PEEK AT THE THIRD BUCKEYE FALLS NOVEL...
Falling Again

Chapter One

Natalie Snyder was used to getting her way. She commanded a room as soon as she walked in. She could negotiate and play politics better than a Clinton. But at the moment, she was involved in the stare-down of the century with a four-year-old. "Give me the bottle, Maddie." Natalie urged, her hand outstretched toward her daughter.

"No!" Shouted the little girl, her blonde curls shaking in protest. "Mine." The last word came out on a whine, and Natalie had to fight an eye roll. Whining was step one of a five-alarm meltdown.

"Maddie," Natalie said, her voice light but firm. "Let Mommy have it."

Maddie looked at her mother, her small head tilted slightly in concentration. "Mine." She repeated, her arms raising the bottle higher.

Natalie could see the chocolate sauce oozing from the nozzle, but she held her breath. "Please, sweetie. I'll make you chocolate milk if I can have the bottle."

Madeline's expression shifted from determined to quizzical, but her fingers still clenched the bottle. "I want to do it." She cried, tears starting to pool in her big, blue eyes.

Breaking eye contact for a second, Natalie looked for reinforcements. Anthony was upstairs getting ready for work, and Otis was nowhere to be seen. Usually their toddler liked to join the chaos, not avoid it. His silence made Natalie nervous, as silence with toddlers was never a good thing. But she didn't have time for that now.

As if taking her mother's broken eye contact as a sign of victory, Madeline raised the bottle of chocolate syrup and squeezed with all her might, her chubby little hands shaking from the force. A fountain of chocolate spewed into the air and covered the girl, the kitchen, and Natalie in chocolate ribbons. Natalie tried to hold back the profanity that escaped her lips, but it was no use. "That's what I get for designing a white kitchen." She groaned as she stomped forward and took the now half-empty bottle from her daughter's hands.

Madeline cried immediately, waving her arms and spreading the chocolate in a 3-foot span around her. "My bottle! It's mine!" She wailed.

"You are in deep trouble young lady," Natalie said as she scooped her daughter up. With her free hand, she tossed the offending bottle into the sink and marched upstairs to the bathroom.

Anthony appeared at the top of the stairs, looking handsome in his gray tailored suit. It brought out the flint in his eyes, but Natalie didn't have time to enjoy the sight. "What the hell happened?" Anthony asked, sidestepping the duo and raising his hands.

Natalie plopped Madeline on the edge of the bathtub and stuck out her index finger. "Don't move a muscle, young lady."

Madeline looked back and forth between her parents and said, "Mommy and Dad both said bad words. You need to put a quarter in the jar. Each." She demanded from her perch. "That's one, two, three, four—" she girl started counting on her fingers while Natalie peeled off her ruined blouse and tossed it in the laundry basket.

Anthony stood still, taking in the sight of his wife in her bra, but he didn't offer to help. Natalie looked down at herself and back at Anthony and frowned. It was the first time she'd been in her bra in front of him for longer than she cared to admit. She caught her reflection in the mirror and hurriedly wrapped a towel around her torso. Was it still considered baby weight if her baby was nearly two-years-old? But Natalie didn't have time to dwell on that now. "Can you please go find Otis? I haven't heard from him in five minutes, which can only mean something bad is happening."

Blinking at her for a moment, Anthony finally nodded and headed for the stairs. Over his shoulder he said, "I can have my mom come over if you need to get out for a meeting or anything. I can't be late for town council."

Natalie looked at her iWatch and groaned. "That'd be nice. I need to get cleaned up before I meet Ginny. Thanks." Turning back to her daughter, she took off her dirty dress and added it to the heap in the laundry basket. "Now Maddie, you need to be a good girl today. Okay? No more messes, and you need to listen to Mommy, Daddy, and Grammie."

Madeline smeared the chocolate syrup on her hands all over her cheeks and giggled. "Look, I'm a mud monster." She raised her hands and growled. If Natalie wasn't already late to work and covered in sugar, she would have laughed. Now all she could muster was a nod before turning on the faucet and plopping her mud monster into the warm water.

DON'T MISS ANOTHER BUCKEYE FALLS STORY

Falling Home

Welcome to Buckeye Falls, Ohio!
'Tis the Season for Second Chances...And this couple is going to need a Christmas Miracle!

When New York transplant Ginny Meyer returns to her small hometown to help her father recover from surgery, she isn't looking for any complications. No Christmas caroling, no cookie decorating, and certainly no time spent with her ex-husband, Max. The trouble is, she's looped into helping with the Christmas Jubilee—and a certain ex is her planning partner. Now all her plans to avoid Max disappear in a puff of tinsel. But she can resist his charms, right?

Max Sanchez has three great loves in his life—his diner, Christmas, and his ex-wife. He's spent two years missing the woman who broke his heart and left town, and he'll use any excuse to spend time with her. Max hopes some holiday cheer, and his famous cheese enchiladas, can help them find their way back together. Buckeye Falls hasn't felt the same since Ginny left, and Max can tell she's warming to the idea of staying in town. Now if only he could get her to stay with him...

With a little help from the residents of Buckeye Falls, this Christmas is bringing more than presents under the tree.

Author Libby Kay's books are perfect for fans of Kristan Higgins' second chance romances or Sharon Sala's smalltown romances. Readers will fall in love with Buckeye Falls, Ohio and the townspeople as they embrace the holiday season. Slip in to this enchanting smalltown and stay awhile! You might just fall in love...

EXCERPT:

Blinking, Ginny begged her eyes to see someone else standing before her. It was as if her memories willed themselves back to life. Beside her, her father perked up and lifted his free hand. "Max, over here." Max turned around, and Ginny felt the air leave her lungs. This was no trick of her mind. It was the real deal. *Well, hell ...*

Time had been good to Max; there was no denying it. His dark hair was longer now, curling at the base of his neck. A few flecks of gray threatened to take over his temples, but he managed to look mature rather than haggard. Instead of the clean-shaven face she remembered, his chiseled jawline was now peppered with a few days of stubble. Suddenly, Ginny understood all the fuss with lumbersexuals.

Max's brown eyes darkened when he saw her, but his steps didn't falter. "Harold, good to see you." He moved one of his shopping bags to his other arm and shook her father's hand. When he turned to her, Ginny felt her breath hitch as he reached out his hand for a shake. *Really? They were in the hand-shaking phase of their relationship?*

Ginny reached out and took his hand, a shot of awareness coursing through her body as his fingers wrapped around hers. "Max," she said his name in greeting, hoping her tone was light, carefree.

"Gin." Max swallowed and squeezed her hand before letting it go. He didn't say anything at first, just studied her. She was glad she had listened to her father about makeup. Bumping into her ex-husband with bedhead and sans mascara would have been mortifying.

Ginny was helpless for a moment, staring at Max like a fool. Perhaps she'd fallen into an alternate universe when she left the turnpike? Maybe her rental car was a time machine where she felt pulled to a man who bruised her heart? A man whose heart was certainly broken by her.

Either oblivious or uncaring of her current slack-jawed state, Max surprised her by stepping closer and giving her a genuine smile. "I'm glad you're back," he said. "It's really good to see you."

In that moment, staring into his warm gaze, Ginny couldn't disagree. Being so close to Max, so close to the worn paths of their past, she felt comfortable. This didn't feel like a foreign place; it felt like home.

Now Available In Ebook And Print Where Books Are Sold

ABOUT THE AUTHOR

Libby Kay lives in the city in the heart of the Midwest with her husband. When she's not writing, Libby loves reading romance novels of any kind. Stories of people falling in love nourish her soul. Contemporary or Regency, sweet or hot, as long as there is a happily ever after she's in love!

When not surrounded by books, Libby can be found baking in her kitchen, binging true crime shows, or on the road with her husband, traveling as far as their bank account will allow.

Writing is a solitary job, and Libby loves to hear from readers. Reach out and review her stories anytime. She'd love to hear from you.

Website: https://www.libbykayauthor.com/
Facebook: @LibbyKayAuthor

Goodreads: Libby Kay

Instagram:
https://www.instagram.com/libbykayauthor/

Bookbub: https://www.bookbub.com/profile/libby-kay